Sherlock Holmes In Song

Words and Music
by Jim Ballinger

Edited by Mark Alberstat

First edition published in 2021
© Copyright 2021
Jim Ballinger

Hardcover ISBN 978-1-78705-942-9
Paperback ISBN 978-1-78705-943-6
ePub ISBN 978-1-78705-944-3
PDF ISBN 978-1-78705-945-0

Published by MX Publishing
335 Princess Park Manor, Royal Drive,
London, N11 3GX
www.mxpublishing.com

Cover design by Brian Belanger

Dedication

To the Bootmakers of Toronto and
the Spence Munros of Halifax

Contents

Introduction

This was never intended to happen. It started as a one-off, an in-joke that got out of hand and took on a life of its own. Here we are, decades later, with a full set of 60 story songs that took almost as long to compose as it took Sir Arthur to write the original stories. And it included a Great Hiatus.

# # # # #

The mists of time have obscured the origins of this project. I had joined the Bootmakers of Toronto in 1978 and over a couple of years vaguely considered the possibility of coming up with a song about some aspect of the Sherlock Holmes world. At a meeting in the autumn of 1980, I suggested gathering together some members of a musical bent to form something which might be called the Speckled Band. That must have got me thinking about the possibility of writing a song (note: it would only be one song) which would retell a story in such great detail that Bootmakers who had not swotted up on the story would have a chance in the quiz (note: despite this, I'm still rubbish at quizzes). The story for the next meeting was The Solitary Cyclist and, sure enough, a folk song of seven verses emerged onto the page. The incoming Meyers (president of the Bootmakers) acquiesced and thus it came to be that at the Bootmaker annual dinner on 31 January 1981 at the Old Mill restaurant in Toronto, trusty guitar in hand, I premiered that song, along with two from Harvey Officer's *A Baker Street Songbook*. The meeting was even written up in the society column of the *Toronto Globe and Mail*. The Solitary Cyclist song was published in *Canadian Holmes* in the summer of 1981. The role of Lassus was created for me on the executive of the Bootmakers.

And so, it continued. The Bootmakers were about two-thirds of their way through the Canon in the Baring-Gould sequence. At almost every meeting I would present a new "story song" along with one or two songs written by others. In 1986 the sequence started over again, this time in order of publication. Most of the songs were written in the 10 days before the meeting, often even less than that. I would start by rereading the story, usually in the two-volume Coles edition pirated from the Doubleday plates, making notes of the names I would have to work into the song. I would then sit down with a wadge of blank paper and try to find a place to start, a rhyming couplet which would set off a cascade of creativity. Usually more than half the song would emerge in that first session, with another a day or two later allowing for completion. Sometimes the melody came with the words, but often it was written afterwards.

After about 15 years of this, I began to lose momentum. By that point I had introduced 46 story songs at Bootmaker meetings. A 47th had been written but a snowstorm prevented me from attending the meeting. However, another project came along. George Vanderburgh of the Battered Silicon Dispatch Box suggested a collection of songs, which became *Singalong with Sherlock Holmes* (1995). It contained about 20 original songs and 80 collected songs from a variety of international sources. I deliberately did not include any story songs as I intended to collect them eventually into the volume you are now holding; little did I know that this would take a further 25 years.

Then in 1999 I had the opportunity to take a job in Britain and the project went on hold, the Great Hiatus. By that point I fully intended to complete the entire run of 60 story songs before I died. The remaining Baker Street dozen songs were constantly nagging me. In 2007 I began to wonder if I would ever be able to write again, so I looked at the list and the first missing song was A Case of Identity. Taking the same approach as previously, within a few hours the song was no longer missing.

Eight years later I took early retirement and no longer had an excuse for procrastination. The planets aligned in January 2016 when Deborah went away for a week to visit her family in true Mary Morstan fashion. A few weeks earlier there had been a radio interview with Joan Baez in which she talked about the brief period in the early 1960s when she lived in Greenwich Village with Bob Dylan during his most creative period. How did he fuel that creativity? Was it drugs? Well, it turned out to be somewhat more prosaic. He would drink coffee all morning, then red wine all afternoon and evening. So, I thought, that's doable, though the wine should be a bit special. I bought a bottle of entry-level Chateauneuf du Pape. On the Tuesday morning I had an extra cup or two of coffee (I'm an "Everything in moderation" type of guy). At about 1 PM I uncorked the bottle, decanted the beeswing, and poured myself a glass. I sat down with a wadge of blank paper and in a couple of hours, The Crooked Man was complete. But it was only mid-afternoon and there was still plenty of wine left. Is there another song in that bottle, I wondered? The next missing song was The Five Orange Pips. I quickly reread it, refilled my glass, and sat down with another wadge of blank paper. A couple more hours and the job was done.

The pace of two songs in one afternoon was never repeated, but progress continued over the next two years even without the stimulus of vintage wine. One of these songs was Shoscombe Old Place. I had started two write it in March 1984 but ran out of time before the meeting; when I came back to it in February 2017 I still had my original notes and initial verses, despite living at 15 addresses in the intervening 33 years. In November 2017 I finished the 60th song, fittingly (and deliberately) His Last Bow.

# # # # #

It was a tacit decision that the songs would be written with original music. This likely occurred for four reasons.

Firstly, it is what I was doing at the time. In the mid- to late-1970s I had been writing satirical songs for revues at university and settings of Biblical texts (how's that for breadth?), all with original music.

Secondly, it continues the tradition of Harvey Officer. I had received a photocopy of Officer's *A Baker Street Song Book* (New York: The Pamphlet House, 1943) from Cameron Hollyer on one of my first visits to the Arthur Conan Doyle Collection at the

Toronto Reference Library. Granted, Officer's most widely known song is "The Road to Baker Street" written to the tune of "On the Road to Mandalay."

Thirdly, it continues the tradition of one of my heroes, Tom Lehrer, whose satirical songs were a holy grail which I pursued. Granted, one of Lehrer's most popular songs is "The Elements", sung to the tune of "I am the very model of a modern major general" from Gilbert and Sullivan's *The Pirates of Penzance*.

Fourthly, and most importantly, it gave me total flexibility in terms of form, metre, and rhyme scheme. And, indeed, I did start work on each song with a blank page and no preconceptions. For the most part. On a few occasions a snippet had occurred to me in advance of the initial formal writing session.

Despite these advantages of original music, there is one massive downside: it makes the song inaccessible beyond the initial audience. At least, until this book came along.

# # # # #

The music encompasses a variety of styles. While many songs could be classed as generic trad folk or folk rock, there are a number of pastiches of familiar styles: Gilbert and Sullivan patter songs (the Modern Major General makes several fleeting appearances), Victorian music hall, and one even verging on punk rock. Several are specific to the topic of the story: sea shanty (Black Peter), rhumba (The Dancing Men, the Sussex Vampire), bouzouki (The Greek Interpreter), country and western (The Three Garridebs), military band (The Naval Treaty), rugby song (The Missing Three-Quarter), and drinking song (The Six Napoleons).

There are also brief quotations of familiar music: "The Bridal Chorus" and "The Wedding March" in The Noble Bachelor, "Alberta Bound" in the Gloria Scott, "Waltzing Matilda" in the Abbey Grange, "The Hornpipe" in the Bruce-Partington Plans, "Matilda" in the Sussex Vampire, and an extended use of "Home on the Range" in A Study in Scarlet. The Musgrave Ritual makes use of Harvey Officer's setting of the chant.

The songs were written to be performed once, by a singer with a guitar. When it came to writing down the notation for posterity, many problems emerged. Verses differed, with eighth notes fitting two syllables to a quarter note in some cases, the presence or absence of pickup notes, etc. In the process of notation of the songs over the last few years, many of these anomalies have been ironed out. Notably, the final dozen songs, written in a leisurely manner post retirement rather than to the deadline of a meeting, tend to be much more regular in their metre. Notation was generated using a package called Sibelius.

Finally, I must acknowledge the influence of Gordon Lightfoot, whose music I have been enjoying for more than 50 years. There is a general influence of his folk ballads, while at least three of the songs are in a definite Lightfoot musical style. And the instrumentation of the YouTube recordings – acoustic guitars and electric bass – reflect early Lightfoot performances. (My YouTube channel is Sherlock Songs.)

To those of you who heard performances at Bootmaker or Spence Munro (Halifax, Nova Scotia) meetings (or ASH, Bimetallic Question or Sherlock Holmes Society of London events), I hope this book reinforces fond memories. And to those for whom this is new, I hope you enjoy it!

Jim Ballinger, MBt
Halifax, Nova Scotia

October, 2021

Section 1:
The Adventures of Sherlock Holmes

A Scandal in Bohemia

by Jim Ballinger

13

Saw the Great De - tec - tive vexed. To her none could hold a can - dle In her Bo - he - mi - an scan - dal.

She's one dame Holmes could-n't han - dle. It's scan-dal ous!_ Scan-dal ous!_

Scan-dal- ous!

A Scandal in Bohemia

It's scandalous!
For a newly-married doctor
To forsake his lovely wife
And, here's what really shocked her,
To resume the bach'lor life
In Bohemian apartments
Overlooking Baker Street
As if to be apart meant
To him nothing indiscreet

It's scandalous!
For a European king
To pay a visit in disguise
As if a normal thing
To wear a mask across the eyes
And to hire a detective
To retrieve a photograph
Out of nothing but invective
It's enough to make one laugh

It's scandalous!
For a drunken-looking groom
When at a wedding ceremony
To vouch for things in whom
He turns out nothing but a phony
The Adler-Norton marriage
Fraught with legal imperfections
They leave in separate carriages
In opposite directions

It's scandalous!
For a Nonconformist parson
To affect a fainting spell
And to follow it with arson:
It's a ticket straight to hell
The object of charade
Is entry to a lady's parlour
And when the smoke is made
In her instinctiveness to snarl her

It's scandalous!
For a wife-deserting medic
To conceal inside his pocket
An object of discredit
In form of a plumber's rocket
Then to throw this little toy
And cry that fire would engulf:
Watson, think about the boy
Who once too often did cry wolf

It's scandalous!
For a Victorian female
To disguise her superb figure
And in effect to be male
And to walk the streets with vigour
To taunt the Great Detective
By saluting him "Good night"
And, what's worse, to be effective
And the victor in the fight

It's scandalous!
For Sherlock Holmes to be defeated
It's scandalous
For a mere woman to win
Irene, alone of all her sex
Saw the Great Detective vexed
To her none could hold a candle
In her Bohemian scandal
She's one dame Holmes couldn't handle
It's scandalous, scandalous,
scandalous!

The Red-Headed League

by Jim Ballinger

Come, all red-head-ed men, You need ne'er work a-gain. The in-cum-bent we seek will earn four pounds a week in the

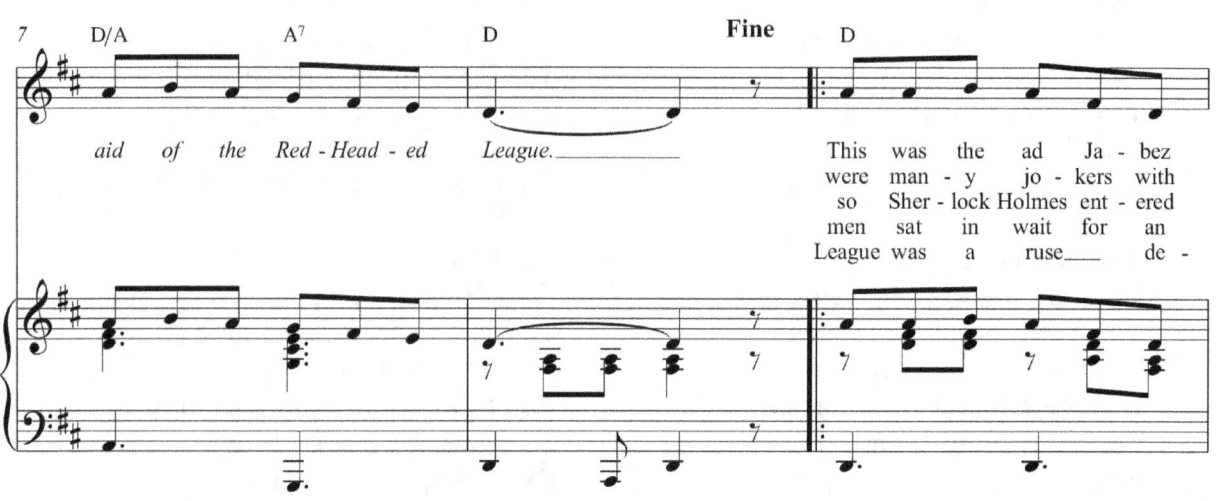

aid of the Red-Head-ed League._____

This was the ad Ja-bez
were man-y jo-kers with so
Sher-lock Holmes ent-ered
men sat in wait for an
League was a ruse__ de-

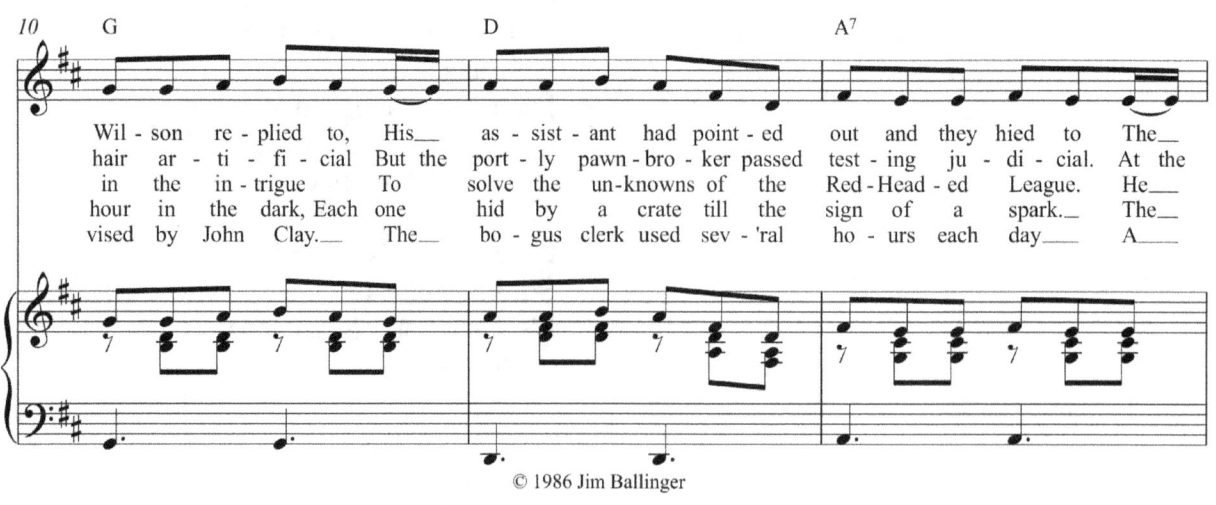

Wil-son re-plied to, His__ as-sist-ant had point-ed out and they hied to The__
hair ar-ti-fi-cial But the port-ly pawn-bro-ker passed test-ing ju-di-cial. At the
in the in-trigue To solve the un-knowns of the Red-Head-ed League. He__
hour in the dark, Each one hid by a crate till the sign of a spark._ The__
vised by John Clay.__ The__ bo-gus clerk used sev-'ral ho-urs each day____ A____

16

The Red-Headed League

Come, all red-headed men
You need ne'er work again
The incumbent we seek
Will earn four pounds a week
In the aid of the Red-Headed League

This was the ad
Jabez Wilson replied to
His assistant had
Pointed out and they hied to
The Pope's Court address
Where a sea of red tresses
Attended the Red-Headed League

There were many jokers
With hair artificial
But the portly pawnbroker
Passed testing judicial
At the labour he balks:
Be a human Xerox???
In employ of the Red-Headed League

Each day, ten till two
Jabez Wilson transcribed
Eight weeks he went through
The A's, near bleary-eyed
Till a note on the door
Said the League was no more
The demise of the Red-Headed League

And so Sherlock Holmes
Entered in the intrigue
To solve the unknowns
Of the Red-Headed League
He first set his mark
On the pawnbroker's clerk
In the case of the Red-Headed League

That evening at ten
At the Baker Street rooms
There gathered four men
Who set out for the tombs
Through locked doors, dark and dank
'Neath the Saxe-Coburg bank
They awaited the Red-Headed League

The men sat in wait
For an hour in the dark
Each one hid by a crate
Till the sign of a spark
The chink in the floor
Opened wider once more
The climax of the Red-Headed League

They captured John Clay
Rising up through the floor
His pal got away
But was caught at the door
The bullion was saved
From a blue-blooded knave
In the end of the Red-Headed League

The League was a ruse
Devised by John Clay
The bogus clerk used
Several hours each day
A tunnel to bore
To the bank from the store
With the aid of the Red-Headed
League

Come, all red-headed men
You need ne'er work again
The incumbent we seek
Will earn four pounds a week
In the aid of the Red-Headed League

A Case of Identity

by Jim Ballinger

♩. = 60

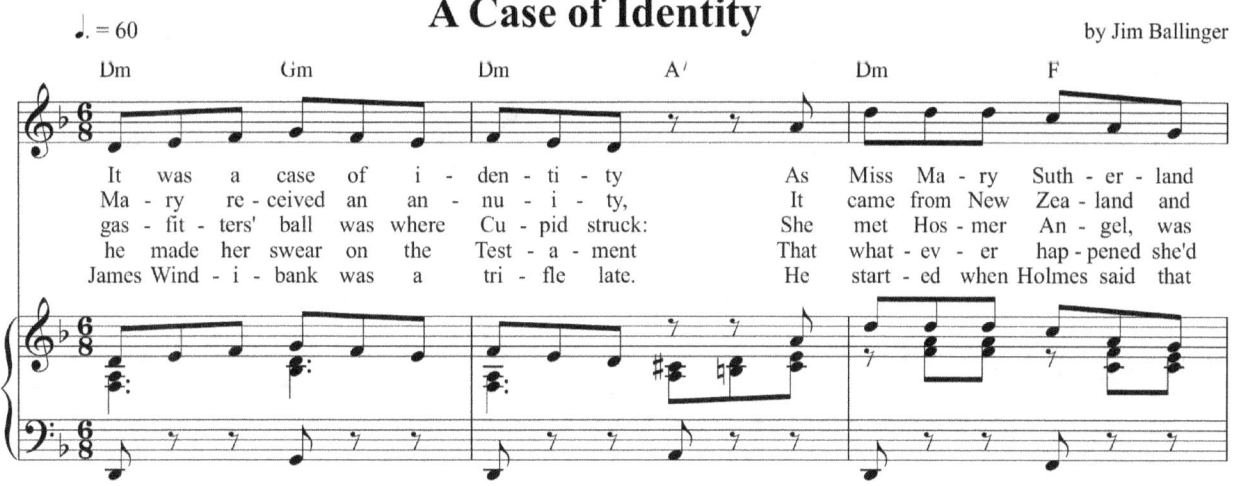

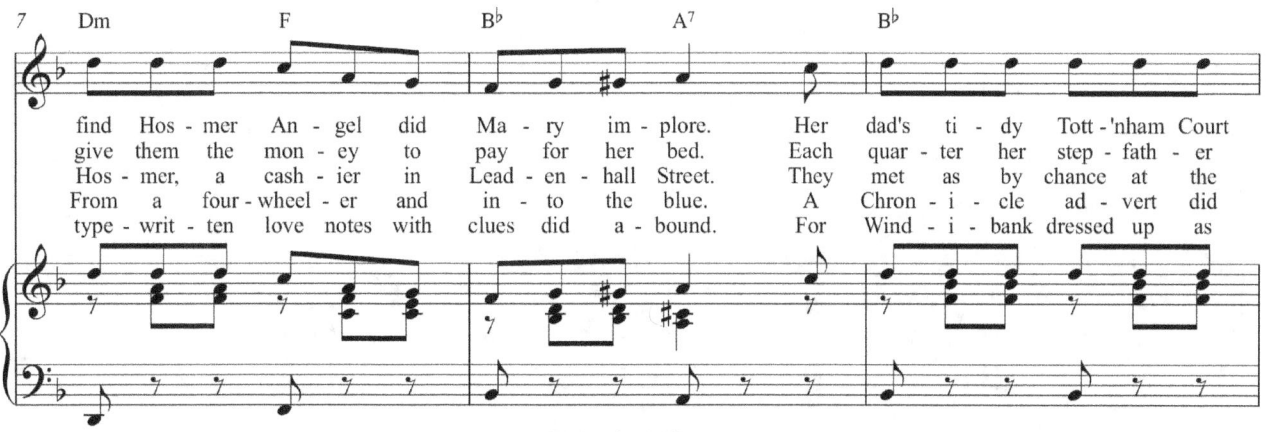

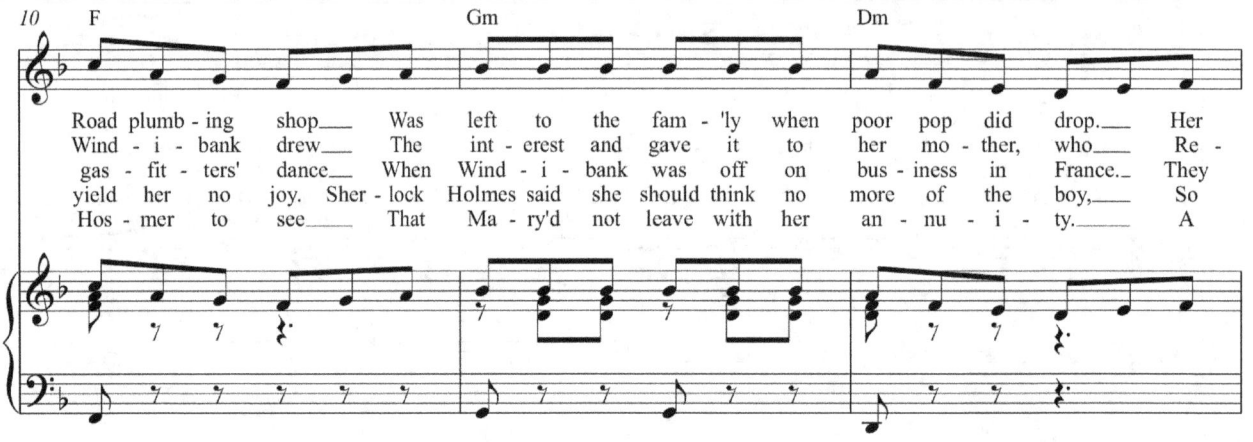

Road plumb - ing shop___ Was left to the fam - 'ly when poor pop did drop.___ Her
Wind - i - bank drew___ The int - erest and gave it to her mo - ther, who___ Re -
gas - fit - ters' dance When Wind - i - bank was off on bus - iness in France.___ They
yield her no joy. Sher - lock Holmes said she should think no more of the boy,___ So

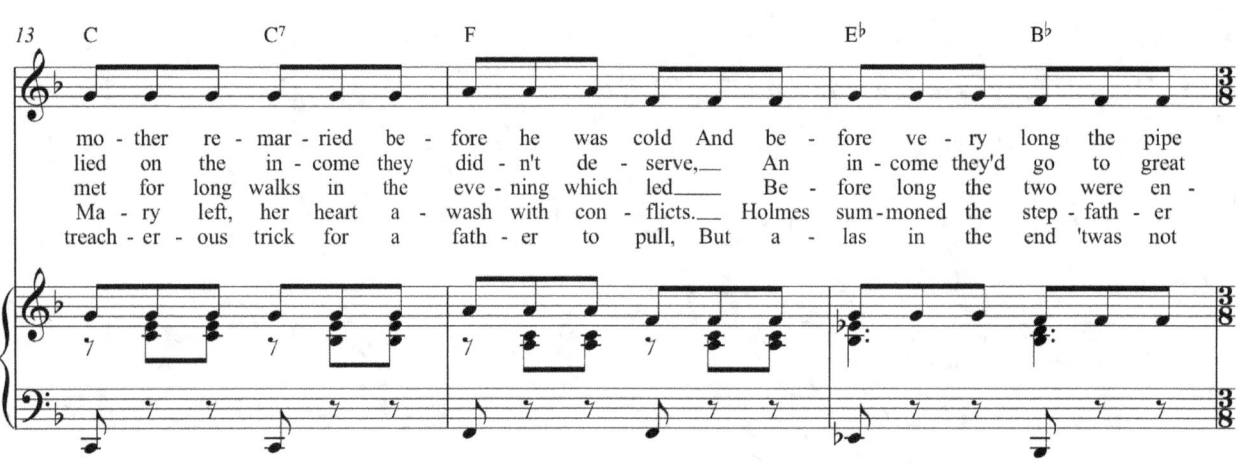

mo - ther re - mar - ried be - fore he was cold And be - fore ve - ry long the pipe
lied on the in - come they did - n't de - serve,___ An in - come they'd go to great
met for long walks in the eve - ning which led___ Be - fore long the two were en -
Ma - ry left, her heart a - wash with con - flicts.___ Holmes sum - moned the step - fath - er

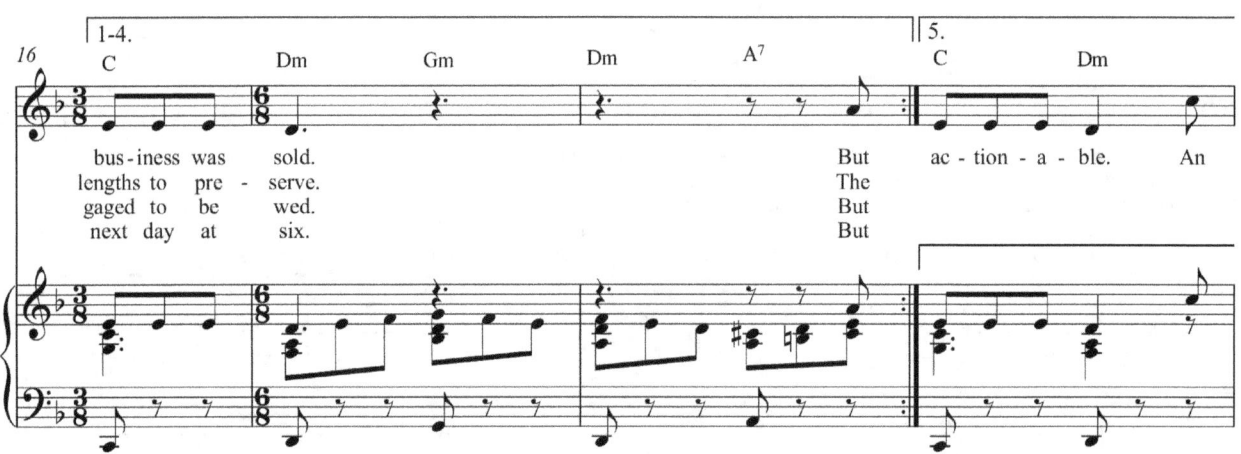

bus - iness was sold. But ac - tion - a - ble. An
lengths to pre - serve. The
gaged to be wed. But
next day at six. But

20

An - gel named Hos - mer had come in her life, An an - gel who'd said he would make her his wife. Poor

short-sight - ed Ma - ry S ne - ver would see that to Holmes it was a Case of I - den - ti - ty.

A Case of Identity

It was a case of identity
As Miss Mary Sutherland burst through the door
Result of the Etherege mystery
To find Hosmer Angel did Mary implore
Her dad's tidy Tottenham Court Road plumbing shop
Was left to the family when poor pop did drop
Her mother remarried before he was cold
And before very long the pipe business was sold

But Mary received an annuity
It came from New Zealand and old uncle Ned
Since she lived at home 'twas her duity
To give them the money to pay board and bed
Each quarter her step-father Windibank drew
The interest and gave it to her mother, who
Relied on the income they didn't deserve
An income they'd go to great lengths to preserve

The gasfitters' ball was where Cupid struck
She met Hosmer Angel, was swept off her feet
And young Mary could not believe her luck
With Hosmer, a cashier in Leadenhall Street
They met as by chance at the gasfitters' dance
When Windibank was off on business in France
They met for long walks in the evening which led
Before long the two were engaged to be wed

But he made her swear on the Testament
That whatever happened she'd always be true
Upon the morn of the wedding he went
From a four-wheeler and into the blue
A Chronicle advert did yield her no joy
Sherlock Holmes said she should think no more of the boy
So Mary left, her heart awash with conflicts
Holmes summoned the step-father next day at six

But James Windibank was a trifle late
He started when Holmes said that Hosmer was found
By locking the door, Holmes had caught the rake
The typewritten love notes with clues did abound
For Windibank dressed up as Hosmer to see
That Mary'd not leave with her annuity
A treacherous trick for a father to pull
But alas in the end 'twas not actionable

An Angel named Hosmer had come in her life
An angel who promised to make her his wife
Poor short-sighted Mary S never would see
That to Holmes it was A Case of Identity

The Boscombe Valley Mystery

by Jim Ballinger

24

Bos-combe Val-ley. Young Al-ice Tur-ner, a friend of Mc-Car-thy, re-tained Sher-lock Holmes and Les-
kil-ler, John Tur-ner, the young la-dy's fath-er, had known the de-ceased in Aus-

trade._ She knew the quar-rel con-cerned their re-la-tion-ship which old Mc-Car-thy saw
tral-ia. Mc-Car-thy, a dev-il in-car-nate, had shown up to black-mail, re-deem-ing his

made. But they loved each oth-er like sis-ter and bro-ther, for it to re-main such was
fail-ure. The screws were turned tight-er by this dir-ty blight-er who want-ed a wife for his

best._____ Like bro-ther and sis-ter he'd scarce e-ven kissed her and fur-ther would make it in-cest.
son._____ This fate for young Al-ice filled Tur-ner with ma-lice, in sec-onds the deed had been done.

The Boscombe Valley Mystery

Have you a couple of days to spare
Come and partake of west country air
Paddington Station from whence we'll sally
Forth to the mystery of Boscombe Valley

There Charles McCarthy has been found dead
Stretched out beside a pool, bashed-in head
He was last seen quarrelling with his son
Found by the same when the deed was done

Young James McCarthy has been arrested
"I didn't kill my Dad," he attested
"We had an argument that day, yes
What it concerned I cannot confess."

Young Alice Turner, a friend of McCarthy
Retained Sherlock Holmes and Lestrade
She knew the quarrel concerned their relationship
Which old McCarthy saw made
But they loved each other like sister and brother
For it to remain such was best
Like brother and sister, he'd scarce even kissed her
And further would make it incest

Sherlock examined the scene of crime
Flat on his face in the dust and grime
There he discovered cigars and tracks
And put Lestrade on the killer's back

The killer, John Turner, the young lady's father
Had known the deceased in Australia
McCarthy, a devil incarnate, had shown up
To blackmail, redeeming his failure
The screws were turned tighter by this dirty blighter
Who wanted a wife for his son
This fate for young Alice filled Turner with malice
In seconds the deed had been done

Within a few months the old man died
Young James McCarthy acquitted when tried
Then James and Alice got deeply pally
After the mystery of Boscombe Valley

The Five Orange Pips

by Jim Ballinger

'Twas a dark and storm-y night when John Op-en-shaw ar-rived in Ba-ker
took a shine to John and in-vit-ed him to man-age the es-
se-ven weeks had passed in a drunk-en stu-por un-cle was found
three or four days passed in an un-fenced chalk-pit John's dad was found
Sher-lock Holmes' ad-vice Op-en-shaw set off for Hor-sham by the

Street. Sher-lock begged him to re-cite the es-sen-tial facts, con-cise and yet com-
tate, But it did-n't last for long, tenth of March in eight-een eight-y three the
dead. As the orange pips had fore-cast, in the un-cle's will John's dad in-her-i-
dead. The in-her-i-tance now passed to John Op-en-shaw him-self, 'twas on his
train. But it did-n't end up nice for he fell in-to the riv-er in the

plete. For his un-cle e-mi-grat-ed to A-mer-i-ca when young, As a
date. For a let-ter came from In-di-a, ac-cord-ing to the stamp, It was
ted. They ex-am-ined the locked at-tic but the let-ters had been burned, And the
head. And for two years and eight months he lived as hap-py as a clam And he
rain. Holmes de-duced the let-ters which con-tained the dead-ly five orange pips Had been

plant-er based in Flo-ri-da a mas-sive for-tune sprung, But he
post-marked Pon-di-cher-ry, that was quite a gal-li-vant. When he
great brass box was emp-ty, save for K K K dis-cerned. And in
thought the curse had passed a-way, no long-er gave a damn. But the
post-ed by a Klans-man who was still a-board a ship. And by

13 Gm⁷   A⁷   F   Gm⁶   A⁷

dis - liked the Re - pub - li - cans, to Eng-land he re - turned, An es - tate near Hor-sham Sus - sex where all
op - ened up the en - vel - ope his face be - gan to change, And his skin turned put - ty col-oured at the
Jan - u - a - ry eight - y - five a let - ter from Dun - dee Which in - struct - ed them to put the pap - ers
blow fell with an en - ve - lope, East Lon-don the post-mark, And its all fam - i - liar con-tents which no
pro - cess of e - lim - i - na - tion that was the Lone Star, But the ship was lost in e - quin - oc - tial

16 A⁷   1. Dm   2,3,4,5. Dm   Dm   Gm   Am⁷

com - pan - y he spurned. Un-cle
con-tents might - y_____ strange. It held five orange pips and the let-ters K K K, And with
on the sun - dial; see It held five orange pips and the let-ters K K K, With con -
long - er seemed a_____ lark. It held five orange pips and the let-ters K K K, Like a
gales on seas a - - - far. And the five orange pips with the let-ters K K K 'board the

21 Dm   Gm   Am⁷   1,2,3. Dm   4. Dm

trem - bling lips Old E - li - as was heard say: "It means death." Af - ter death.
tempt he dripped, we can't have tom-fool - er - y. It means death. Af - ter
rab - bit gripped by a snake, can't get a - way. It means death. And on
Lone Star ship from fate could not get a - way. It meant

28

The Five Orange Pips

'Twas a dark and stormy night
When John Openshaw arrived in Baker Street
Sherlock begged him to recite
The essential facts, concise and yet complete
For his uncle emigrated to America when young
As a planter based in Florida a massive fortune sprung
But he disliked the Republicans, to England he returned
An estate near Horsham Sussex where all company he spurned

Uncle took a shine to John
And invited him to manage the estate
But it didn't last for long
Tenth of March in 1883 the date
For a letter came from India, according to the stamp
It was postmarked Pondicherry, that was quite a gallivant
When he opened up the envelope his face began to change
And his skin turned putty coloured at the contents mighty strange

It held five orange pips
And the letters KKK
And with trembling lips
Old Elias was heard say
"It means death"

After seven weeks had passed
In a drunken stupor uncle was found dead
As the orange pips had forecast
In the uncle's will John's dad inherited
They examined the locked attic but the letters had been burned
And the great brass box was empty, save for KKK discerned
And in January '85 a letter from Dundee
Which instructed them to put the papers on the sundial; see

It held five orange pips
And the letters KKK
With contempt he dripped
We can't have tomfoolery
It means death

After three or four days passed
In an unfenced chalk pit John's dad was found dead
The inheritance now passed
To John Openshaw himself, 'twas on his head
And for two years and eight months he lived as happy as a clam
And he thought the curse has passed away, no longer gave a damn
But the blow fell with an envelope, East London the postmark
And its all familiar contents which no longer seemed a lark

It held five orange pips
And the letters KKK
Like a rabbit gripped
By a snake, can't get away
It means death

And on Sherlock Holmes' advice
Openshaw set off for Horsham by the train
But it didn't end up nice
For he fell into the river in the rain
Holmes deduced the letters which contained the deadly five orange pips
Had been posted by a Klansman who was still aboard a ship
And by process of elimination that was the Lone Star
But the ship was lost in equinoctial gales on seas afar

And the five orange pips
With the letters KKK
'board the Lone Star ship
From fate could not get away
It meant death

The Man with the Twisted Lip

by Jim Ballinger

31

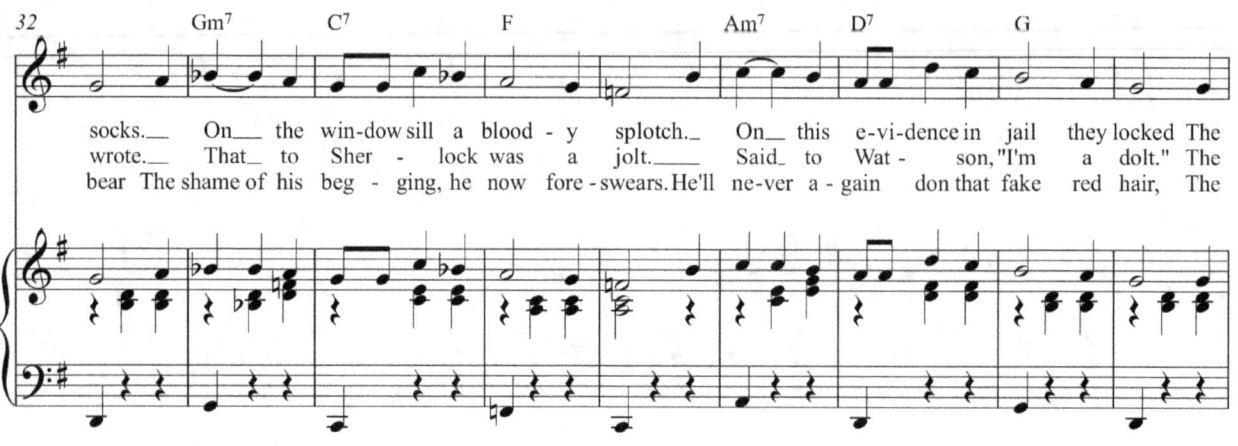

socks.___ On___ the win-dow sill a blood - y splotch.___ On___ this e-vi-dence in jail they locked The
wrote.___ That___ to Sher - lock was a jolt.___ Said___ to Wat - son, "I'm a dolt." The
bear The shame of his beg - ging, he now fore - swears. He'll ne-ver a - gain don that fake red hair, The

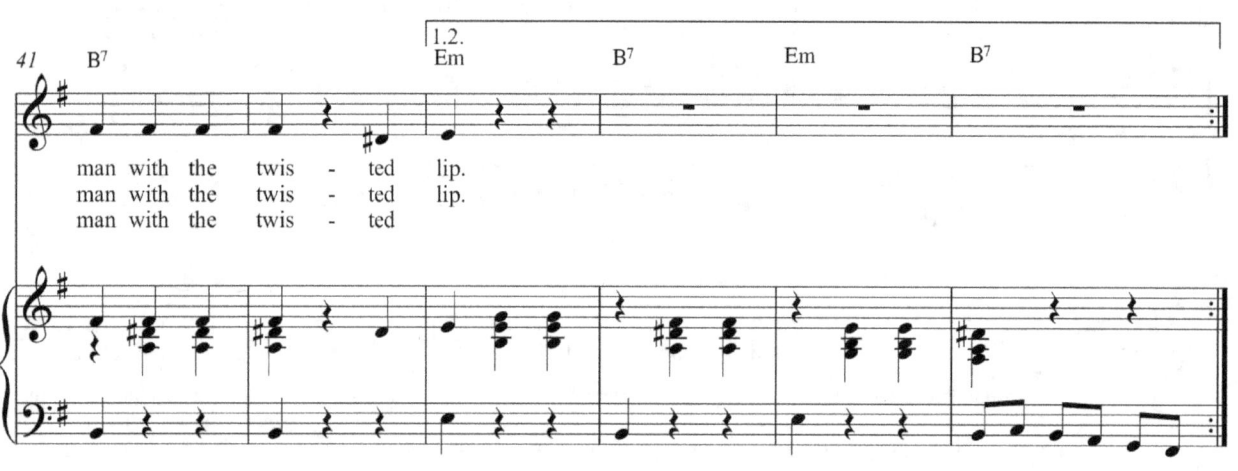

man with the twis - ted lip.
man with the twis - ted lip.
man with the twis - ted

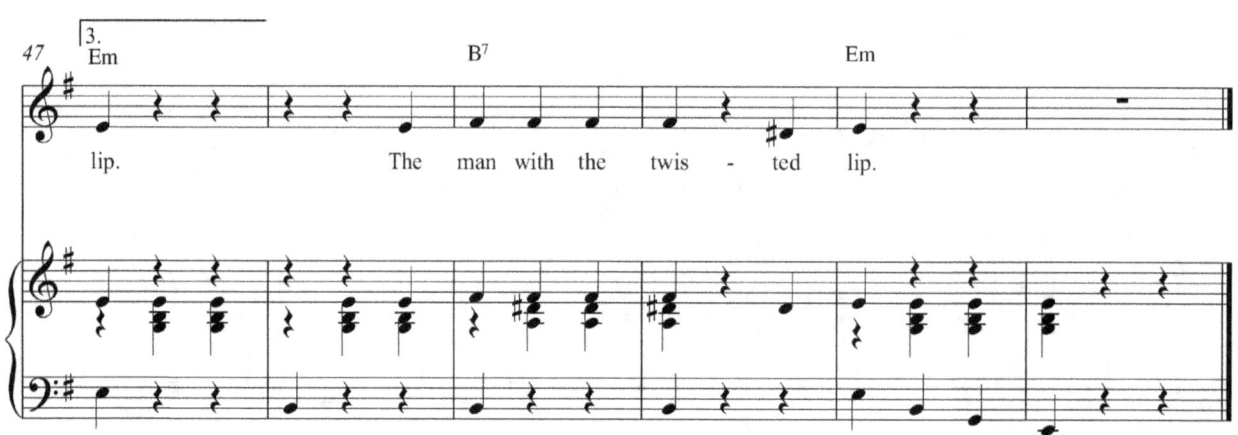

lip.   The man with the twis - ted lip.

The Man with the Twisted Lip

Mrs Neville St Clair
Saw her husband at the window of an opium den
But when she got upstairs
She found no-one but a beggar, 'twas the vilest of men
In the room were some building blocks
A present for her son
Her husband's watch and hat, boots and socks
On the window-sill a bloody splotch
On this evidence in jail they locked
The man with the twisted lip

When the tide had gone out
They found Neville St Clair's jacket weighted down with loose change
His corpse was nowhere about
But the next day there came something that was even more strange
Neville's wife received a note
Posted that very day
"Don't be frightened", Neville wrote
That to Sherlock was a jolt
Said to Watson, "I'm a dolt"
The man with the twisted lip

Holmes and Watson set out
For the Bow Street police station where the beggar was in grip
Holmes extinguished all doubt
With a bath sponge filled with water he untwisted the lip
The beggar turned out to be St Clair
More lucrative than honest work
He didn't want his children to bear
The shame of his begging, he now foreswears
He'll never again don that fake red hair
The man with the twisted lip

The Blue Carbuncle

by Jim Ballinger

34

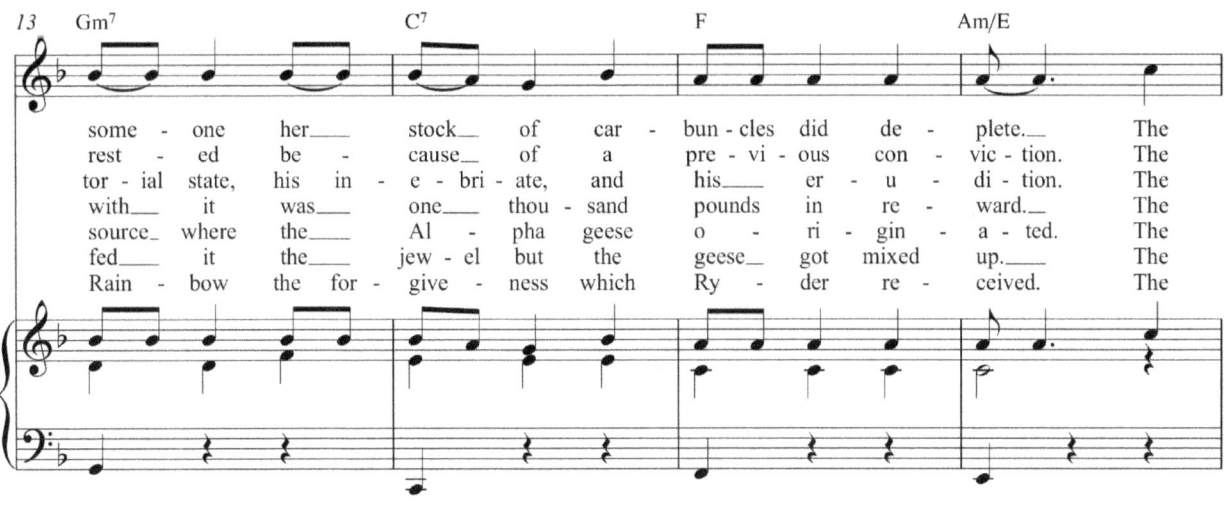

some - one her___ stock___ of car - bun - cles did de - plete.___ The
rest - ed be - cause___ of a pre - vi - ous con - vic - tion. The
tor - ial state, his in - e - bri - ate, and his___ er - u - di - tion. The
with___ it was___ one___ thou - sand pounds in re - ward.___ The
source_ where the___ Al - pha geese o - ri - gin - a - ted. The
fed___ it the___ jew - el but the geese___ got mixed up.___ The
Rain - bow the for - give - ness which Ry - der re - ceived. The

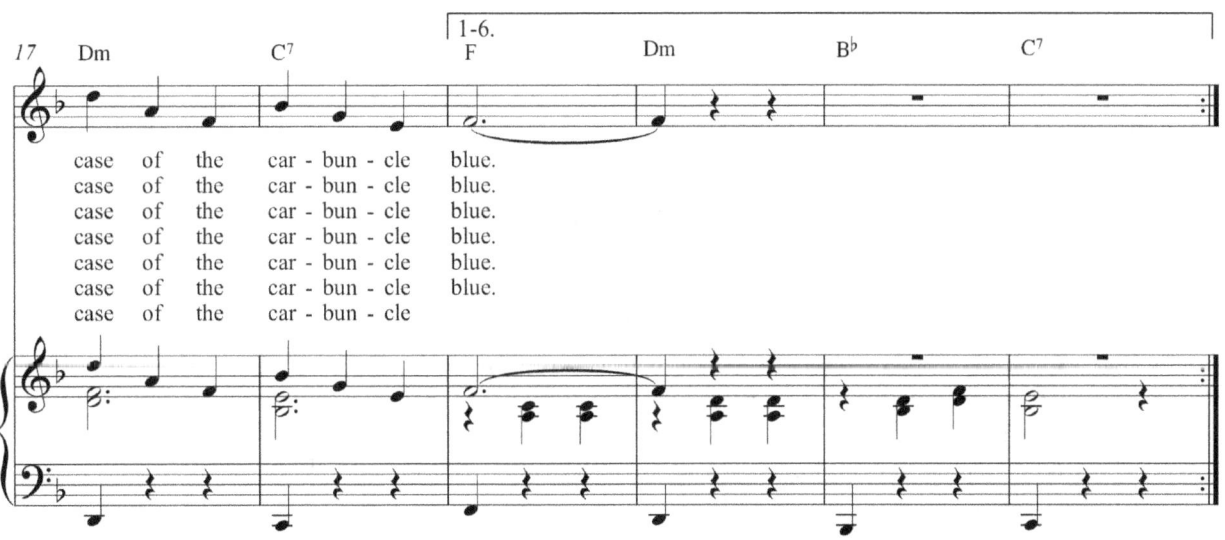

| 1-6. |
case of the car - bun - cle blue.
case of the car - bun - cle blue.
case of the car - bun - cle blue.
case of the car - bun - cle blue.
case of the car - bun - cle blue.
case of the car - bun - cle blue.
case of the car - bun - cle

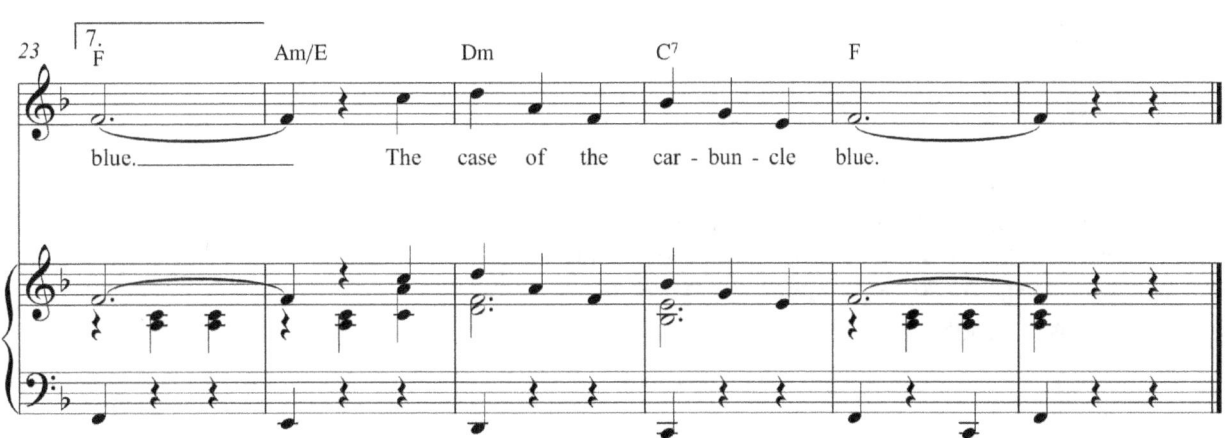

7.
blue._____ The case of the car - bun - cle blue.

The Blue Carbuncle

Blue was the colour of the carbuncle which disappeared
From the Hotel Cosmopolitan on December twenty-two
The Countess of Morcar was out of her suite
When someone her stock of carbuncles did deplete
The case of the carbuncle blue

Red was the colour of the Countess Morcar's countenance
Until they found a suspect who in prison they threw
John Horner, a plumber, had been doing some fixin'
Was arrested because of a previous conviction
The case of the carbuncle blue

Black was the colour of the felt hat discovered
By Peterson, commissionaire, when its owner turned and flew
From it Sherlock Holmes deduced its owner's condition
His sartorial state, his inebriate, and his erudition
The case of the carbuncle blue

White was the colour of the goose that laid the golden egg
When Mrs Peterson was preparing it to stew
The jewel was found as the crop she explored
And with it was one thousand pounds in reward
The case of the carbuncle blue

Pink was the colour of the racing forum Breckinridge
Did carry in his pocket at his Covent Garden venue
In the form of a lost wager Holmes extricated
The source where the Alpha geese originated
The case of the carbuncle blue

Yellow was the colour of the stripe on James Ryder
Who'd stolen the jewel with the lady's maid, too
He'd chosen the Christmas goose on which he'd sup
And fed it the jewel but the geese got mixed up
The case of the carbuncle blue

Green was the colour of the Christmas tree at Baker Street
Golden was the colour of the cooked goose's hue
White was the wine which in the ice bucket breathed
Rainbow the forgiveness which Ryder received
The case of the carbuncle blue

The Speckled Band

by Jim Ballinger

37

father, Grimes-by Roy-lott, fol-lowed He-len up___ to Lon-don To warn Holmes not to
Holmes and Wat-son spent the night in that room (with-out He-len)_____ Sat till nigh three

med-dle in his plan._____ He knot-ted up___ a po-ker, which Holmes
thir-ty in the gloom._____ Sud-den-ly Holmes lashed out with his

own strength soon had un done, And Holmes and Wat-son left for Stoke Mo-ran._____ In-
cane and start-ed yel-lin', Soon drowned out by a shriek from the next room.

Coda

Band. The Ssss - - peck-led Band.

The Speckled Band

Her name was Julia Stoner and she was soon to be wed
She'd heard at night a whistle as she lay upon her bed
Then one night she screamed wildly and proceeded to drop dead
It was the speckled band

Her sister went to Sherlock Holmes 'cause what's a girl to do
For she became betrothed and then she heard the whistle too
She feared her death was imminent and that it would be due
To the speckled band

Her father, Grimesby Roylott, followed Helen up to London
To warn Holmes not to meddle in his plan
He knotted up a poker, which Holmes own strength soon had undone
And Holmes and Watson left for Stoke Moran

Inspecting the dead sister's room, the bed clamped to the floor
A bell-pull not connected to a bell, and there was more
A ventilator to the next room, what could it be for?
Maybe the speckled band

Holmes and Watson spent the night in that room (without Helen)
Sat till nigh three thirty in the gloom
Suddenly Holmes lashed out with his cane and started yelling
Soon drowned out by a shriek from the next room

Entering, they found Roylott, a band around his head
Seated on a chair, his eyes the fixed stare of the dead
The band was a swamp adder, Holmes soon back to its vault led
The speckled band

The Engineer's Thumb

by Jim Ballinger

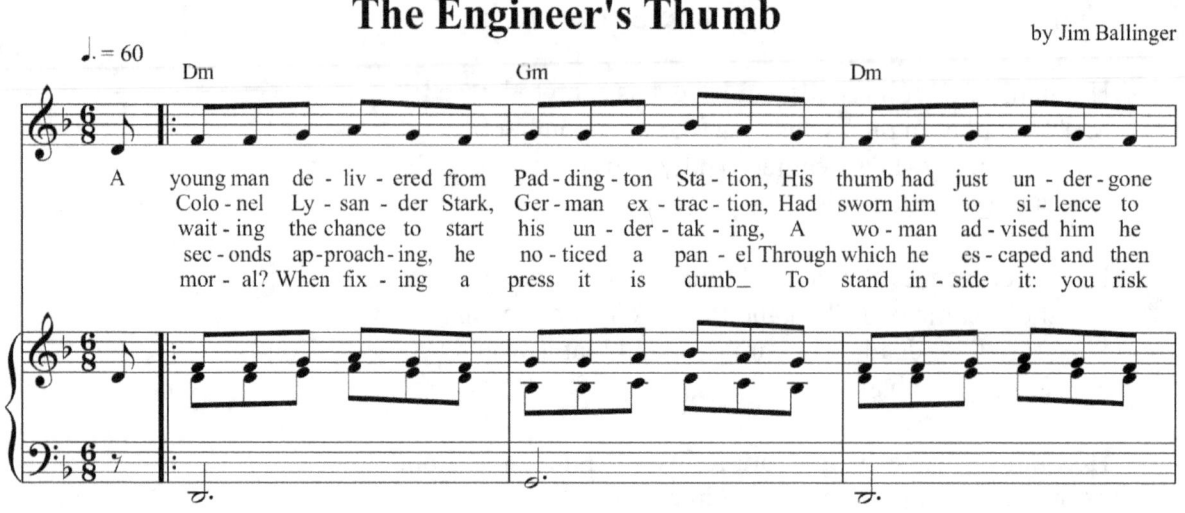

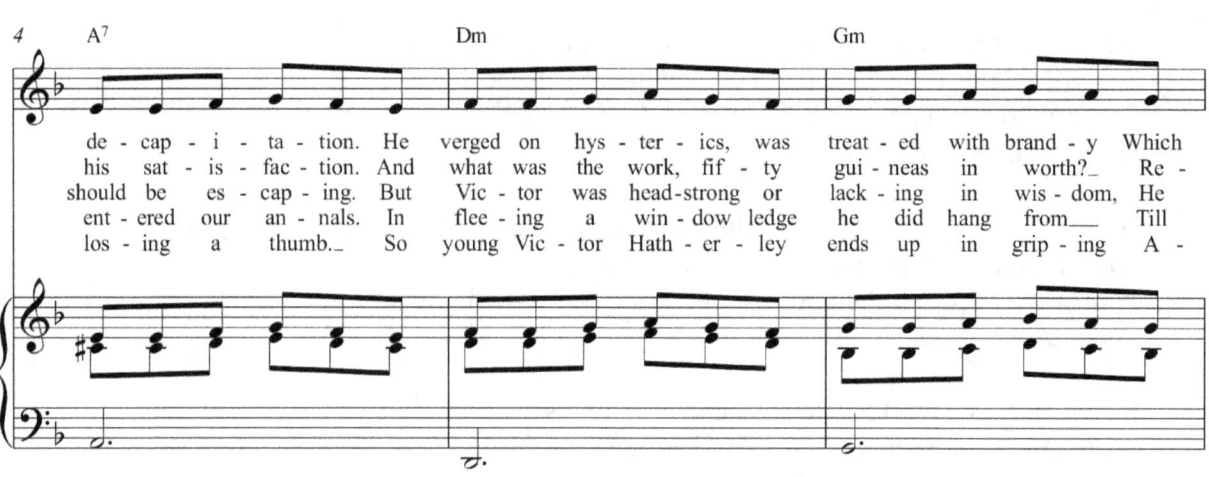

young Vic - tor Hath - er - ly, versed in hy - draul - ics, Re - count - ed the tale of his
Ey - ford, in Berk - shire, a few miles from Read - ing, He was at e - lev - en - fif -
fixed it in no time, what thanks did the man make? He turned on the press to squish
wak - ing next morn - ing, not far from the sta - tion, Re - ceiv - ing from Wat - son, then

e - ven - ing's fro - lics. In bus - i - ness for two years, the tak - ings were skin - ny, Then
teen that night head - ing. A fresh horse and car - riage were there at the sta - tion And
Vic to a pan - cake. They say cur - i - ous - i - ty 'twas killed the cat; Well,
Sher - lock, li - ba - tion. Re - turn - ing with help, the house burnt to the ground. The

of - fered for one eve - ning's work fif - ty gui - neas. A
drove for an ho - ur to their des - tin - a - tion. While
Vic learned his les - son in one min - ute flat. Last
mur - der - ous count - er - feit - ers ne - ver found. The

Coda

that pro-found thought we have fin - al - ly come To the end of the case of the En - gin-eer's Thumb.

41

The Engineer's Thumb

A young man delivered from Paddington Station
His thumb had just undergone decapitation
He verged on hysterics, was treated with brandy
Which good Dr Watson did chance to have handy

For young Victor Hatherley, versed in hydraulics
Recounted the tale of his evening's frolics
In business for two years, the takings were skinny
Then offered for one evening's work fifty guineas

A Colonel Lysander Stark, German extraction
Had sworn him to silence to his satisfaction
And what was the work, fifty guineas in worth?
Repair a machine to compress fuller's earth

To Eyford, in Berkshire, a few miles from Reading
He was at eleven fifteen that night heading
A fresh horse and carriage were there at the station
And drove for an hour to their destination

While waiting the chance to start his undertaking
A woman advised him he should be escaping
But Victor was headstrong or lacking in wisdom
He soon found himself hard at work on the piston

He fixed it in no time, what thanks did the man make?
He turned on the press to squish Vic to a pancake
They say curiousity 'twas killed the cat
Well Vic learned his lesson in one minute flat

Last seconds approaching, he noticed a panel
Through which he escaped and then entered our annals
In fleeing, a window ledge he did hang from
Till Stark with a meat cleaver chopped off his thumb

Awaking next morning, not far from the station
Receiving from Watson then Sherlock libation
Returning with help, the house burnt to the ground
The murderous counterfeiters never found

The moral? When fixing a press it is dumb
To stand inside it: you risk losing a thumb
So young Victor Hatherley ends up in griping
About all the problems he'll have in hitch hiking

With that profound thought we have finally come
To the end of the case of the Engineer's Thumb

The Noble Bachelor

by Jim Ballinger

she dis - ap - peared. Not an aus - pi - cious be - gin - ning, 'twas clear. Les -

♩ = 80

trade came to in - vest - i - gate the mys - t'ry at Lan - cas - ter Gate. He
Hat - ty, af - ter her de - par - ture, was seen walk - ing in Hyde Park With
Sher - lock Holmes be - gan his search with the strange man at the church.

learned a girl named Flo - ra Mil - lar Tried to in - fil - trate the vil - la.
Flo - ra Mil - lar of Al - leg - ro, Straight in - to the jail she did go.
Through a bill for ho - tel fare, Holmes traced the man to Gor - don Square.

Claimed that she was a - mour - euse Of Lord Ro - bert St Si - mon, But
Les - trade dragged the Ser - pen - tine, No bo - dy did it bring. An -
For the wife of Frank Hay Moul - ton was Hat - ty Do - ran.

Les-trade thought this young dans-euse was simp - ly so - cial climb - in'.____
oth - er trea - sure he did find: her wed-ding dress and ring.
Long a - go wed in the gold - en Cal - i - for - nia land.

Ro - bert St Si - mon, the most for - tun - ate of men:

The No - ble Bach - e - lor was free to____ woo a - gain.

The Noble Bachelor

Robert St Simon, Hatty Doran
St George's, Hanover Square was the plan
The wedding breakfast, Lancaster Gate
St Simon ended the day sans a mate
During the service Hatty did change
Dropped her bouquet to a gentleman strange
During the breakfast she disappeared
Not an auspicious beginning, 'twas clear

Lestrade came to investigate
The mystery at Lancaster Gate
He learned a girl named Flora Millar
Tried to infiltrate the villa
Claimed that she was amoureuse
Of Lord Robert St Simon
But Lestrade thought this young danseuse
Was simply social climbin'

Hatty, after her departure
Was seen walking in Hyde Park
With Flora Millar of Allegro
Straight into the jail she did go
Lestrade dragged the Serpentine
No body did it bring
Another treasure he did find
Her wedding dress and ring

Sherlock Holmes began his search
With the strange man from the church
Through a bill for hotel fare
Holmes traced the man to Gordon Square
For the wife of Frank Hay Moulton
Was Hatty Doran
Long ago wed in the golden
California land

Robert St Simon, the most fortunate of men
The noble bachelor was free to woo again

The Beryl Coronet

by Jim Ballinger

He was

tall and port - ly, well dressed as he ran down Bak - er Street__ For
trust - ing of the of - fice safe, Al took the boot - y home__ And
Ar - thur would - n't say__ a - noth - er word a - bout the jewels. His

niece and Sir George Burn - well had been hav - ing an af - fair.__ When

Al - ex - and - er Hold - er was a bank - er, not ath lete. A cli - ent most il - lust - ri - ous had
told his son and niece of the co - lat - er - al and loan. 'Twas no sur - prise he woke that night, dis-
fath - er called on Sher - lock Holmes 'cause Scot - land Yard were fools.____ Holmes ex - am - ined scene of crime, then
George heard of the cor - o - net, he could - n't leave it there. But Ar - thur tried to stop the theft which

bor - rowed fif - ty thou And as sec - ur - i - ty__ the ber - yl cor - o - net en - dowed. Not
cov - er - ing his son__ Was wrest - ling with the cor - o - net, in
went out in dis - guise. He spent a long hard day__ at work and came back with the prize. Al's
Ma - ry did a - bet, And in the scuf - fle George got hurt, as

The Beryl Coronet

He was tall and portly, well-dressed, as he ran down Baker Street
For Alexander Holder was a banker, not athlete
A client most illustrious had borrowed fifty thou
And as security the beryl coronet endowed

Not trusting of the office safe, Al took the booty home
And told his son and niece of the collateral and loan
'Twas no surprise he woke that night, discovering his son
Was wrestling with the coronet, in fact had torn off one

Arthur, you villain, you thief
How dare you touch that coronet and bring your father grief
You blackguard, destroyer, you louse
If that's the way you feel about it, Dad, I'll leave your house

Arthur wouldn't say another word about the jewels
His father called on Sherlock Holmes 'cause Scotland Yard were fools
Holmes examined scene of crime, then went out in disguise
He spent a long hard day at work and came back with the prize

Al's niece and Sir George Burnwell had been having an affair
When George heard of the coronet, he couldn't leave it there
But Arthur tried to stop the theft which Mary did abet
And in the scuffle George got hurt, as did the coronet

Arthur, I must make amends
You took the blame to cover for your cousin and your friend
How noble, my doubts I regret
I hope I'll never see again the beryl coronet

The Copper Beeches

by Jim Ballinger

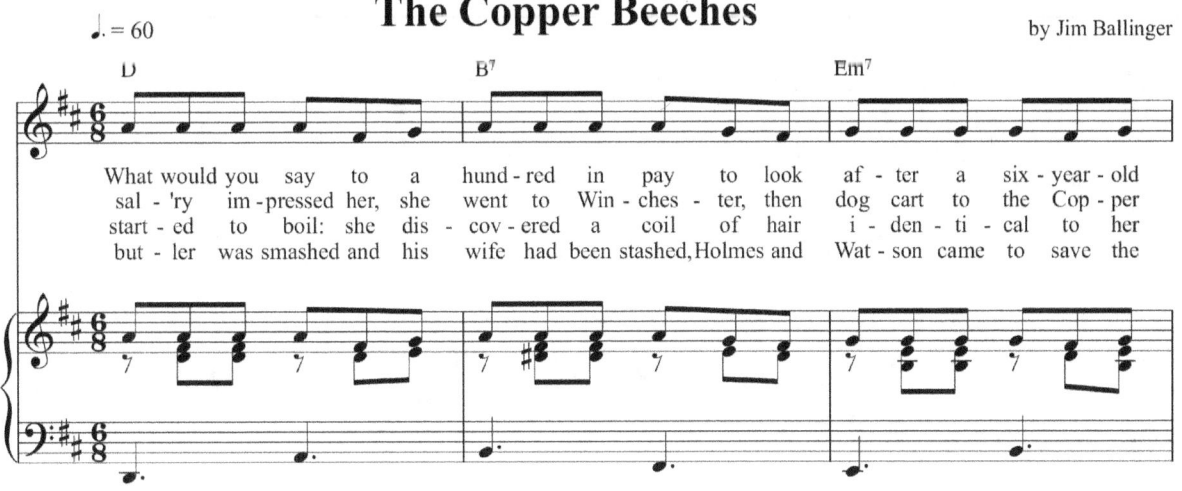

What would you say to a hund-red in pay to look af-ter a six-year-old
sal-'ry im-pressed her, she went to Win-ches-ter, then dog cart to the Cop-per
start-ed to boil: she dis-cov-ered a coil of hair i-den-ti-cal to her
but-ler was smashed and his wife had been stashed, Holmes and Wat-son came to save the

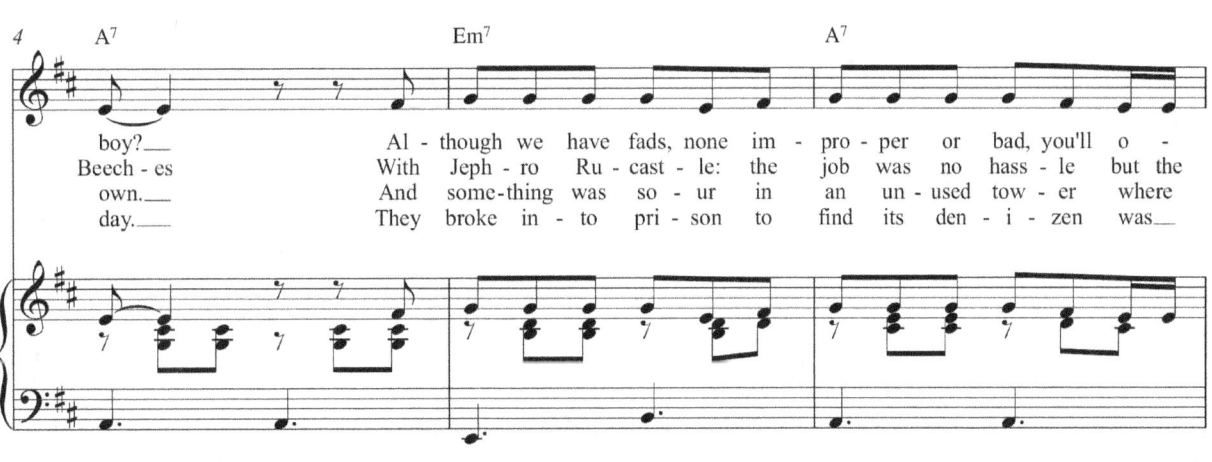

boy?__ Al-though we have fads, none im-pro-per or bad, you'll o-
Beech-es With Jeph-ro Ru-cast-le: the job was no hass-le but the
own.__ And some-thing was so-ur in an un-used tow-er where
day.__ They broke in-to pri-son to find its den-i-zen was__

bey us while in our em-ploy.__ Now,_ girl, be a sport, won't you
child won't re-tain what she teach-es. They_ made her sit down in an e-
some-one was locked up a-lone.__ 'Twas_ time to en-treat some_ help
al-read-y tak-en a-way.__ But Ru-cast-le came back, by__ his
cast-le had hid-den__ his

51

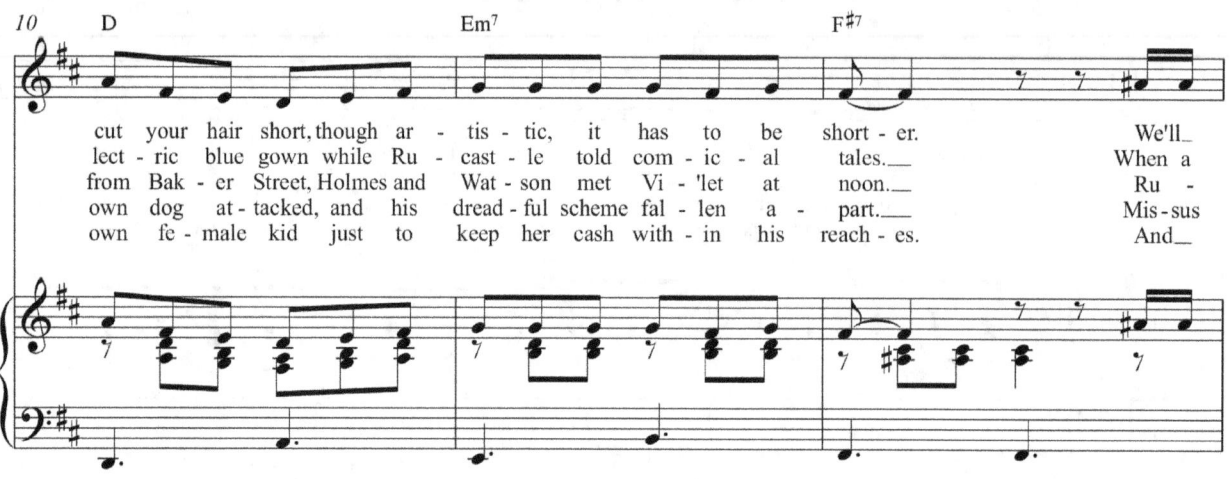

cut your hair short, though ar - tis - tic, it has to be short - er. We'll
lect - ric blue gown while Ru - cast - le told com - ic - al tales.__ When a
from Bak - er Street, Holmes and Wat - son met Vi - 'let at noon.__ Ru -
own dog at - tacked, and his dread - ful scheme fal - len a - part.__ Mis - sus
own fe - male kid just to keep her cash with - in his reach - es. And__

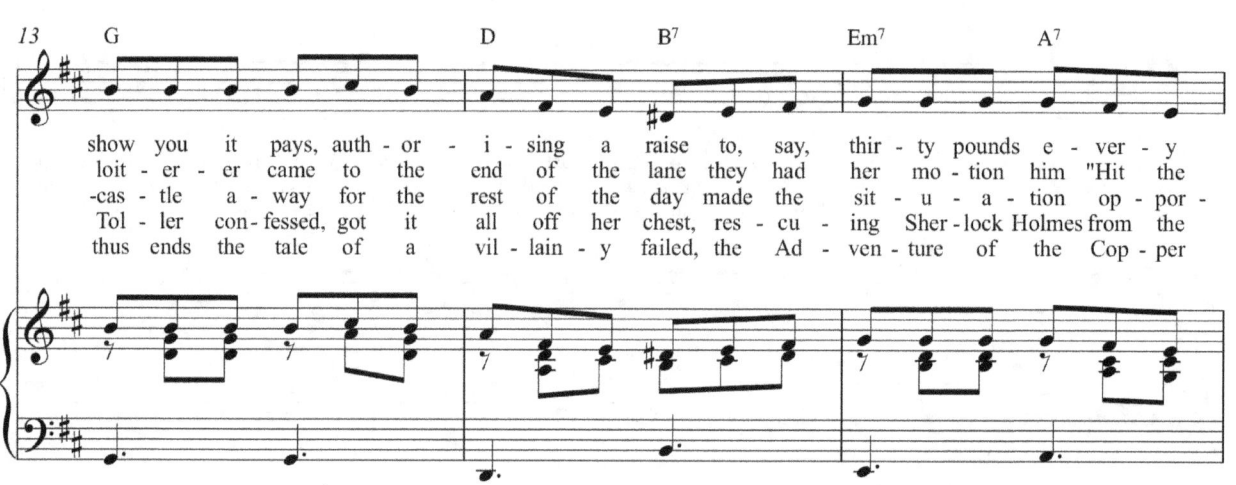

show you it pays, auth - or - i - sing a raise to, say, thir - ty pounds e - ver - y
loit - er - er came to the end of the lane they had her mo - tion him "Hit the
-cas - tle a - way for the rest of the day made the sit - u - a - tion op - por -
Tol - er con - fessed, got it all off her chest, res - cu - ing Sher - lock Holmes from the
thus ends the tale of a vil - lain - y failed, the Ad - ven - ture of the Cop - per

quart - er.
trail."   The   dark.   Ru - Beech - es.____
tune.__   Things
              When the

52

The Copper Beeches

What would you say
To a hundred in pay
To look after a six-year-old boy
Although we have fads
None improper or bad
You'll obey us while in our employ
Now, girl, be a sport
Won't you cut your hair short
Though artistic, it has to be shorter
We'll show you it pays
Authorising a raise
To, say, thirty pounds every quarter

The sal'ry impressed her
She went to Winchester
Then dog-cart to the Copper Beeches
With Jephro Rucastle;
The job was no hassle
But the child won't retain what she
teaches
They made her sit down
In an electric blue gown
While Rucastle told comical tales
When a loiterer came
To the end of the lane
They had her motion him "Hit the trail"

Things started to boil:
She discovered a coil
Of hair identical to her own

And something was sour
In an unused tower
Where someone was locked up alone
'Twas time to entreat
Some help from Baker Street
Holmes and Watson met Vi'let at noon
Rucastle away
For the rest of the day
Made the situation opportune

When the butler was smashed
And his wife had been stashed
Holmes and Watson came to save the
day
They broke into prison
To find its denizen
Was already taken away
But Rucastle came back
By his own dog attacked
And his dreadful scheme fallen apart
Mrs Toller confessed
Got it all off her chest
Rescuing Sherlock Holmes from the
dark

Rucastle had hidden
His own female kid
Just to keep her cash within his reaches
And thus ends the tale
Of a villainy failed
The adventure of the Copper Beeches

Section 2:
The Memoirs of
Sherlock Holmes

Silver Blaze

by Jim Ballinger

56

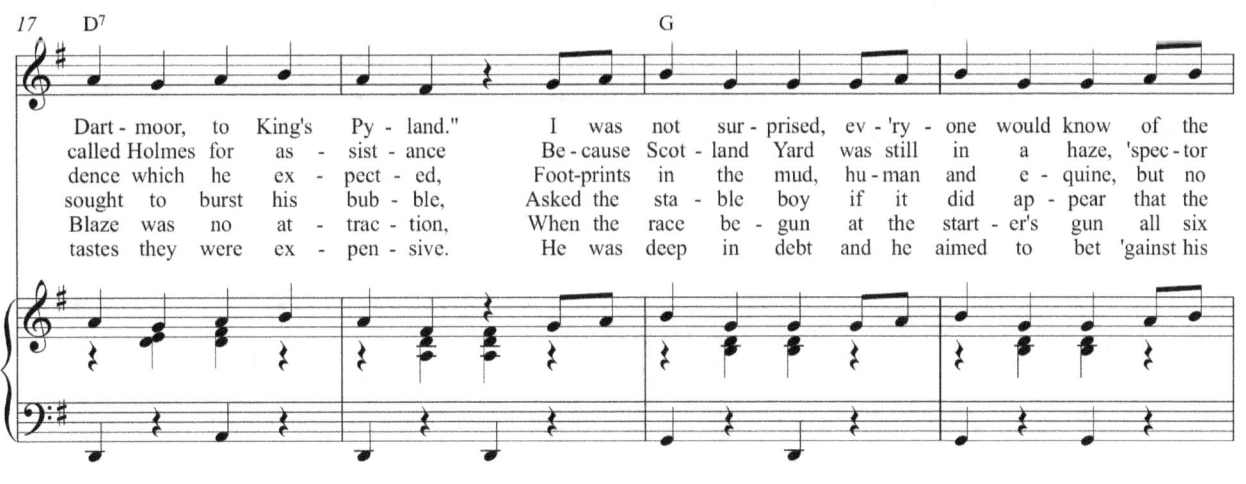

17 D⁷ / G

Dart - moor, to King's Py - land." I was not sur - prised, ev -'ry - one would know of the
called Holmes for as - sist - ance Be - cause Scot - land Yard was still in a haze, 'spec - tor
dence which he ex - pect - ed, Foot - prints in the mud, hu - man and e - quine, but no
sought to burst his bub - ble, Asked the sta - ble boy if it did ap - pear that the
Blaze was no at - trac - tion, When the race be - gun at the start - er's gun all six
tastes they were ex - pen - sive. He was deep in debt and he aimed to bet 'gainst his

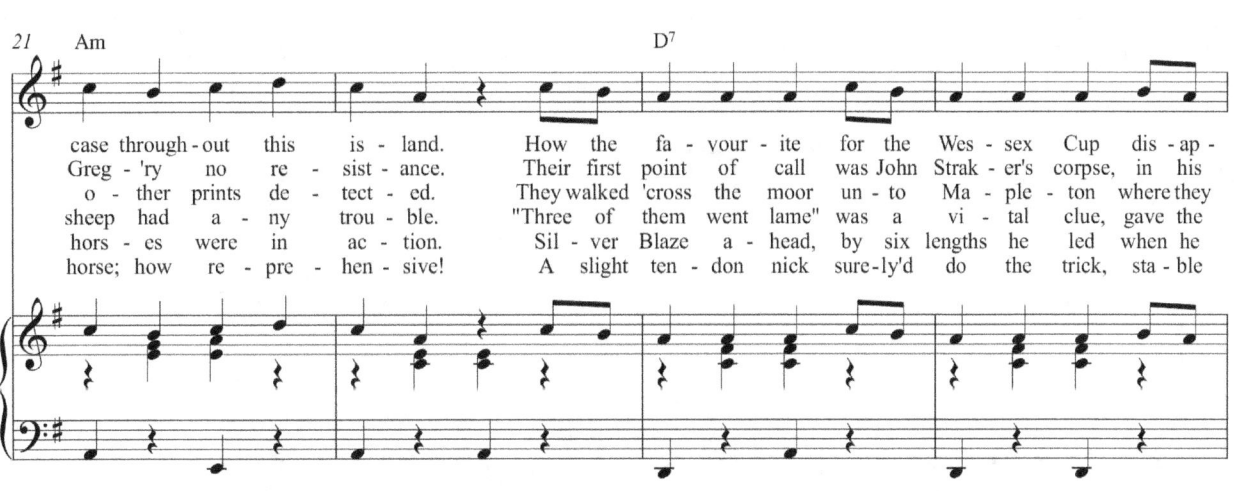

21 Am / D⁷

case through - out this is - land. How the fa - vour - ite for the Wes - sex Cup dis - ap -
Greg - 'ry no re - sist - ance. Their first point of call was John Strak - er's corpse, in his
o - ther prints de - tect - ed. They walked 'cross the moor un - to Ma - ple - ton where they
sheep had a - ny trou - ble, "Three of them went lame" was a vi - tal clue, gave the
hors - es were in ac - tion. Sil - ver Blaze a - head, by six lengths he led when he
horse; how re - pre - hen - sive! A slight ten - don nick sure - ly'd do the trick, sta - ble

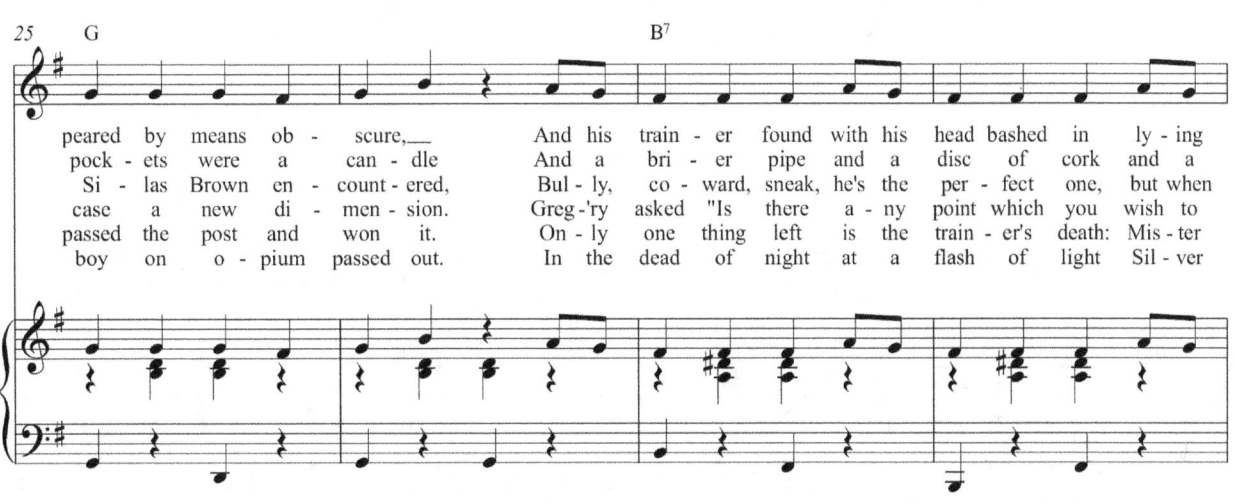

25 G / B⁷

peared by means ob - scure,___ And his train - er found with his head bashed in ly - ing
pock - ets were a can - dle And a bri - er pipe and a disc of cork and a
Si - las Brown en - count - ered, Bul - ly, co - ward, sneak, he's the per - fect one, but when
case a new di - men - sion. Greg -'ry asked "Is there a - ny point which you wish to
passed the post and won it. On - ly one thing left is the train - er's death: Mis - ter
boy on o - pium passed out. In the dead of night at a flash of light Sil - ver

29

1,2,3,5. Em   4,6. Em   ♩ = 120

dead up - on the moor.   Colo-nel   ten - tion?"   The   cu-ri-ous in - ci - ent___ of the dog in the night
knife with iv -'ry han - dle.   At the   lashed out.
bluff was called he flound-ered.   Colo-nel
draw to my at -
Holmes, tell us who done it.   Stra-ker
Blaze in in-stinct

35   D   Em

___time,   The cu-ri-ous in- ci - ent___ of the dog in the night_time.   But the dog did no-thing,

40   D   Em

But the dog did no-thing.   That is the cu - ri-ous in - ci - dent.

43   1.   2.

Came the

Silver Blaze

The curious incident of the dog in the night time
The curious incident of the dog in the night time
But the dog did nothing, but the dog did nothing
That is the curious incident

"I'm afraid, Watson, I shall have to go
Out to Dartmoor, to King's Pyland"
I was not surprised, everyone would know
Of the case throughout this island
How the favourite for the Wessex Cup
Disappeared by means obscure
And his trainer found with his head bashed up
Lying dead upon the moor

Colonel Ross it was who owned Silver Blaze
And he called Holmes for assistance
Because Scotland Yard was still in a haze
'spector Greg'ry no resistance
Their first point of call was John Straker's corpse
In his pockets were a candle
And a brier pipe and a disc of cork
And a knife with iv'ry handle

At the scene of crime Sherlock Holmes did find
Evidence which he expected
Footprints in the mud, human and equine
But no other prints detected
They walked 'cross the moor unto Mapleton
Where they Silas Brown encountered
Bully, coward, sneak, he's the perfect one
But when bluff was called he floundered

Colonel Ross had been rather cavalier
Sherlock sought to burst his bubble
Asked the stable boy if it did appear
That the sheep had any trouble
"Three of them went lame" was a vital clue
Gave the case a new dimension
Greg'ry asked "Is there any point which you
Wish to draw to my attention?"

The curious incident of the dog in the night time
The curious incident of the dog in the night time
But the dog did nothing, but the dog did nothing
That is the curious incident

Came the day of race, at the starting place
Silver Blaze was no attraction
When the race begun at the starter's gun
All six horses were in action
Silver Blaze ahead, by six lengths he led
When he passed the post and won it
Only one thing left is the trainer's death
Mr Holmes, tell us who done it

Straker was a cad, misteress he had
And her tastes they were expensive
He was deep in debt and he aimed to bet
'gainst his horse; how reprehensive!
A slight tendon nick surely'd do the trick
Stable boy on opium passed out
In the dead of night at a flash of light
Silver Blaze in instinct lashed out

The curious incident of the dog in the night time
The curious incident of the dog in the night time
But the dog did nothing, but the dog did nothing
That is the curious incident

The Yellow Face

by Jim Ballinger

Three years a - go he'd met and wed a___ wid - ow from the States.___ Her
Ef - fie took a vil - la and made___ Nor - bur - y their home. The be -
caught his wife while sneak - ing out in the mid - dle of the night.___ Her
a - tion could not be re - sist - ed,___ once more she gave in.___ On
hus - band in the States had come from Af - ri - can de - scent.___ Their

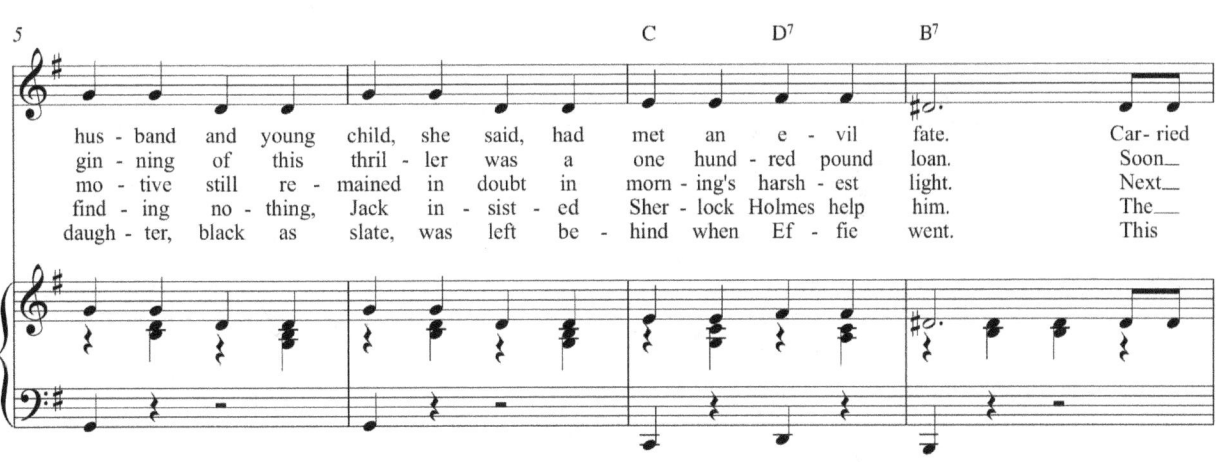

hus - band and young child, she said, had met an e - vil fate. Car - ried
gin - ning of this thril - ler was a one hund - red pound loan. Soon___
mo - tive still re - mained in doubt in morn - ing's harsh - est light. Next___
find - ing no - thing, Jack in - sist - ed Sher - lock Holmes help him. The___
daugh - ter, black as slate, was left be - hind when Ef - fie went. This

off by ty - phoid fe - ver said cer - tif - i - cate of death. This
af - ter on an e - vening stroll past a cot - tage long for rent The
day she paid a call up - on the cot - tage 'cross the field But
se - ven o' - clock train brought Holmes and___ Wat - son for the chase. On
sec - ret from Jack Mun - ro kept for___ fear of his dis - grace. Con -

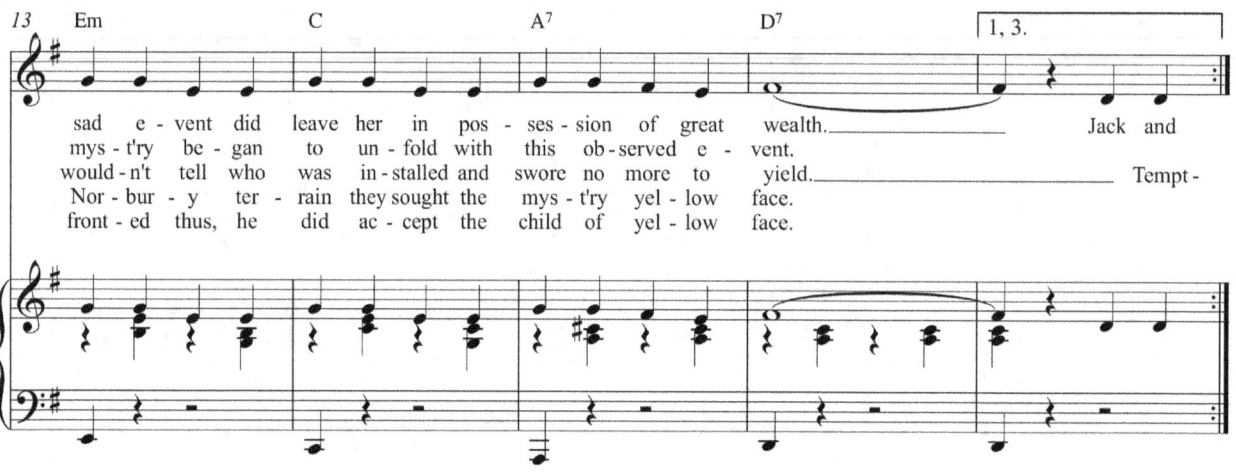

sad e - vent did leave her in pos - ses - sion of great wealth._____ Jack and
mys - t'ry be - gan to un - fold with this ob - served e - vent.
would - n't tell who was in - stalled and swore no more to yield._____ Tempt -
Nor - bur - y ter - rain they sought the mys - t'ry yel - low face.
front - ed thus, he did ac - cept the child of yel - low face.

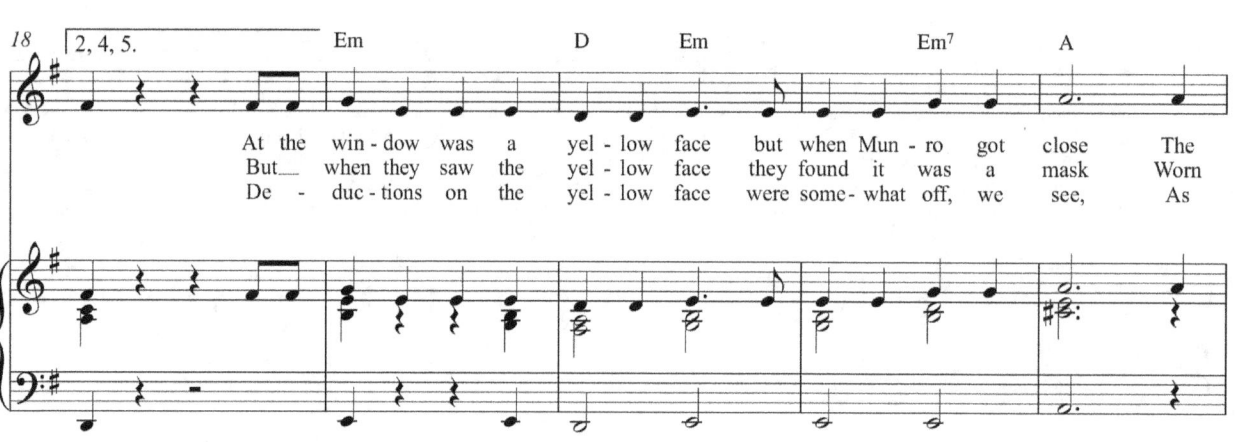

At the win - dow was a yel - low face but when Mun - ro got close The
But__ when they saw the yel - low face they found it was a mask Worn
De - duc - tions on the yel - low face were some - what off, we see, As

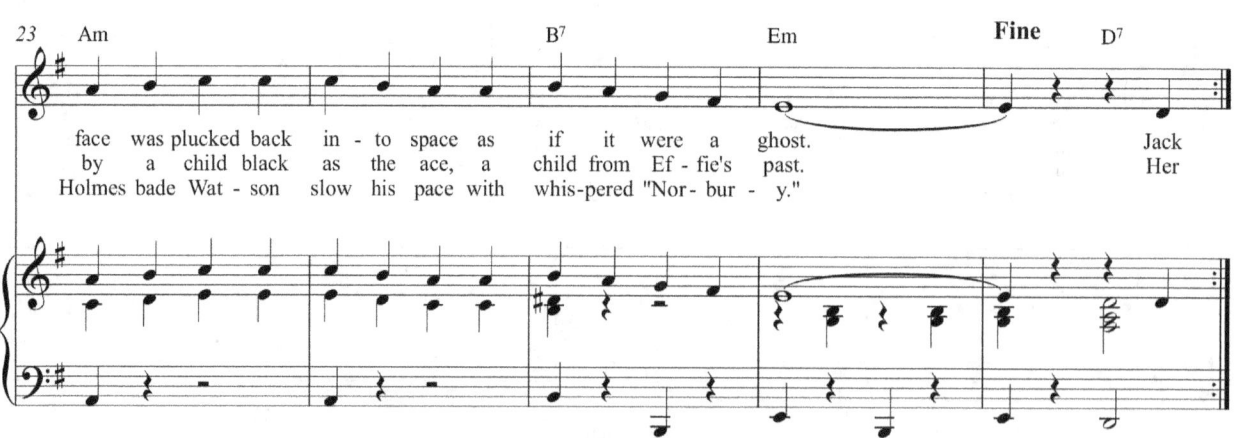

face was plucked back in - to space as if it were a ghost. Jack
by a child black as the ace, a child from Ef - fie's past. Her
Holmes bade Wat - son slow his pace with whis - pered "Nor - bur - y."

62

The Yellow Face

Three years ago he'd met and wed
A widow from the States
Her husband and young child, she said
Had met an evil fate
Carried off by yellow fever
Said certificate of death
This sad event did leave her
In possession of great wealth

Jack and Effie took a villa
And made Norbury their home
The beginning of this thriller
Was a one hundred pound loan
Soon after on an evening stroll
Past a cottage long for rent
The myst'ry began to unfold
With this observed event

At the window was a yellow face
But when Munro got close
The face was plucked back into space
As if it were a ghost

Jack caught his wife while sneaking
out
In the middle of the night
Her motive still remained in doubt
In morning's harshest light
Next day again she paid a call
On the cottage 'cross the field
But wouldn't tell who was installed
And swore no more to yield

Temptation could not be resisted
Once more she gave in
On finding nothing, Jack insisted
Sherlock Holmes help him
The seven o'clock train
Brought Holmes and Watson for the
chase
On Norbury terrain
They sought the mystery yellow face

But when they saw the yellow face
They found it was a mask
Worn by a child black as the ace
A child from Effie's past

Her husband in the States
Had come from African descent
Their daughter black as slate
Was left behind when Effie went
This secret from Jack Munro kept
For fear of his disgrace
Confronted thus, he did accept
The child of yellow face

Deductions on the yellow face
Were somewhat off, we see
As Holmes bade Watson slow his pace
With whispered "Norbury"

The Stockbroker's Clerk

by Jim Ballinger

The Stockbroker's Clerk

My name is Hall Pycroft, a stockbroker's clerk
At Coxon and Woodhouse I formerly worked
Until a loan failure made to Venezuela
Left me on the street, door to door on sore feet

To Mawson and Williams I applied through the mail
And was offered a job on a higher wage scale
That night after dinner, this bloke, Arthur Pinner
Made an offer I couldn't refuse

To manage the Franco-Midland Hardware Co
One hundred and thirty-four branches in tow
At double the pay, so I said, what the hay
The next day I scrammed by train to Birmingham

I met Pinner's brother in unfurnished rooms
He gave me a job which the next days consumed
By list to explore Parisien hardware stores
It was shades of "The Red-Headed League"

Next time I met Pinner I saw his gold tooth
'Twas just like his brother's; I called in a sleuth
We confronted this faker while reading his paper
He made some excuse and attempted the noose

A cracksman named Beddington had taken my place
At Mawson's where no-one had e'er seen my face
He tried to abscond with US railway bonds
But an observant cop forced the felon to stop
He was soon in a cell for a murder as well
His brother had tried to commit suicide
I'll go back to work as a stockbroker's clerk
Or maybe a stockbroker's clerk

The "Gloria Scott"

by Jim Ballinger

67

The "Gloria Scott"

"You never have heard me talk of Victor Trevor?"
Asked Sherlock of Watson, who answered, "No, never."
"The only friend I made in two years of college
Though I was not sociable, that I'll acknowledge"

At his invitation, I spent my vacation
With his dad, a man of wealth and consideration
One day there appeared a small wizened old sailor
Named Hudson, whose coming made old Trevor paler

"Some two months passed till Victor sent me a wire
Which bade me return for his dad's health grew dire
But it was too late when back home we had ridden
His last breath told where his confession was hidden"

"My name isn't Trevor, it's James Armitage
When young I endeavoured to augment my wage
Embezzled and caught when the auditors found
'Board the "Gloria Scott" we were Australia bound

Australia bound, Australia bound
It's good to be Australia bound

"The very next cell held one Jack Prendergast
Who'd defrauded as well but had held the loot fast
Disguised as a chaplain avoiding close scrutiny
His friend killed the captain and started a mutiny

"A group of eight wanted no part of this blood shed
We drifted undaunted by which way we should head
An explosion behind us that sounded like thunder
One man we did find but the rest had gone under

"The survivor was Hudson who blackmailed his saviours
When they were in England in genteel behaviour
His goal was to see that they never forgot
They'd been Australia bound on the "Gloria Scott"
And so Sherlock Holmes did tell Watson the plot
Of the extraordin'ry case of the "Gloria Scott"

The Musgrave Ritual

by Jim Ballinger

70

The Musgrave Ritual

Reginald Musgrave called on Sherlock Holmes
Acquaintance from college with specialised knowledge
To resolve a myst'ry at his Hurlstone home
A butler named Brunton for whom they were huntin'
Musgrave had caught Brunton at two in the morning
In ritual myst'ry from family hist'ry
This infamous conduct cut short his career
And three mornings later Brunton disappeared

Whose was it? He who is gone
Who shall have it? He who will come
Where was the sun? Over the oak
Where was the shadow? Under the elm

Holmes went to Hurlstone, the Musgrave seat
A long-missing elm had distance to tell 'im
He followed its shadow for ninety-six feet
His marker confrontin' another by Brunton
North by ten and by ten, east by five and by five
South by two and by two, west by one and by one
And under meant down a stone stair to the cellar
Wherein was discovered the curious feller

What shall we give for it? All that is ours
Why should we give it? For the sake of the trust

Brunton unravelled the ritual's clues
The maid he had conned to help lift the flagstone
But when the maid realised how she had been used
She kicked the support and entombed her cohort
The tomb contained coins and some metal debris
The coins were authentic, the First Charles' identic
And although the metal bits were tumble-down
The ritual identified them as the crown
Though battered and shapeless that diadem now
It one time encircled the royal Stuarts' brow

The Reigate Squires

by Jim Ballinger

Verse 1:
Wat - son be - came wor - ried as Holmes' deep fa - tigue grew great - er. They spent a week in Sur - rey at the home of Col - onel Hay - ter. But near - by was a break - in at the home of mag - nate Act - on. The odd as - sort - ment tak - en left no clues po - lice could act on. The

Verse 2:
next night things went fur - ther near - by at the Cun - ning - ham's,__ The burg - lar turned to mur - der and shot Wil - liam the coach - man.__ The lo - cal p'lice in - spect - or came to Sher - lock Holmes for aid,__ And so the Great De - tect - or saw his hol - i - day way - laid.__ The

Verse 3:
Cun - ning - hams claimed they had seen the mur - der - ous es - cap - er. The vic - tim's grip re - tained a lit - tle frag - ment of torn pap - er. The par - tial mes - sage seemed to in - di - cate a ren - dez - vous.__ The light in Holmes' eye gleamed at where the rest of it got to.__ Holmes

Verse 4:
had to fake col - lapse to stop the cop re - veal - ing all.__ An - other seem - ing lapse got sam - ples of the vil - lain's scrawl.__ A Wat - son mis - hap al - lowed Holmes to search the den of smok - ing From whence came muf - fled cries and groans. They res - cued Holmes from chok - ing. The

Verse 5:
Cun - ning - hams robbed Act - on's home for leg - al doc - u - ments But coach - man Bill had tracked 'em, want - ing black - mail re - com - pense. They lured him, shot him, but cast not the note in - to the fi - re. This o - ver - sight re - vealed the plot and trapped the Rei - gate Squi - res.

Fine

73

The Reigate Squires

Watson became worried
As Holmes' deep fatigue grew greater
They spent a week in Surrey
At the home of Colonel Hayter
But nearby was a break-in
At the home of magnate Acton
The odd assortment taken
Left no clues police could act on

The next night things went further
Nearby at the Cunningham's
The burglar turned to murder
And shot William the coachman
The local p'lice inspector
Came to Sherlock Holmes for aid
And so the Great Detector
Saw his holiday waylaid

The Cunninghams claimed
They had seen the murderous escaper
The victim's grip retained
A little fragment of torn paper
The partial message seemed
To indicate a rendez-vous
The light in Holmes' eye gleamed
At where the rest of it got to

Holmes had to fake collapse
To stop the cop revealing all
Another seeming lapse
Got samples of the villain's scrawl
A Watson mishap allowed Holmes
To search the den of smoking
From whence came muffled cries and groans
They rescued Holmes from choking

The Cunninghams robbed Acton's home
For legal documents
But coachman Bill had tracked 'em
Wanting blackmail recompense
They lured him, shot him, but cast not
The note into the fire
This oversight revealed the plot
And trapped the Reigate Squires

The Crooked Man

by Jim Ballinger

Col-onel Barc-lay of the Roy-al Mun-ster Ir-ish reg-i-
Then a dread-ful cry from him, a pierc-ing scream from her, a
Sher-lock searched for foot-prints on the lawn, of cul-prit 'twas a
On re-turn-ing from the Watt Street Mis-sion meet-ing as they
Af-ter thir-ty years by chance they met, Wood to her home was

ment Was the vic-tim of ap-par-ent mur-der fol-low-ing a fur-ious arg-u-
thud, When the coach-man en-tered he found Barc-lay stone dead in a pool of his own
feast, His com-pan-ion was an un-known cur-tain-climb-ing car-ni-vor-ous stoat-like
planned, Nan-cy re-cog-nised a fear-some grey haired crink-led puck-ered with-ered crook-ed
led, With his mon-goose, Ted-dy, Barc-lay re-cog-nised Wood and im-med-iate-ly dropped

|1,2,3.
ment. For the man. *The crook-ed man,__ the*
blood. Sher-lock dead.
beast. 'Twas Miss

|4,5.

crook-ed man,__ Oh, the crook-ed man.__ The crook-ed man,__ the crook-ed man,__

76

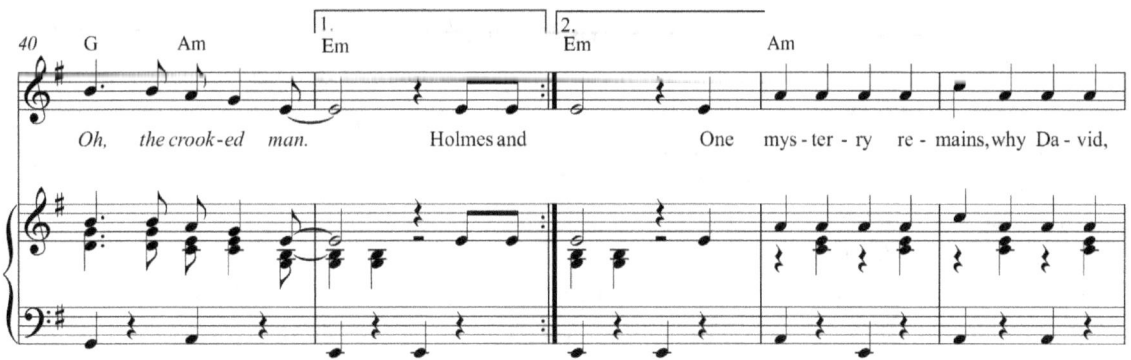

Oh, the crook-ed man. Holmes and One mys-ter-ry re-mains, why Da-vid,

not James, pray do tell. Though my know-ledge is a tri-fle rust-y it's in first or

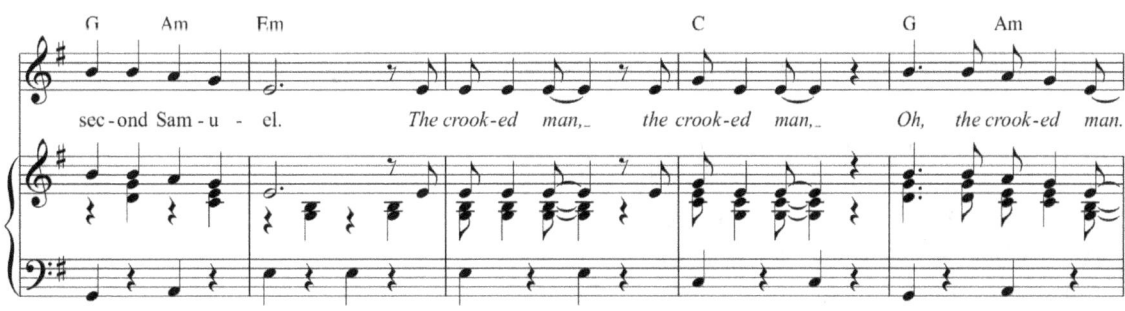

sec-ond Sam-u-el. *The crook-ed man,_ the crook-ed man,_ Oh, the crook-ed man.*

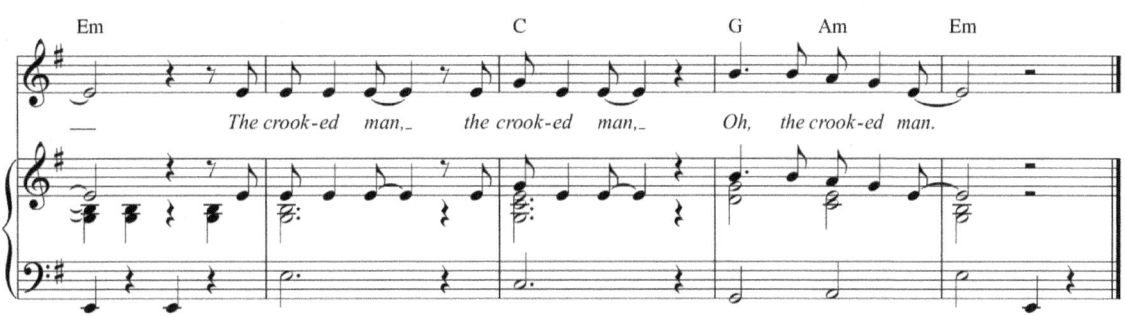

The crook-ed man,_ the crook-ed man,_ Oh, the crook-ed man.

The Crooked Man

With his wife and servants safe in bed
Doctor Watson smoked his pipe and read
Till the doorbell clanged: now what could that portend?
Not a medical emergency
It was Sherlock Holmes he there did see
Looking for a place where he the night could spend
Colonel Barclay of the Royal Munster Irish regiment
Was the victim of apparent murder following a furious argument

For the Colonel's wife Nancy Barclay
From the Watt Street Mission charity
She retired to the morning-room for tea
Colonel Barclay joined her in a state
And the maid o'erheard them altercate
Nancy shouted "You coward!" repeatedly
Then a dreadful cry from him, a piercing scream from her, a thud
When the coachman entered he found Barclay stone dead in a pool of his own blood

Sherlock Holmes first talked to Jane the maid
Who had overheard the quarrel played
She remembered something odd about the names
Although much was low and not precise
She heard Nancy utter "David" twice
Even though her husband's Christian name was James
Sherlock searched for footmarks on the lawn, of culprit 'twas a feast
His companion was an unknown curtain-climbing carnivorous stoat-like beast

'Twas Miss Morrison next interviewed
She was full of common sense and shrewd
She had promised Nancy nothing would be said
But with Nancy's mouth by illness closed
It absolved the promise, she disclosed
What had happened Monday night e'er James was dead
On returning from the Watt Street Mission meeting as they planned
Nancy recognised a fearsome grey haired crinkled puckered withered crooked man

The crooked man, the crooked man
Oh, the crooked man
The crooked man, the crooked man
Oh, the crooked man

Holmes and Watson went to Hudson Street
Where they Mr Henry Wood did meet
And he told them how the mystery had played
Back in India Wood and Barclay
Were both suitors of sweet Nancy D
Until Wood by Barclay cruelly was betrayed
After thirty years by chance they met, Wood to her home was led
With his mongoose Teddy, Barclay recognised Wood and immediately dropped dead

The crooked man, the crooked man
Oh, the crooked man
The crooked man, the crooked man
Oh, the crooked man

Just one mystery remains, why David, not James, pray do tell
Though my knowledge is a trifle rusty it's in first or second Samuel

The crooked man, the crooked man
Oh, the crooked man
The crooked man, the crooked man
Oh, the crooked man

The Resident Patient

by Jim Ballinger

80

The Resident Patient

I tell you the story of Percy Trevelyan
A bit of a wet fish and scarcely a hellion
Who showed such great promise before graduation
But went into practice with a resident patient
And this Mister Blessington set up his rooms
In Brook Street and income three-quarters consumed

One evening he saw an old noble from Russia
Whose son had come with him, a giant, a crusher
The old man went in cataleptic attack
But just five minutes later when Percy came back
With a remedy he found the two men had flewn
And Blessington cried they'd been into his room

Early next morning old Blessington died
With a rope 'round his neck but 'twas not suicide
For Holmes with the aid of cigars reconstructed
The quasi-judicial proceedings conducted
That night, a tribunal made up of three men
Their verdict: the Blessington chap was condemned

Holmes identified them as the Worthingdon gang
Of bank robbers convicted when Blessington sang
One Cartwright was hung and the others did time
Upon their release was revenge on their mind
Despite a programme of witness relocation
Which failed in the case of the Resident Patient

The Greek Interpreter

by Jim Ballinger

82

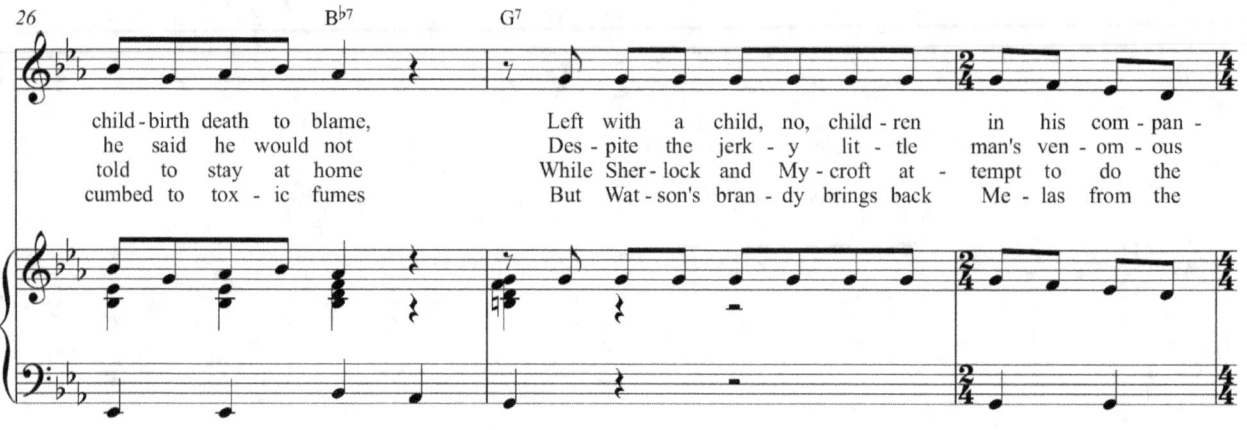

child-birth death to blame,
he said he would not
told to stay at home
cumbed to tox - ic fumes

Left with a child, no, child-ren in his com-pan-
Des - pite the jerk - y lit - tle man's ven - om - ous
While Sher-lock and My-croft at - tempt to do the
But Wat-son's bran - dy brings back Me - las from the

y.
threats.
rest.
brink.

Coda

But Wat-son dis - a - grees, says "It's all Greek to me!"

The Greek Interpreter

Art in the blood is wont to take the strangest forms
As Holmes reveals a brother heretofore unknown
In observation and deduction he excels
Mycroft has no ambition and no energy
He is contented with his lodgings in Pall Mall
And working in Whitehall and its bureaucracy

So Holmes and Watson visit Club Diogenes
Where talking is forbidden, makes them most displeased
Sherlock and Mycroft play the observation game
A soldier, recently discharged, artillery
A recent widower, a childbirth death to blame
Left with a child, no, children in his company

For Mister Melas, Mycroft's neighbour in Pall Mall
Had an extraordinary narrative to tell
Two evenings earlier a Mister Latimer
Had called upon him a translation to request
They rode by carriage for two hours, maybe more
And where they ended up was anybody's guess

When they arrived at a secluded country house
Poor Melas encountered a second fearsome louse
Then an emaciated prisoner was brought
And Melas translated the captors' vile request
When asked to sign the papers, he said he would not
Despite the jerky little man's venomous threats

Melas devised a means the story to make clear
He added questions which the captors did not hear
He found Kratides was the starving captive's name
He hailed from Athens but that was the last thing told
Into the room a tall dark woman, Sophy, came
Which terminated the interrogation cold

They paid five sovereigns and reinforced the fright
Left him on Wandsworth Common in the dead of night
He told his narrative to neighbour Mycroft Holmes
Who placed an advert quickly in the daily press
The Greek interpreter was told to stay at home
While Sherlock and Mycroft attempt to do the rest

An answer to the advert promptly came to them
The lady's living at The Myrtles, Beckenham
They go for Melas but the villains got there first
On reaching Scotland Yard, Inspector Gregson's there
The warrant takes an hour, Sherlock fears the worst
They take the train from London Bridge, no time to spare

They reach The Myrtles but the windows are all dark
Our birds have flown, the nest is empty, Sherlock barked
They found Kratides and Melas locked in a room
The poisonous charcoal atmosphere, a gasping stink
Poor old Kratides has succumbed to toxic fumes
But Watson's brandy brings back Melas from the brink

Young Sophy got involved with Harold Latimer
Her brother Paul arrived from Greece to rescue her
Months afterward a clipping came from Buda-Pesth
Two Englishmen were stabbed in mortal injury
The Grecian girl could solve the mystery, Holmes suggests
But Watson disagrees, says "It's all Greek to me"

The Naval Treaty

by Jim Ballinger

Percy Phelps need-ed Sher-lock's help to find the Na-val Treat-y. Nine
in nine weeks there had been no leaks, the Treat-y had not sur-faced. The
fi-an-cée had a part to play in trap-ping those con-spir-ing. She
Sher-lock Holmes could not re-sist a touch of the dram-a-tic. The

weeks he'd lain with a fe-vered brain at-tend-ed by his sweet-ie. The
thief is ill or the price is still too low to suit his pur-pose. The
had to stay in the room all day and lock it when re-tir-ing. Then
Treat-y lay on a break-fast tray, the sight made Phelps ec-

doc-u-ment had dis-ap-peared from For-eign Of-fice rooms.___ The com-
first night Per-cy slept a-lone a burg-lar tried to break in, But___
Sher-lock kept a lone-ly vi-gil un-til two o'-clock.___ Jo-seph

88

The Naval Treaty

Young Percy Phelps
Needed Sherlock's help
To find the Naval Treaty
Nine weeks he's lain
With a fevered brain
Attended by his sweetie
The document had disappeared
From Foreign Office room
The commissionaire and wife were there
To witness Percy's doom

But in nine weeks
There had been no leaks
The Treaty had not surfaced
The thief was ill
Or the price was still
Too low to suit his purpose
The first night Percy slept alone
A burglar tried to break in
But he'd not quaffed his sleeping draught
And so nothing was taken

His fiancée
Had a part to play
In trapping those conspiring
She had to stay
In the room all day
And lock it when retiring
Then Sherlock kept a lonely vigil
Until two o'clock
Joseph Harrison
Was the guilty one
And in the trap got caught

But Sherlock Holmes could not resist
A touch of the dramatic
The Treaty lay
On a breakfast tray
The sight made Phelps ecstatic
He'd found the Naval Treaty
He'd get to wed his sweetie
He'd found the Naval Treaty

The Final Problem

by Jim Ballinger

morn-ing I jumped in the third han-som cab__ And rode to the end of the Low-ther Ar-cade,__ I
to-ri-a Sta-tion with mo-ments to spare,_ A pri-vate com-part-ment but Holmes was no-where. An
train to New-ha-ven, a boat 'cross the Chan-nel, Then Brus-sels and Stras-bourg ap-peared in my an-nals. A

dashed to the o-ther end, quart-er to nine, And hopped in a brougham with the driv-er as-signed.___ Vic
a-ged I-ta-lian priest, so I sur-mised, Turned out to be Holmes in a-
wi-re from Lon-don said he had es-caped, The dread Mo-ri-ar-ty's re-

no-ther dis-guise.___ Clear-ing the sta-tion on our south-east route, The e-vil Pro-fes-sor in

hung-ry pur-suit, He hir-ed a spe-cial and told them to hur-ry But we dis-em-barked and hid

91

at Can - ter - bur - y.___ A venge would a - wait.___ We made our jour-ney o - ver-land to Meir-in - gen in Switz-er-land And put up at the En - gl-isch - er Hof. 'Twas run by Pe - ter Steil - er eld - er, In - tel - li - gent Engl-ish speak-ing fel - ler, On his ad - vice the next day we set off To view the falls of Reich-en - bach, A tor - rent hurled twixt coal-black rocks, And there we stood, our minds re - mote, Un - til a Swiss lad brought a note. An

Eng-lish la - dy in dis-tress wants a doc - tor on the N H S And as I turned to tend to this I

saw Holmes gaze at the a - byss. When I got back to our ho - tel there was no la - dy, sick or well, I

re - a - lised the note had been a trick. I ran back to the dread-ed falls And

D.S. al fine

searched in vain, I called and called, I saw a sight which turned me cold and sick.

93

The Final Problem

It is with a heavy heart I take up my pen
To write these words about the best and wisest of men
Last record of his singular gifts by which he was distinguished
To state the facts about his life and how it was extinguished

He walked in my consulting-room one evening in Spring
Looking paler, thinner, and afraid of something
Of air-guns, he replied, because the net had been entwined
About Professor Moriarty, the Napoleon of crime

Next morning I jumped in the third hansom cab
And rode to the end of the Lowther Arcade
I dashed to the other end, quarter-past nine
And hopped in a brougham with the driver assigned

Victoria Station with moments to spare
A private compartment, but Holmes was nowhere
An aged Italian priest, so I surmised
Turned out to be Holmes in another disguise

Clearing the station on our south-east route
The evil Professor in hungry pursuit
He hired a special and told them to hurry
But we disembarked and hid at Canterbury

A train to Newhaven, a boat 'cross the Channel
Then Brussels and Strasbourg appeared in my annals
A wire from London said he had escaped
The dread Moriarty's revenge would await

We made our journey over land
To Meiringen in Switzerland
And put up at the Englischer Hof
'Twas run by Peter Steiler elder
Intelligent, English-speaking feller
On his advice the next day we set off

To view the falls of Reichenbach
A torrent hurled twixt coal-black rocks
And there we stood, our minds remote
Until a Swiss lad brought a note
An English lady in distress
Wants a doctor on the NHS
And as I turned to tend to this
I saw Holmes gaze at the abyss

When I got back to our hotel
There was no lady, sick or well
I realized the note had been a trick
I ran back to the dreaded falls
And searched in vain, I called and called
I saw a sight which turned me cold and sick

There I saw his Alpine-stock and cigarette case
Together with a note about the end of the chase
Holmes and Moriarty drowned, I made my way alone
Still Holmes remains the best and wisest man I've ever known

Section 3:
The Return of Sherlock Holmes

The Empty House

by Jim Ballinger

Verse 1 (line under staves):

The emp-ty house in Ba-ker Street that faced two two one B, The emp-ty house in Ba-ker Street where

Colo-nel Seb-as-tian Mo-ran con-duct-ed his vile, fiend-ish plan: A-venge Pro-fes-sor Mor-i-ar-i-ty. Hon 'ra-

ble Ron-ald A-dair, per-fect teeth and per-fect hair, Spent the e-v'ning at his club, the Ba-ga-
Wat-son though that he'd solve the Park Lane Mys-ter-y, Took a stroll a-cross Hyde Park to have a
Holmes sur-vived the Falls, ne-ver in the chasm at all, And he'd dodged the rocks from Mor-i-ar-ty's

telle, Where he played some rounds of whist (and got mod-er-ate-ly pissed) Where he
look. And not watch-ing where he walked clum-sy Doc-tor Wat-son knocked Down an
friend. He made Flo-rence in a week, on-ly My-croft did he speak To pro-
caught. Dropped the cab at Cav'n-dish Square, car-ried on by foot from there, Through the
gun. He took care-ful aim and shot, Holmes sprang ti-ger-like and brought Him to

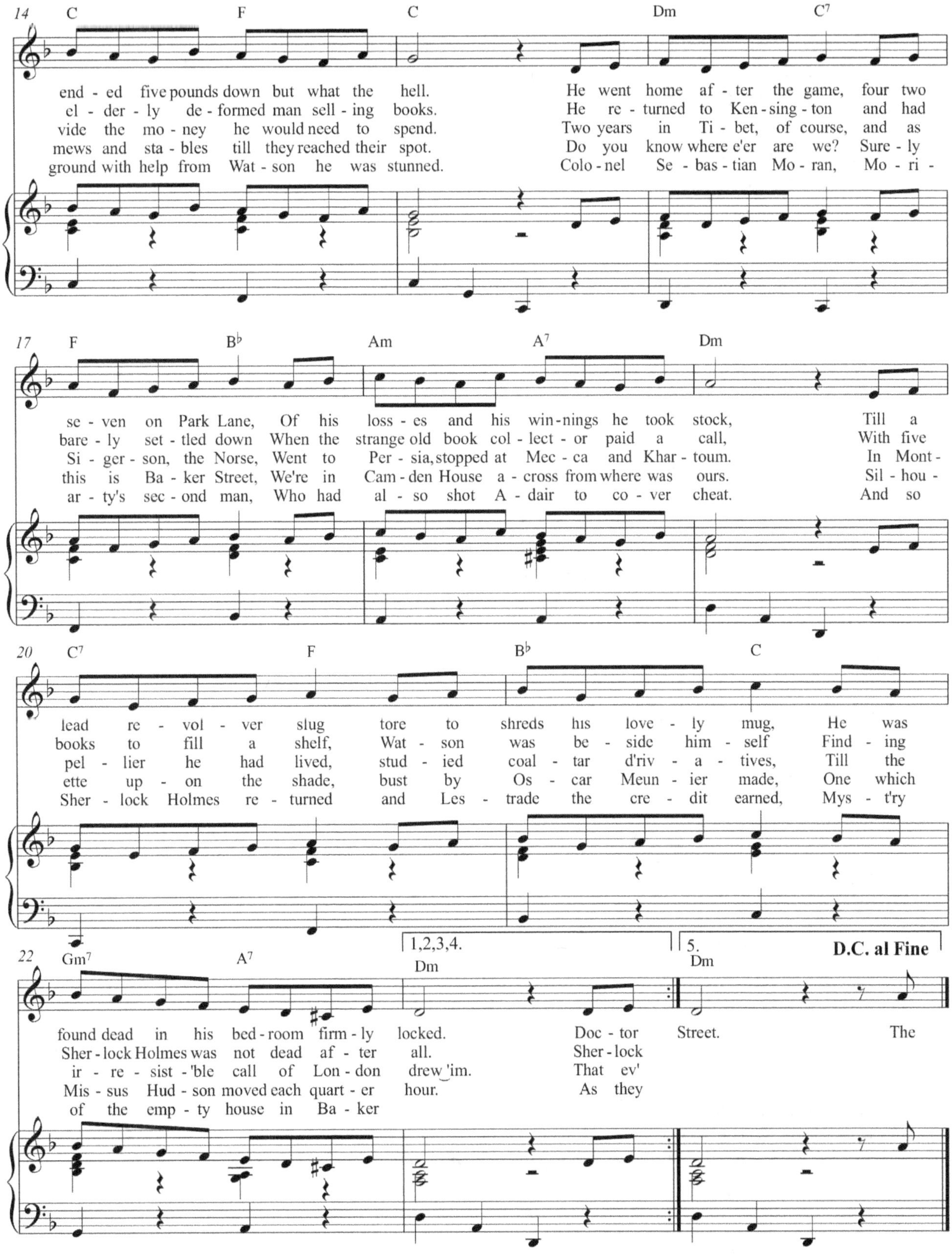
14
C F C Dm C7
end - ed five pounds down but what the hell. He went home af - ter the game, four two
el - der - ly de - formed man sell - ing books. He re - turned to Ken - sing - ton and had
vide the mo - ney he would need to spend. Two years in Ti - bet, of course, and as
mews and sta - bles till they reached their spot. Do you know where e'er are we? Sure - ly
ground with help from Wat - son he was stunned. Colo - nel Se - bas - tian Mo - ran, Mo - ri -
17
F B♭ Am A7 Dm
se - ven on Park Lane, Of his loss - es and his win - nings he took stock, Till a
bare - ly set - tled down When the strange old book col - lect - or paid a call, With five
Si - ger - son, the Norse, Went to Per - sia, stopped at Mec - ca and Khar - toum. In Mont -
this is Ba - ker Street, We're in Cam - den House a - cross from where was ours. Sil - hou -
ar - ty's sec - ond man, Who had al - so shot A - dair to co - ver cheat. And so
20
C7 F B♭ C
lead re - vol - ver slug tore to shreds his love - ly mug, He was
books to fill a shelf, Wat - son was be - side him - self Find - ing
pel - lier he had lived, stud - ied coal - tar d'riv - a - tives, Till the
ette up - on the shade, bust by Os - car Meun - ier made, One which
Sher - lock Holmes re - turned and Les - trade the cre - dit earned, Mys - t'ry
22
Gm7 A7
1,2,3,4.
Dm
5.
Dm
D.C. al Fine
found dead in his bed - room firm - ly locked. Doc - tor Street. The
Sher - lock Holmes was not dead af - ter all. Sher - lock
ir - re - sist - 'ble call of Lon - don drew 'im. That ev'
Mis - sus Hud - son moved each quart - er hour. As they
of the emp - ty house in Ba - ker

The Empty House

The empty house in Baker Street
That faced 221B
The empty house in Baker Street
Where Colonel Sebastian Moran
Conducted his vile, fiendish plan:
Avenge Professor Moriar-i-ty

Honourable Ronald Adair
Perfect teeth and perfect hair
Spent the evening at his club, the Bagatelle
There he played some rounds of whist
(And got moderately pissed)
Where he ended five pounds down but what the hell

He went home after the game
Four-two-seven on Park Lane
Of his losses and his winnings he took stock
Till a lead revolver slug
Tore to shreds his lovely mug
He was found dead in his bedroom firmly locked

Doctor Watson thought that he'd
Solve the Park Lane Mystery
Took a stroll across Hyde Park to have a look
And not watching where he walked
Clumsy Doctor Watson knocked
Down an elderly deformed man selling books

He returned to Kensington
And had barely settled down
When the strange old book collector paid a call
With five books to fill a shelf
Watson was beside himself
Finding Sherlock Holmes was not dead after all

Sherlock Holmes survived the Falls
Never in the chasm at all
And he'd dodged the rocks from Moriarty's friend
He made Florence in a week
Only Mycroft did he speak
To provide the money he would need to spend

Two years in Tibet, of course
And as Sigerson, the Norse
Went to Persia, stopped at Mecca and Khartoum
In Montpellier he had lived
Studied coal-tar derivatives
Till the irresistible call of London drew 'im

That evening at half-past nine
It was just like the old times
The adventure till the criminal is caught
Dropped the cab at Cavendish Square
Carried on by foot from there
Through the mews and stables till they reached their spot

Do you know where'er are we?
Surely this is Baker Street
We're in Camden House across from where was ours
Silhouette upon the shade
Bust by Oscar Meunier made
One which Mrs Hudson moved each quarter hour

As they waited in the gloom
An old man entered the room
With a walking-stick that turned into a gun
He took careful aim and shot
Holmes sprang tiger-like and brought
Him to ground with help from Watson he was stunned

Colonel Sebastian Moran
Moriarty's second man
Who had also shot Adair to cover cheat
And so Sherlock Holmes returned
And Lestrade the credit earned
Mystery of the empty house in Baker Street

The empty house in Baker Street
That faced 221B
The empty house in Baker Street
Where Colonel Sebastian Moran
Conducted his vile, fiendish plan:
Avenge Professor Moriar-i-ty

The Norwood Builder

by Jim Ballinger

bach - e - lor, law -yer, Free - mas - on, asth - ma - tic: all that Holmes de -duced in a glance_____ From the
he had named me heir to his prop - er - ty though my fam - 'ly had grown out of touch;_____ But
walk - ing -stick sur -faced, its mur - der - ous pur -pose at - test - ed by trac - es of blood;_____ In -
no - thing new turned up at Nor -wood, some burned up old but - tons sup -port -ed Les - trade,_____ But
shock would have killed her. That damn Nor -wood Build -er would take a new i - den - ti - ty. And it

sheaf in my pock - et, my breath - ing er - rat - ic, my watch -chain, and bad - ly creased
I had as -sured him I'd not breathe a word that I stood to in - her - it so
spec - tor Les - trade and his C. I. D. squad dumped me quick - ly in gaol with a
worked like a charm till he did him - self harm when he add - ed that thumb -print of

|1.|2, 4.| To next strain |3, 5.| **D.C.**

pants. much.____ Last thud.
odd._____ Next me.

ev -'ning a house -keep - er named Mis - sus Lex - ing - ton showed me where sup - per was laid;_____ And
morn -ing did come and the print of a thumb was dis - cov - ered where I'd hung my hat;_____ Les -

The Norwood Builder

Oh I am the unhappy John Hector Macfarlane
Arrested but innocent still
A Norwood house-maker named Jonas Oldacre
Has written me into his will

One morning I burst in on Watson and Holmes
The police followed me from the train
I wanted to tell the events that befell me
Before Lestrade clapped me in chains
A bachelor, lawyer, Freemason, asthmatic
All that Holmes deduced in a glance
From the sheaf in my pocket, my breathing erratic
My watch-chain and badly-creased pants

Yesterday Jonas Oldacre approached me
To put his will in legal shape
He asked me to dine the same evening at nine
When he left my mouth was still agape
For he had named me heir to his property
Though my family had grown out of touch
I had assured him I'd not breathe a word
That I stood to inherit so much

Last evening a housekeeper named Mrs Lexington
Showed me where supper was laid
Afterward, Jonas Oldacre took me to the safe
Where his papers all stayed
'Twas getting toward midnight when we finally finished
And I tried to locate my cane
He said it would turn up and that I could claim it
When next I would visit again

This morning I read that Oldacre was dead
Victim of what seemed like homicide
His wood-pile on fire, charred bones on the pyre
And spattered blood showed he had died
My walking-stick surfaced, its murderous purpose
Attested by traces of blood
Inspector Lestrade of the CID squad
Dumped me quickly in gaol with a thud

Oh I am the unhappy John Hector Macfarlane
Arrested but innocent still
A Norwood house-maker named Jonas Oldacre
Has written me into his will

Sherlock Holmes took on my case and he looked
First to Blackheath where my folks did dwell
My Mum knew Oldacre, he once tried to make her
His wife, till she said "Go to hell"
But nothing more turned up at Norwood, some burned up
Old buttons supported Lestrade
But still Sherlock Holmes could feel it in his bones
That the story contained something odd

Next morning did come and the print of a thumb
Was discovered where I'd hung my hat
Lestrade was elated, his case further weighted
But Holmes was like the Cheshire Cat
He knew that the print was not there yesterday
And all doubt was removed by this fake
He set a small fire to smoke out his quarry
And who emerged? Jonas Oldac – re!

The old builder spoke: "It was only a joke
And after all, no harm's been done"
But Holmes knew the plot and revenge would be gotten
By framing his old sweetheart's son
The shock would have killed her; that damn Norwood Builder
Would take a new identity
And it worked like a charm till he did himself harm
When he added that thumb-print of me

Oh I now am the happy John Hector Macfarlane
Soon back to solicitor's tomes
Inspector Lestrade's police quickly had me released
Thanks to Mr Sherlock Holmes

The Dancing Men

by Jim Ballinger

At-tend the tale of Hil-ton Cu - bitt,_ Re-cip - i - ent of dan cing men,
A had_ Be-fore the dan-cing fig-ures come,
jo - ker_ By keep-ing vi - gil dark and mute,
mur - der,_ For Hil-ton Cu-bitt was shot dead,
pres - sion_ That it would be a heav-y date.

A tale with mur-der to con-clude it,_ Re-sult-ing from "cher-chez la
And short-ly Sher-lock in his way had_ To cu - ri-os - i - ty suc-
But El - sie said some-thing a - woke her_ And then she would-n't let him
And El - sie when some-thing had stirred her_ Re-ceived a bul - let in the
When trapped, he of-fered a con-fes - sion_ His El - sie to ex - hon - or -

femme." In Lon-don he met a ter-ri - fic_ Young wo-man from the U S
cumbed. The lit - tle hei - ro-glyphs were done while El - sie and Hil-ton were a-
shoot. Cu - bitt had sworn to give his wife her_ Sec - re - cy on her ear-ly
head. Sher-lock be-gan in-vest-i-gat - ing,_ The gar-den held the prints of
ate. This is the end-ing of the sa - ga, To read-ers is this mo-ral

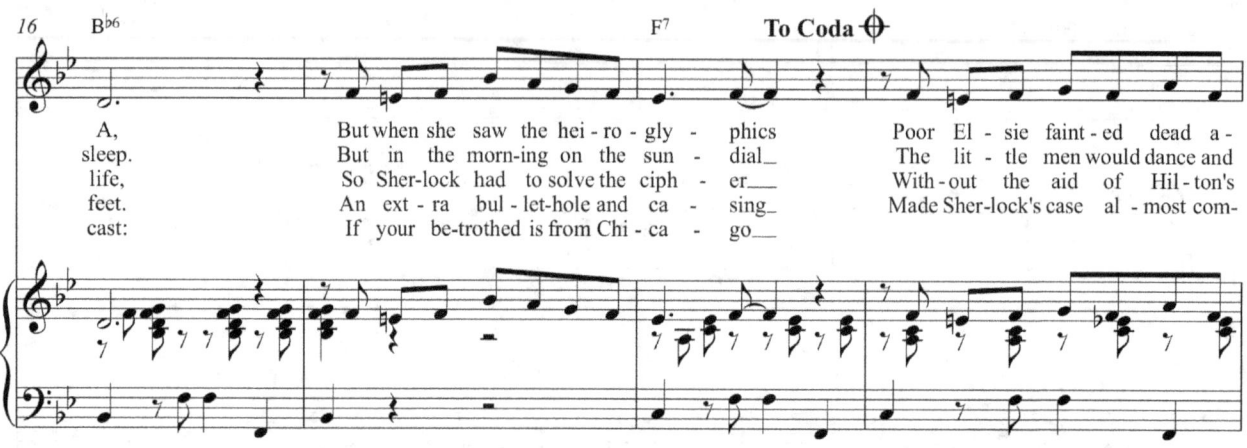

16 B♭6   F⁷   **To Coda** ⊕

A,   But when she saw the hei-ro-gly-phics   Poor El-sie faint-ed dead a-
sleep.   But in the morn-ing on the sun-dial__   The lit-tle men would dance and
life,   So Sher-lock had to solve the ciph-er__   With-out the aid of Hil-ton's
feet.   An ex-tra bul-let-hole and ca-sing__   Made Sher-lock's case al-most com-
cast: If your be-trothed is from Chi-ca-go__

20 B♭6   G♭

way.   To com-pre-hend the dan-cing gnomes, Cu-bitt ap-pealed to Sher-lock
leap.   He by the post-al ser-vice sent A tra-cing of each pro-nounce
wife.   But Sher-lock fin'l-ly broke the code And to his cli-ent's fine a-
plete.   For his fi-na-le Sher-lock wrote In dan-cing men a lit-tle

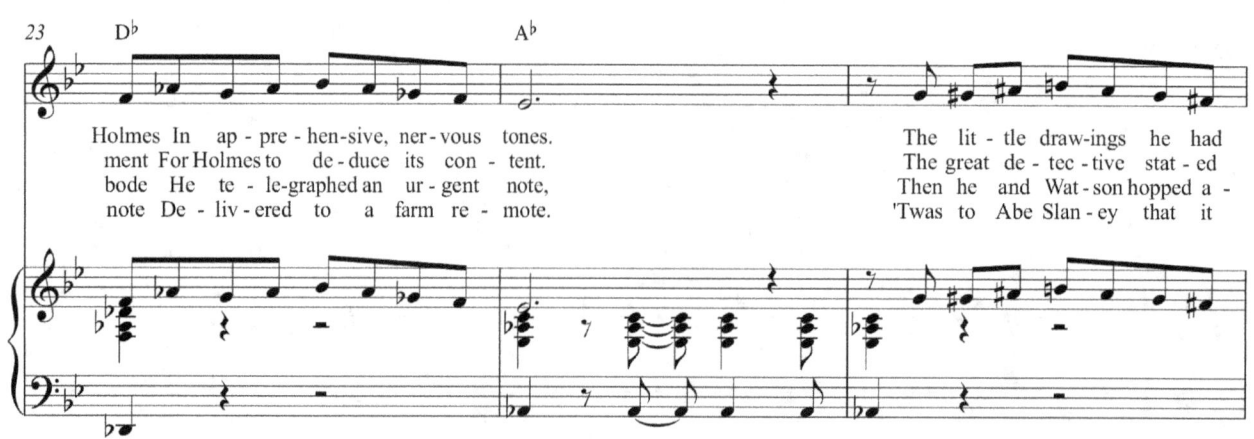

23 D♭   A♭

Holmes In ap-pre-hen-sive, ner-vous tones.   The lit-tle draw-ings he had
ment For Holmes to de-duce its con-tent.   The great de-tec-tive stat-ed
bode He te-le-graphed an ur-gent note,   Then he and Wat-son hopped a-
note De-liv-ered to a farm re-mote.   'Twas to Abe Slan-ey that it

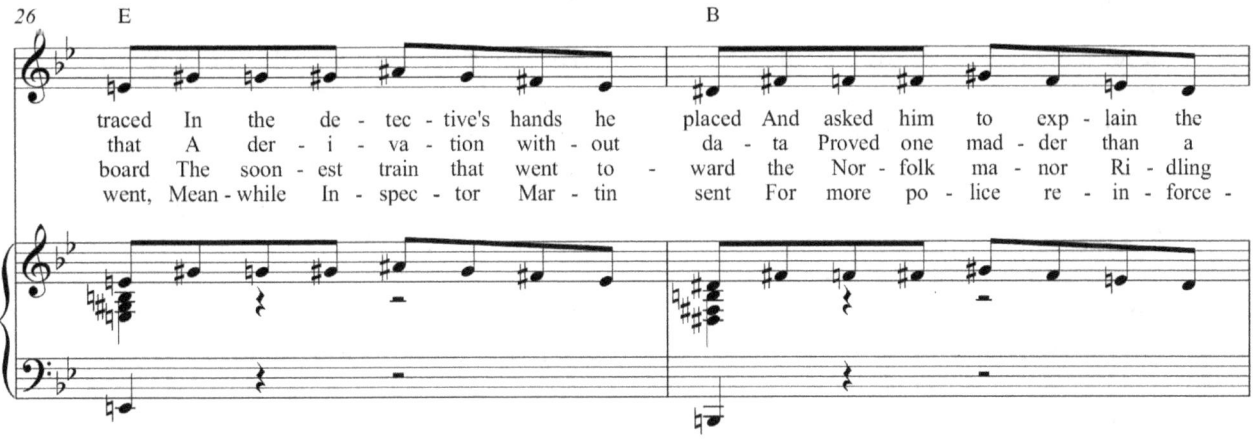

traced In the de - tec - tive's hands he placed And asked him to exp - lain the
that A der - i - va - tion with - out da - ta Proved one mad - der than a
board The soon - est train that went to - ward the Nor - folk ma - nor Ri - dling
went, Mean - while In - spec - tor Mar - tin sent For more po - lice re - in - force -

case.
hat - ta.
Thorpe.
ments.

A let - ter from the U S
One night old Hil - ton saw the
When they ar - rived it was to
Abe Slan - ey came with the im -

Coda

Be sure to look in - to her past.

109

The Dancing Men

Attend the tale of Hilton Cubitt
Recipient of dancing men
A tale with murder to conclude it
Resulting from "cherchez la femme"

In London he'd met a terrific
Young woman from the USA
But when she saw the hieroglyphics
Poor Elsie fainted dead away

To comprehend the dancing gnomes
Cubitt appealed to Sherlock Holmes
In apprehensive, nervous tones
The little drawing he had traced
In the detective's hands he placed
And asked him to explain the case

A letter from the USA had
Before the dancing figures come
And shortly Sherlock in his way had
To curiosity succumbed

The little hieroglyphs were done while
Elsie and Hilton were asleep
But in the morning on the sundial
The little men would dance and leap

He by the postal service sent
A tracing of each pronouncement
For Holmes to deduce its content
The great detective stated that a
Derivation without data
Proved one madder than a hatter

One night old Hilton saw the joker
By keeping vigil dark and mute
But Elsie said something had woke her
And then she wouldn't let him shoot

Cubitt had sworn to give his wife her
Secrecy on her early life
So Sherlock had to solve the cypher
Without the aid of Hilton's wife

But Sherlock fin'lly broke the code
And to his client's fine abode
He telegraphed an urgent note
Then he and Watson hopped aboard
The soonest train that went toward
The Norfolk manor Ridling Thorpe

When they arrived it was to murder
For Hilton Cubitt was shot dead
And Elsie when something had stirred her
Received a bullet in the head

Sherlock began investigating
The garden held the prints of feet
An extra bullet-hole and casing
Made Sherlock's case almost complete

For his finale Sherlock wrote
In dancing men a little note
Delivered to a farm remote
'Twas to Abe Slaney that it went
Meanwhile Inspector Martin sent
For more police reinforcements

Abe Slaney came with the impression
That it would be a heavy date
When trapped, he offered a confession
His Elsie to exonerate

This is the ending of the saga
To readers is this moral cast
If your betrothed is from Chicago
Be sure to look into her past

The Solitary Cyclist

by Jim Ballinger

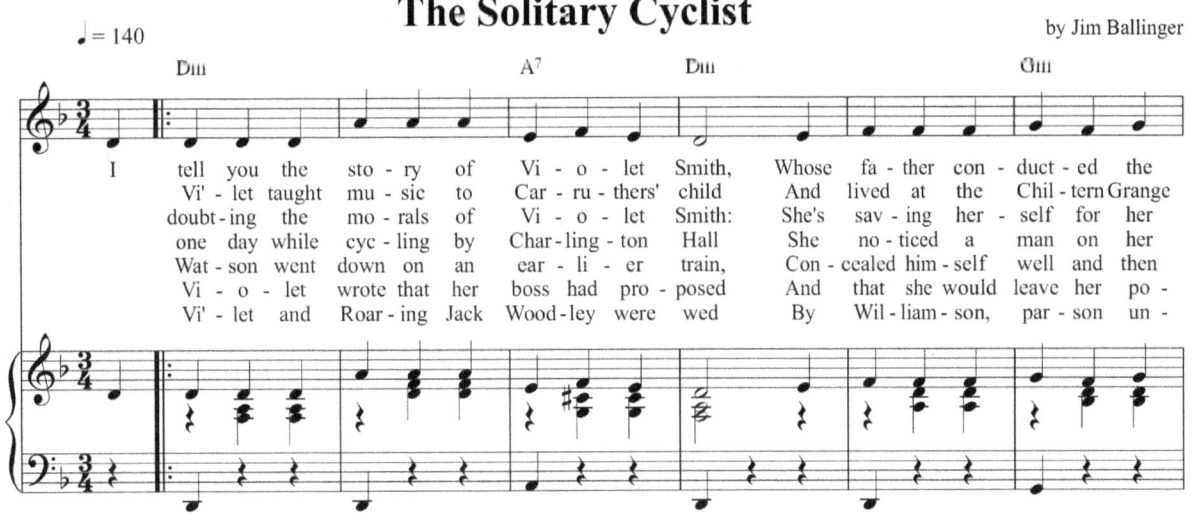

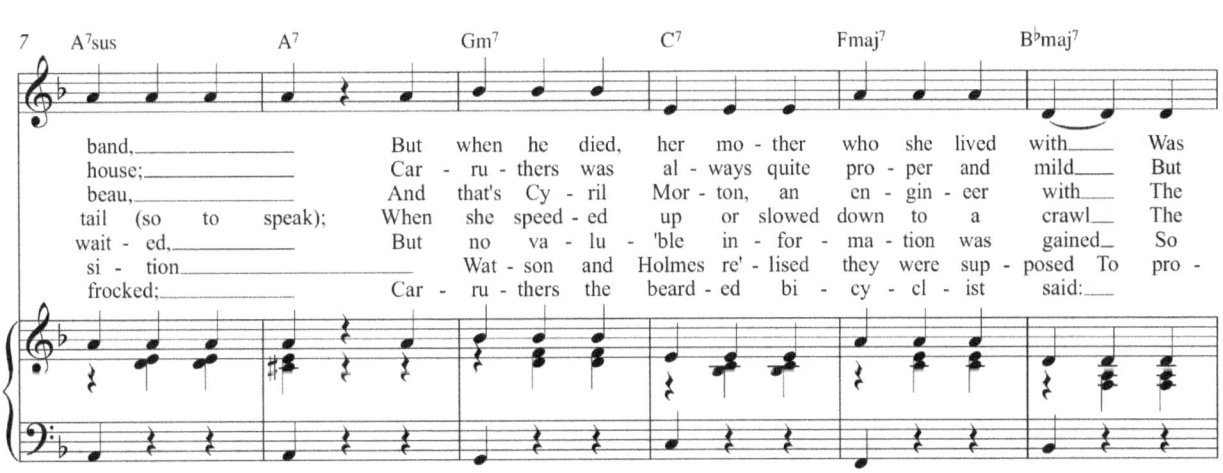

111

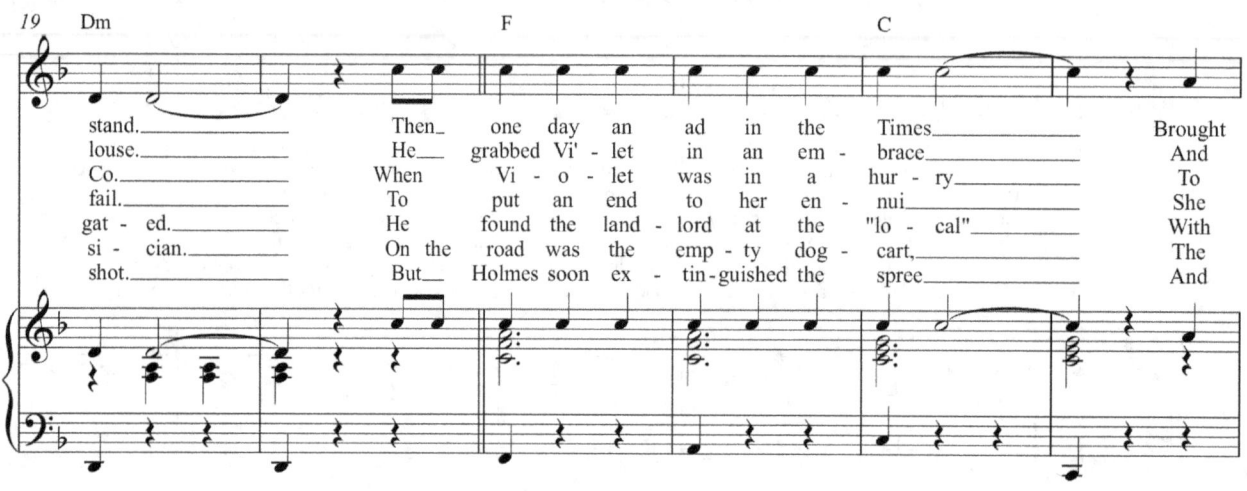

19. (Dm) stand. / (F) Then one day an ad in the Times (C) Brought
louse. / He grabbed Vi'-let in an em-brace And
Co. / When Vi-o-let was in a hur-ry To
fail. / To put an end to her en-nui She
gat-ed. / He found the land-lord at the "lo-cal" With
si-cian. / On the road was the emp-ty dog-cart, The
shot. / But Holmes soon ex-tin-guished the spree And

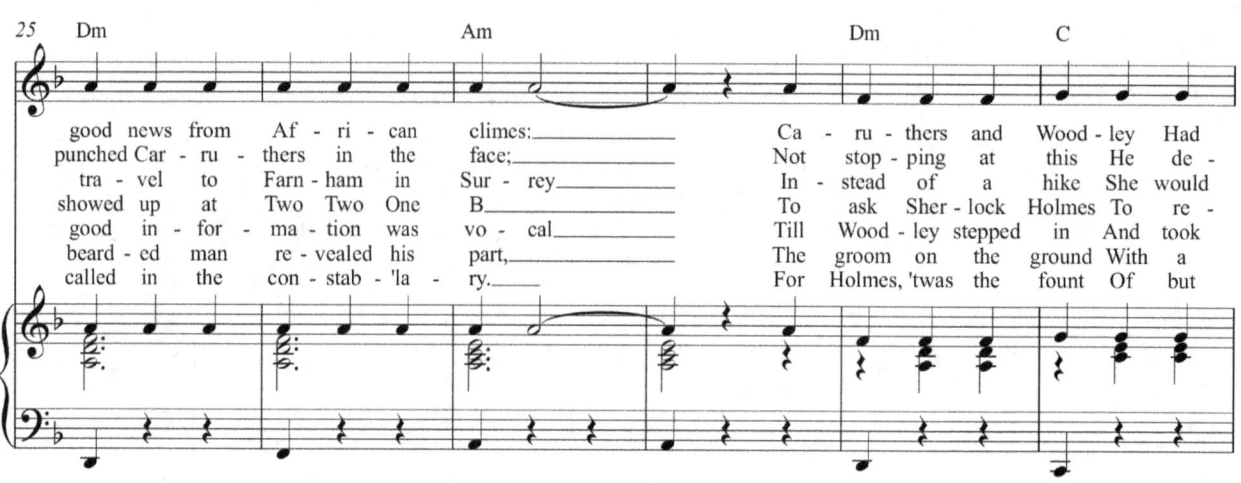

25. (Dm) good news from Af-ri-can climes: (Am) Ca-ru-thers and Wood-ley (Dm) Had (C)
punched Car-ru-thers in the face: Not stop-ping at this He de-
tra-vel to Farn-ham in Sur-rey In-stead of a hike She would
showed up at Two Two One B To ask Sher-lock Holmes To re-
good in-for-ma-tion was vo-cal Till Wood-ley stepped in And took
beard-ed man re-vealed his part, The groom on the ground With a
called in the con-stab-'la-ry. For Holmes, 'twas the fount Of but

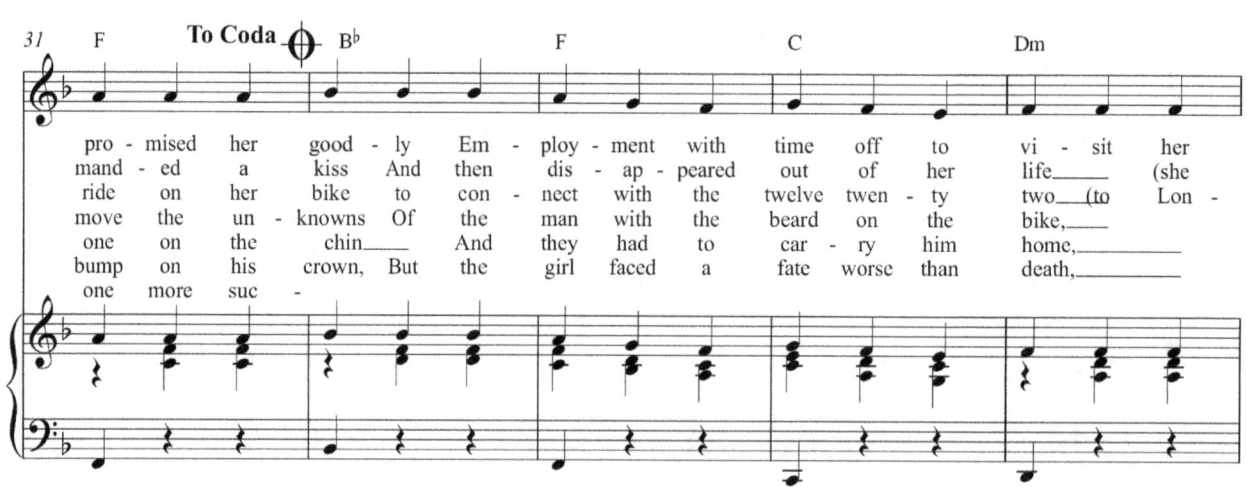

31. (F) pro-mised her good-ly Em- **To Coda** (Bb) ploy-ment with (F) time off to (C) vi-sit her (Dm)
mand-ed a kiss And then dis-ap-peared out of her life (she
ride on her bike to con-nect with the twelve twen-ty two (to Lon-
move the un-knowns Of the man with the beard on the bike,
one on the chin And they had to car-ry him home,
bump on his crown, But the girl faced a fate worse than death,
one more suc -

112

The Solitary Cyclist

I tell you the story of Violet Smith
Whose father conducted the band
But when he died, her mother who she lived with
Was left having no leg to stand on
Left with no leg on which to stand

Then one day an ad in The Times
Brought good news from African climes:
Carruthers and Woodley
Had promised her goodly
Employment with time off to visit her mom
With time off to visit her mom

So Vi'let taught music to Carruthers' child
And lived at the Chiltern Grange house
Carruthers was always quite proper and mild
But Woodley was really a louse
Oh that Woodley was really a louse

He grabbed Vi'let in an embrace
And punched Carruthers in the face
Not stopping at this
He demanded a kiss
And then disappeared out of her life (she thought)
He disappeared out of her life

No doubting the morals of Violet Smith
She's saving herself for her beau
And that's Cyril Morton, an engineer with
The Midland Electrical Co (at Coventry)
Midland Electrical Co

When Violet was in a hurry
To travel to Farnham in Surrey
Instead of a hike
She would ride on her bike
To connect with the 12:22 (to London)
Connect with the 12:22

Then one day while cycling by Charlington Hall
She noticed a man on her tail (so to speak)
When she speeded up or slowed down to a crawl
The man did the same without fail, he did
The man did the same without fail

To put an end to her ennui
She showed up at 221B
To ask Sherlock Holmes
To remove the unknowns
Of the man with the beard on the bike
Yes, the man with the beard on the bike

So Watson went down on an earlier train
Concealed himself well and then waited
But no valu'ble information was gained
So Holmes himself investigated
Yes, Sherlock Holmes investigated

He found the landlord at the "local"
With good information was vocal
Till Woodley stepped in
And took one on the chin
And they had to carry him home
Yes, they had to carry him home

When Violet wrote that her boss had proposed
And that she would leave her position
Watson and Holmes realised they were supposed
To protect the bicycling musician
Yes, protect the bicycling musician

On the road was the empty dog-cart
The bearded man revealed his part
The groom on the ground
With a bump on his crown
But the girl faced a fate worse than death
Yeth, the girl faced a fate worse than death

For Vi'let and Roaring Jack Woodley were wed
By Williamson, parson unfrocked
Carruthers the bearded bicyclist said
"No, she's your widow" and shot
Yes, Roaring Jack Woodley was shot

But Holmes soon extinguished the spree
And called in the constabulary
For Holmes 'twas the fount of but one more success
And Watson's account soon appeared in the press
The audience liked by deduction and might
How Holmes rescued the girl on the bike
He rescued the girl on the bike

The Priory School

by Jim Ballinger

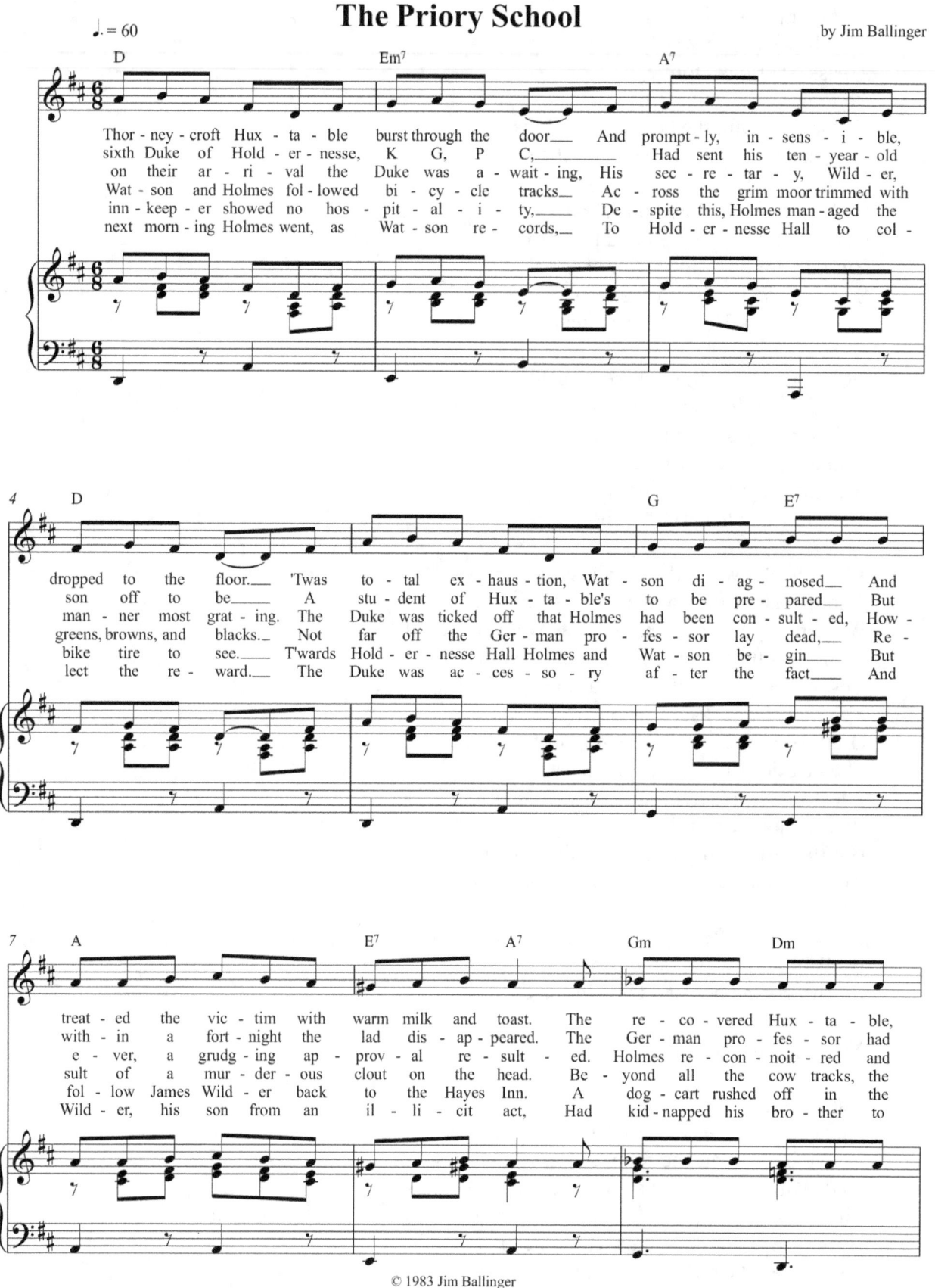

crim - son with shame, Pro - claim - ing him - self a liv - ing te - le - gramme. To
dis - ap - peared too, Per - haps on his bike the young Lord he pur - sued. Tracks
drew up a map, Some gip - sies were dis - cov - ered with the lad's cap, And
bike trace a - gain Led on 'cross the moor to the Fight - ing Cock Inn, Right
dark - en - ing gloom, A new - com - er was sent to a first - floor room. The
le - git - i - mise His claim to in - her - it the Hold - er - nesse prize. And

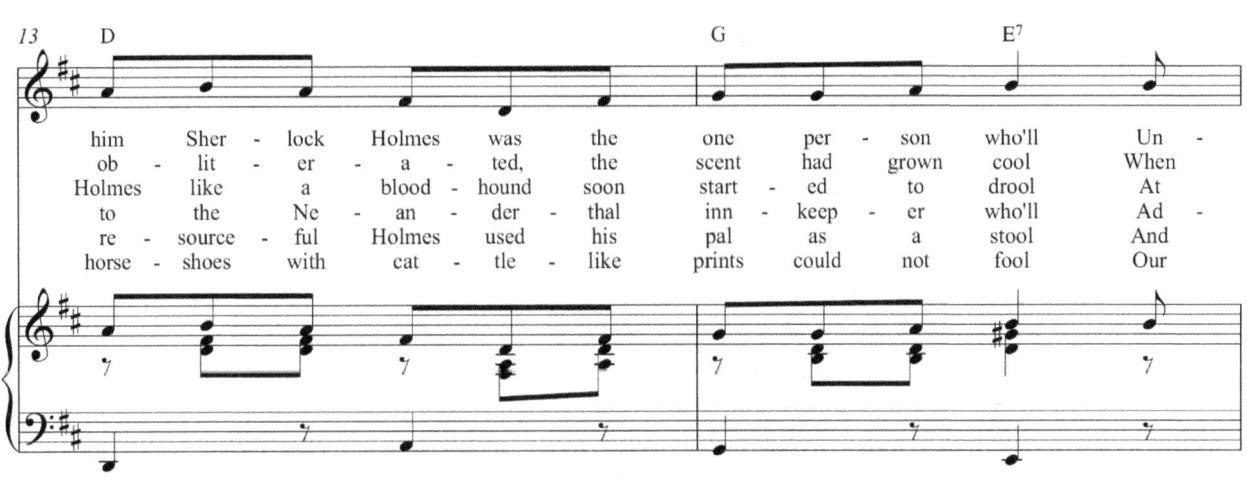

him Sher - lock Holmes was the one per - son who'll Un -
ob - lit - er - a - ted, the scent had grown cool When
Holmes like a blood - hound soon start - ed to drool At
to the Ne - an - der - thal inn - keep - er who'll Ad -
re - source - ful Holmes used his pal as a stool And
horse - shoes with cat - tle - like prints could not fool Our

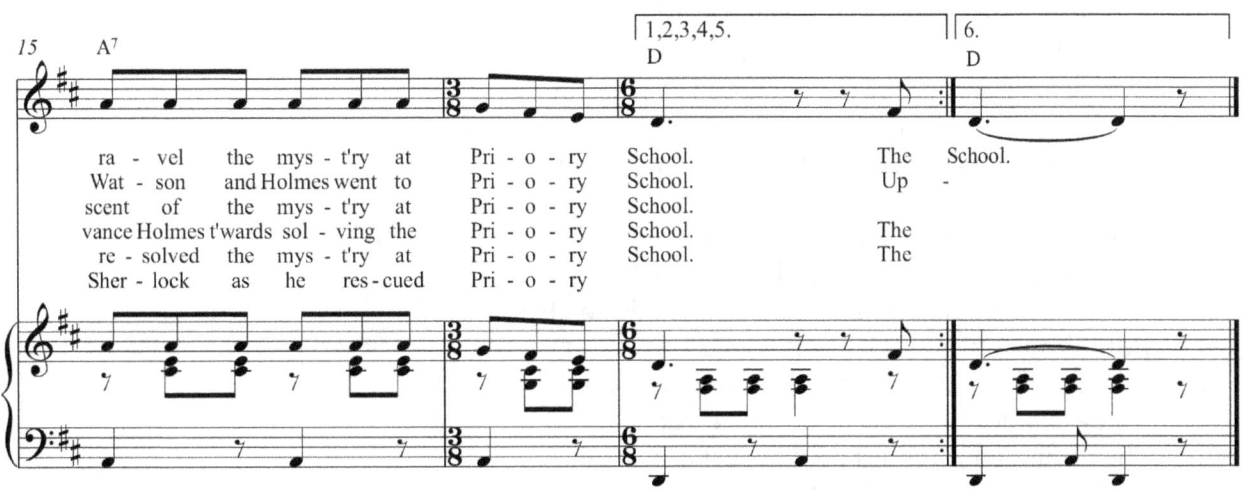

ra - vel the mys - t'ry at Pri - o - ry School. The School.
Wat - son and Holmes went to Pri - o - ry School. Up -
scent of the mys - t'ry at Pri - o - ry School.
vance Holmes t'wards sol - ving the Pri - o - ry School. The
re - solved the mys - t'ry at Pri - o - ry School. The
Sher - lock as he res - cued Pri - o - ry

The Priory School

Thorneycroft Huxtable burst through the door
And promptly, insensible, fell to the floor
'Twas total exhaustion, Watson diagnosed
And treated the victim with warm milk and toast
The recovered Huxtable, crimson with shame
Proclaiming himself a living telegramme
To him Sherlock Holmes was the one person who'll
Unravel the myst'ry at Priory School

The sixth Duke of Holdernesse, KG, PC
Had sent his ten-year-old son off to be
A student at Huxtable's to be prepared
But within a fortnight the lad disappeared
The German professor had disappeared too
Perhaps on his bike the young Lord he pursued
Tracks obliterated, the scent had grown cool
When Watson and Holmes went to Priory School

Upon their arrival the Duke was awaiting
His secretary, Wilder, manner most grating
The Duke was ticked off that Holmes had been consulted
However, a grudging approval resulted
Holmes reconnoitred and drew up a map
Some gipsies were discovered with the lad's cap
And Holmes like a bloodhound soon started to drool
At scent of the myst'ry at Priory School

Watson and Holmes followed bicycle tracks
Across the grim moor trimmed with greens, browns, and blacks
Not far off the German professor lay dead
Result of a murderous clout on the head
Beyond all the cow tracks, the bike trace again
Led on 'cross the moor to the Fighting Cock Inn
Right to the Neanderthal innkeeper who'll
Advance Holmes towards solving the Priory School

The innkeeper showed no hospitality
Despite this, Holmes managed the bike tire to see
Towards Holdernesse Hall Holmes and Watson begin
But follow James Wilder back to the Hayes Inn
A dog-cart rushed off in the darkening gloom
A newcomer was sent to a first-floor room
The resourceful Holmes used his pal as a stool
And resolved the myst'ry at Priory School

The next morning Holmes went, as Watson records
To Holdernesse Hall to collect the reward
The Duke was accessory after the fact
And Wilder, his son from an illicit act
Had kidnapped his brother to legitimise
His claim to inherit the Holdernesse prize
And horseshoes with cattle-like prints could not fool
Our Sherlock as he rescued Priory School

Black Peter

by Jim Ballinger

Verse lyrics:

Pe-ter Car - ey__ sailed in__ search of whales, he spent most of his life at sea.__ He was cap-tain of the "Sea U - ni - corn" in eight-y three and re - tired to Wood-man's Lee.__ He__ drank like a fish and when he got pished he would chase his wife and beat her. He__ once set his wrath on a

Hop - kins re-treat - ed to Ba - ker Street to__ ask for__ help from Sher - lock. When de - tec - tives__ three went to Wood - Man's Lee they found some - one forced the door lock. They__ kept watch that night with the door in sight, he re - turned to force the locks.__ 'Twas the Nel - li - gan lad, Pe-ter'd

Sher-lock's digs o - ver scram - bled eggs they__ in - ter - viewed three sail - ors. The__ first two were de-ferred, then__ en - ter the third, 'twas__ Pat - rick Cairns, the whal - er. He was big and__ tough e - ven in hand - cuffs, it took three men to sub - due him. Holmes con - grat - u - lat - ed his

120

Black Peter

Peter Carey sailed in search of whales
He spent most of his life at sea
He was captain of the "Sea Unicorn" in '83
And retired to Woodman's Lee

He drank like a fish and when he got pished
He would chase his wife and beat her
He once set his wrath on a man of the cloth
They all knew him as Black Peter

One night his daughter heard him slaughtered
In his cabin in the woods
He met his doom with a steel harpoon
Bluebottles, flies, and blood

The clues in the room were a bottle of rum
With two dirty glasses beside it
A notebook and tobacco pouch
With initials PC inside it

His beard was as black as a pile of coal
And so was his temper and so was his soul
He sailed seven seas till he got too old
And retired to Woodman's Lee -- Black Peter

Stanley Hopkins retreated to Baker Street
To ask for help from Sherlock
When detectives three went to Woodman's Lee
They found someone forced the door lock

They kept watch that night with the door in sight
He returned to force the locks
'Twas the Neligan lad, Peter'd killed his dad
And marketed his stocks

Young Neligan said Black Peter was dead
Before he reached the cabin
But no other suspect could be detected
So Hopkins had to nab him

But Holmes wasn't sure, set a trap to lure
The killer to his bait
Sent some telegrams to complete his plans
While Stanley Hopkins ate

His beard was as black as a pile of coal
And so was his temper and so was his soul
He sailed seven seas till he got too old
And retired to Woodman's Lee -- Black Peter

At Sherlock's digs over scrambled eggs
They interviewed three sailors
The first two were deferred, then enter the third
'Twas Patrick Cairns the whaler

He was big and tough even in handcuffs
It took three men to subdue him
Holmes congratulated his Scotland Yard mate
The killer came right to him

Cairns knew Pete from the Dundee fleet
And had seen the murder happen
With blackmail in mind he set out to find
The retired rich sea captain

Peter let him in three sheets to the wind
With murder in his eyes
But Cairns contends it was self-defence
Left his baccy-pouch behind

So what have we all learned from this?
The moral is plain to see:
You can never, never, never
Never trust a PC

His beard was as black as a pile of coal
And so was his temper and so was his soul
He sailed seven seas till he got too old
And retired to Woodman's Lee -- Black Peter

Charles Augustus Milverton

by Jim Ballinger

Charles Augustus Milverton

Charles Augustus Milverton
My name strikes terror in the heart
Of any man or, worse, a woman
Who has fallen in my grasp
Charles Augustus Milverton
For many lives were thrown away
By people who refused to pay
I always have the final laugh
Charles Augustus Milverton
Charles Augustus Milverton

I'm Charles Augustus Milverton
And of my life I sing
I'm called the worst man in London
Of blackmailers the king
From treacherous valets and maids
I purchase documents
Embarrassing when trump is played
At judicious moments

The threat of family ruin
Makes them cough up princely sums
The all dance to the tune
Which I gleefully do hum
I have been called my many names
Called of a bitch the son
But that is all part of the game
For Charles A Milverton

I pay a call on Sherlock Holmes
Who's acting as an agent
For Lady Eva Blackwell's moans
Concerning her engagement
Some letters to a country sport
(She filled his every want)
Would show the Earl of Dovercourt
She's not a debutante

My price is seven thousand quid
But Lady Eve won's meet it
And I refuse her lower bid
And with drawn gun I beat it
Now, Holmes and Watson, hugs and kisses?
Scandal there, me thought
It's such a bloody shame that Missus
Hudson can't be bought

The night in question I do not
Retire at ten-thirty
For there are letters to be bought
With secrets dark and dirty
The veilèd maid at last is there
With letter compromising
The foolish young Countess d'Albert
But comes a twist surprising

The maid removes her veil revealing
Not a maid at all
In fact, a former victim feeling
Bitter from her fall
Her hand emerges from her coat
I hear a dreadful sound
Each pistol shot I hear her gloat
Take that, and that, you hound

Charles Augustus Milverton
As I lie dying on the floor
Two men who hid behind the curtains
Burn the contents of my safe
Charles Augustus Milverton
Before my man breaks down the door
The two masked trespassers are certain
To have made a clean escape
Charles Augustus Milverton
Charles Augustus Milverton

The Six Napoleons

by Jim Ballinger

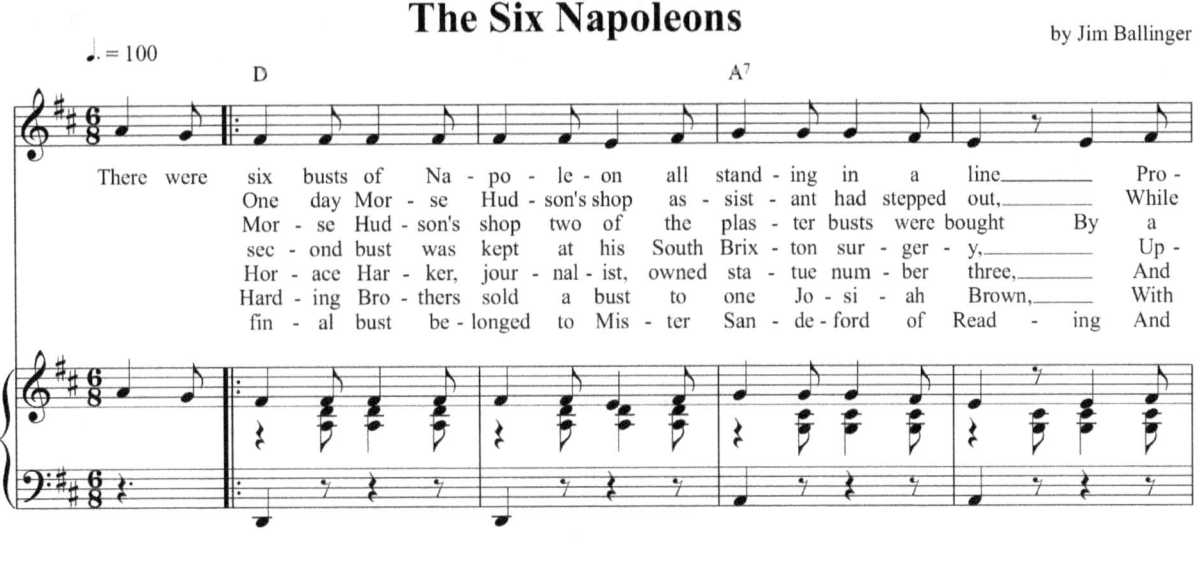

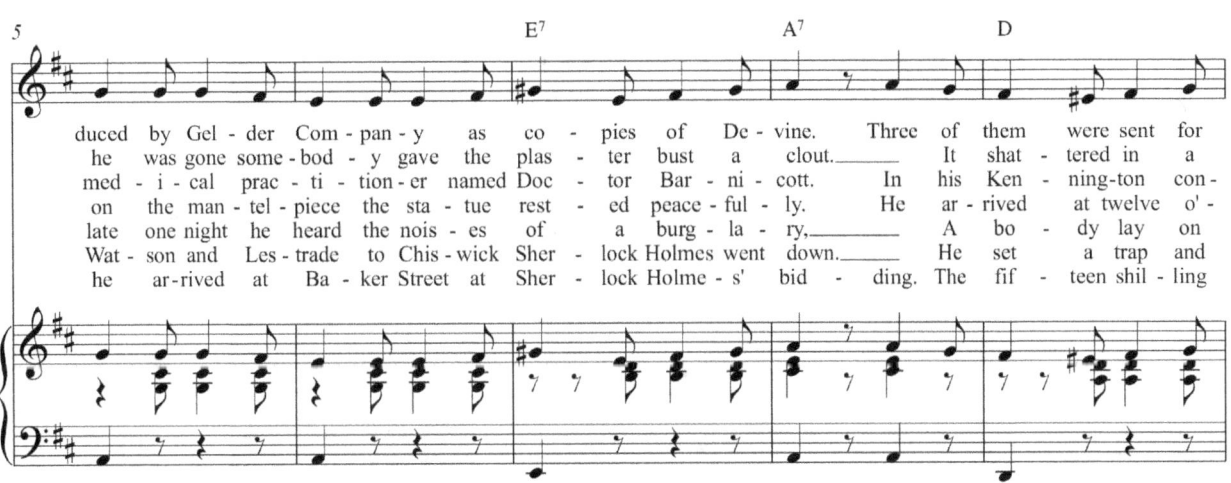

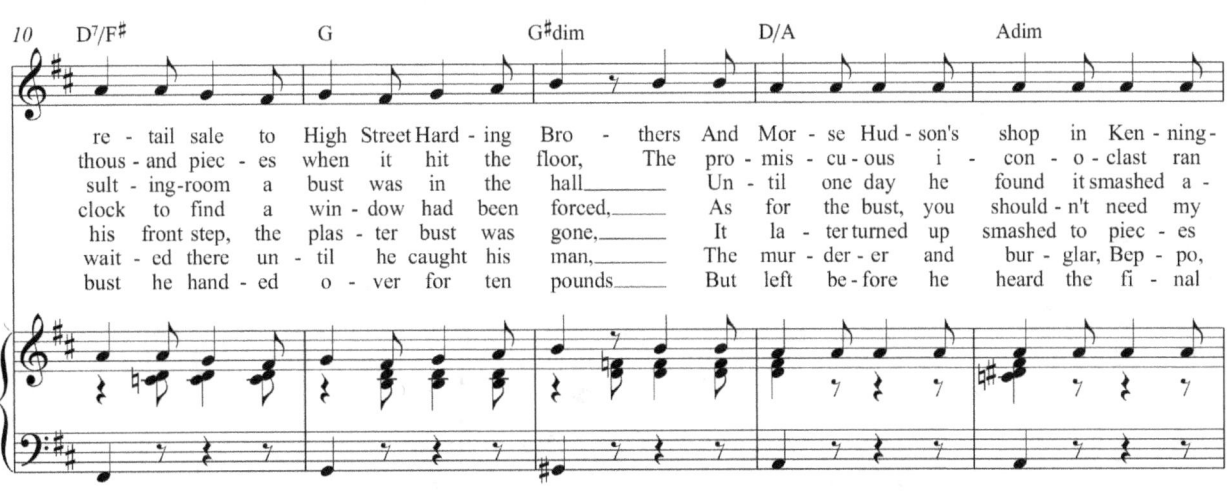

129

The Six Napoleons

There were six busts of Napoleon all standing in a line
Produced by Gelder Company as copies of Devine
Three of them were sent for retail sale to High Street Harding Brothers
And Morse Hudson's shop in Kennington would sell the others

The Emperor's stern face
With furrowed brow and gaze transfixed
As Sherlock Holmes would solve the case
Of the Napoleonic six

One day Morse Hudson's shop assistant had stepped out
While he was gone somebody gave the plaster bust a clout
It shattered in a thousand pieces when it hit the floor
The promiscuous iconoclast ran safely out the door

The case brought by Lestrade
To solve it Sherlock Holmes would strive
He would catch the daring sod
Who brought the number down to five

From Morse Hudson's shop two of the plaster busts were bought
By a medical practitioner named Dr Barnicot
In his Kennington consulting-room a bust was in the hall
Until one day he found it smashed against the garden wall

Napoleonic treasures
Right from ceiling down to floor
Less the one of cheapest measure
Leaving us with only four

A second bust was kept at his South Brixton surgery
Upon the mantelpiece the statue rested peacefully
He arrived at twelve o'clock to find a window had been forced
As for the bust, you shouldn't need my help to guess the worst

You shouldn't need my help to guess
How many left there be
From former four there is one less
The answer must be three

Horace Harker, journalist, owned statue number three
And late one night he heard the noises of a burglary
A body lay on his front step, the plaster bust was gone
It later turned up smashed to pieces on a neighbour's lawn

The victim had a photograph
To Sherlock 'twas a clue
He planned to have the final laugh
And save bust number two

The Harding Brothers sold a bust to one Josiah Brown
With Watson and Lestrade to Chiswick Sherlock Holmes went down
He set a trap and waited there until he caught his man
The murderer and burglar, Beppo, walked into their hands

But not before the bust was bust
As Beppo had his fun
The fifth straight bust had bit the dust
Which left us only one

The final bust belonged to Mr Sandeford of Reading
And he arrived at Baker Street at Sherlock Holmes's bidding
The fifteen-shilling bust he handed over for ten pounds
But left before he heard the final plaster-smashing sound

The black pearl of the Borgias
Was inside the final bust
As Sherlock Holmes rewards us
For awarding him our trust

And on a literary note
My little song is done
As Agatha Christie once wrote:
"And then there were none!"

The Three Students

by Jim Ballinger

133

Hil - ton
The dis -

For the pap - ers were moved from their place on the ta - ble, some
on - ly three stu - dents who were on the same stairs and so

wood - shav - ings proved that a draft was un - a - ble to ac - count where they lay. There was
Holmes thought it pru - dent to start quest - ion - ing there. It was Gil - chrsit on first floor, on the

al - so a lump made of saw - dust and clay and the tu - tor was
next Dau - lat Ras; Miles Mc - La - ren burst forth most pro - fane on the

stumped. There were last. So when

D.S. al Fine

134

The Three Students

Mr Hilton Soames
Called on Sherlock Holmes
As he studied early charters
To avoid a scandal
If Holmes would handle
A myst'ry at his quarters
The exam was due for the Fortesque
Scholarship which Soames taught
Greek in
And the test must be kept in secrecy
But it seems someone was peekin'

Hilton looked for goofs
In the galley proofs
In a chapter for translation
But while he was out
For a glass of stout
(Claiming tea was his libation)
His long trusted servant
Was unobservant
And left the office open
And the evidence that this negligence
Led to scandal sent Soames mopin'

For the papers were moved
From their place on the table
Some wood-shavings proved
That a draft was unable
To account where they lay
There was also a lump
Made of sawdust and clay
And the tutor was stumped

There were only three students
Who were on the same stairs
And so Holmes thought it prudent
To start questioning there
It was Gilchrist on first floor
On the next, Daulat Ras
Miles McLaren burst forth
Most profane on the last

So when Hilton Soames
Whined to Sherlock Holmes
He was told to keep his shirt on
Things would be set right
By the morning light
And of that Sherlock was certain
At the crack of dawn
Sherlock was long gone
Then took Watson without breakfast
He had solved the case
Of exam disgrace
And was off to save Soames neck fast

The distraught tutor
Called for Bannister
Sherlock knew the man was lying
When young Gilchrist came
And saw his dismay
He broke down and started crying
But his plan to flee to the colonies
Satisfied the jurisprudents
And they headed straight
For their breakfast plates
Closed the case of the Three Students

The Golden Pince-Nez

by Jim Ballinger

'Twas a night not fit for man nor beast when to
path by which no - one had passed but some
searched for foot-steps by the walk and found
Sher - lock helped pick up the stash he saw
Holmes the ev - i - dence gave she, "Take it

Bak - er Street came the po - lice. Young In - spec - tor Hop - kins on the case of a
one had trod - den on the grass, so young Hop - kins said, which Holmes would call be - ing
scratch - es on the ta - ble lock. The in - vest - ig - a - tion starts to bloom in Pro -
foot - prints in the bed of ash and a wo - man out of hid - ing stirred show - ing
to the Rus - sian Em - bas - sy." She had tak - en poi - son, sank a - way, nev - er

mur - der at Yox - ley Old Place.
cer - tain of no - thing at all.
fes - sor Co ram's own bed - room.
the pro - fes - sor it was her.
more to wear the gold pince - nez.

Fine

A sec - ret - a - ry named Wil - lough - by Smith in the
Go - ing back to where the case com - menced there was
When in there the first thing Sher - lock saw: cig - a -
For the kil - ler was the old man's wife. Back in

neck was stabbed and found near death by a maid named Su - san just as he mur-mured
one piece of firm ev - i - dence: in the mur - dered man's right hand there lay clasped a
rettes from Al - ex - an - dri - a. He be - gan to mad - ly smoke and pace, spread-ing
Rus - sia, mar - ried late in life, there had he his wife and friends be - trayed. They all

"The pro - fes - sor, it was she." There were on - ly two ways
pair of gold - en - rimmed pince - nez. And from these could Sher - lock
ash - es all o - ver the place. They re - turned af - ter the
went to jail, he got a - way. He had tak - en with him

out of there: the pro - fes - sor's bed - room up the stairs and the oth - er mat - ted
Holmes in - fer a des - crip - tion of the mur - der - er: her re - fine - ment, pos - ture,
old man's lunch ('twas a big one, as per Sher - lock's hunch) where that care - less Sher - lock
ev - i - dence of a pa - ci - fist friend's in - no - cence. From Si - ber - i - a it

cor - ri - dor led di - rect - ly to the gar - den door._____ And a
and her face, so they set off for Yox - ley Old Place._____ Where they
did up - set the en - ti - re box of cig - a - rettes._____ And while
could re - prieve, so to Eng - land she came to re - trieve._____ And to

137

The Golden Pince-Nez

'Twas a night not fit for man nor beast
When to Baker Street came the police
Young Inspector Hopkins on the case
Of a murder at Yoxley Old Place

A secretary named Willoughby Smith
In the neck was stabbed and found near death
By a maid named Susan just as he
Murmured "The professor, it was she"

There were only two ways out of there
The professor's bedroom up the stairs
And the other matted corridor
Led directly to the garden door

And a path by which no-one had passed
But someone had trodden on the grass
So young Hopkins said, which Holmes would call
Being certain of nothing at all

Going back to where the case commenced
There was one piece of firm evidence
In the murdered man's right hand there lay
Clasped a pair of golden-rimmed pince-nez

And from these could Sherlock Holmes infer
A description of the murderer
Her refinement, posture, and her face
So they set off for Yoxley Old Place

Where they searched for footsteps by the walk
And found scratches on the table lock
The investigation starts to bloom
In Professor Coram's own bedroom

When in there the first thing Sherlock saw
Cigarettes from Alexandria
He began to madly smoke and pace
Spreading ashes all over the place

They returned after the old man's lunch
('Twas a big one, as per Sherlock's hunch)
Where that careless Sherlock did upset
The entire box of cigarettes

And while Sherlock helped pick up the stash
He saw footprints in the bed of ash
And a woman out of hiding stirred
Showing the professor it was her

For the killer was the old man's wife
Back in Russia, married late in life
There had he his wife and friends betrayed
They all went to jail, he got away

He had taken with him evidence
Of a pacifist friend's innocence
From Siberia it could reprieve
So to England she came to retrieve

And to Holmes the evidence gave she
"Take it to the Russian Embassy"
She had taken poison, sank away
Never more to wear the gold pince-nez

The Missing Three-Quarter

by Jim Ballinger

"Please a-wait me, Ter-ri-ble mis-for-tune, Right wing three-quart-er mis-sing, In-dis-pen-si-ble to-mor-row."

Such was the te-le-gram from Cy-ril O-ver-ton,
Ar-thur H Staun-ton, the ris-ing young for-ger, nor
rooms at the inn o-ver-look-ing the Arm-strong shack,

skip-per of Tri-ni-ty Col-leg-e's team. Young Stan-ley Hop-kins thought
one Hen-ry Staun-ton whom Holmes saw well hung. This was God-frey Staun-ton, the
Sher-lock at-temp-ted to fol-low his prey. In-ver-ness fly-ing, he

his sto-ry o-ver done and so to Sher-lock coach Cy-ril did steam. For
Cam-bridge three-quart-er, who could pass or tack-le or drib-ble or run. He
cyc-led and kept long back but Arm-strong saw him and broke up the play. Each

31 Bm   D   D⁷/F♯   G   G♯dim

unc - le,   was   spot - ted,   a   te - le - graph clerk gave Holmes   in - fo   he sought - ed,   to
sit - ting,   half kneel - ing,   young Staun - ton   was racked by   the   sobs   he   was feel - ing,   "Con -

34 A⁷   E⁷   A⁷   Bm   F♯⁷

wit: who was that ur - gent   te - le - gram for?____   Wat - son and Holmes went to   Cam - bridge to - ge - ther, asked
sump - tion be done" was all   Wat - son could say.   For   such was the case   of the   mis - sing three quart - er,   he

38   Bm   D   D⁷/F♯   G   G♯dim

me - di - cine's Dean, Les - lie Arm - str - ong, whe - ther he   could help, but soon reached the   end   of   his   te - ther and
se - cret - ly   mar - ried his   land - la - dy's daught - er,   pro - tect his in - he - ri - tance till sick - ness got her and

42   D   A⁷   1. D   2. D

un - ce - re - mon - ious - ly   showed them the   door.   With   play.
he ar - rived in her last   mi - nute of

142

The Missing Three-Quarter

"Please await me
Terrible misfortune
Right wing three-quarter missing
Indispensable tomorrow"

Such was the telegram from Cyril Overton
Skipper of Trinity College's team
Young Stanley Hopkins thought his story over done
And so to Sherlock coach Cyril did steam
For match against Oxford the squad was in London
And just settled at Bentley's private hotel
Abruptly their chances of winning came undone
Without Godfrey Staunton their game's shot to hell

Not Arthur B Staunton, the rising young forger
Nor one Henry Staunton whom Holmes saw well hung
This was Godfrey Staunton, the Cambridge three-quarter
Who could pass or tackle or dribble or run
He disappeared from the hotel in the company
Of a bewhiskered, disquieted man
If Sherlock can't find him the team doesn't have any
Hope; without Staunton they're not worth a damn

At the hotel Sherlock found message blotted
And Lord Mount-James, Staunton's rich uncle, was spotted
A telegraph clerk gave Holmes info he soughted
To wit: who was that urgent telegram for?
Watson and Holmes went to Cambridge together
Asked medicine's dean, Leslie Armstrong, whether
He could help, but soon reached the end of his tether
And unceremoniously showed them the door

With rooms at the inn overlooking the Armstrong shack
Sherlock attempted to follow his prey
Inverness flying, he cycled and kept long back
But Armstrong saw him and broke up the play
Each pass intercepted, each receiver covered
Holmes put on the blitz with a threadbare device
A draghound named Pompey pursued and discovered
The missing three-quarter who'd paid such a price

A girl on the bed with her eyes toward the ceiling
Lay peaceful in death while, half sitting, half kneeling
Young Staunton was racked by the sobs he was feeling
"Consumption be done" was all Watson could say
For such was the case of the Missing Three-Quarter
He secretly married his landlady's daughter
Protect his inheritance till sickness got her
And he arrived in her last minute of play

The Abbey Grange

by Jim Ballinger

She was a young girl from Aus-tra-lia, her first time a-way from home. Her name was Ma-ry
Eust-ace was a drunk-ard of the most un-plea-sant kind. Their life at Ab-bey
spect-or Stan-ley Hop-kins asked if Sher-lock Holmes would aid, So Holmes and Wat-son

Fra-ser with her trus-ty maid in tow. The ship, Rock of Gib-ral-tar, Ad-el-aide-South-amp-ton
Grange was hell but mar-riage vows do bind. His wife's dog with pet-rol-e-um he drenched and set a-
caught the ear-ly morn-ing Kent-ish train. The sto-ry seemed con-vinc-ing from the la-dy and her

bound. First of-fi-cer, Jack Crok-er, was the first male friend she found._____ For
light And threw a glass de-can-ter at the maid, Ther-e-sa Wright._____ And
maid But the bee-swing in the wine glass-es a-lert-ed Sher-lock's brain._____ He

once in Lon-don, star-ry-eyed, she met Sir Eus-tace Brack-en-stall and soon be-came his gol-den bride and
so Jack Crock-er chanced near-by to hear of Ma-ry's dread-ful plight. He went to see her on the sly till
tracked down Cap-tain Crock-er and con-vinced him to con-fess__ to the truth a-bout the pok-er__ and

25

E7   **A**   **Bm**   **F#m**

moved to Ab - bey Grange.   Her trust - y maid, The - re - sa Wright, went with them down to   Mar - sham, Kent, where
she'd see him no   more.   A - bout to set sail,   he in - sist - ed   that she see him   one last time. The
his role in the   piece.   With Wat - son as the   ju - ry and with Sher - lock as the judge, the Brit - ish

31

Bm   **Em7**   **A7**   **1.** **D**   **2.** **D**

soon their hon - ey - moon de - light in - to a night - mare changed._____ Sir door._____ Al -
girl, though she at   first re - sist - ed,   op - ened the French
pub - lic need not wor - ry though the kill - er is   re -

38

F#m   **Bm**

though their love was   in - no - cent, Sir Eus - tace found them there that night, He called his wife the   vil - est name and
maid had heard her   la - dy scream and came down to   in - vest - i - gate. To - geth - er they de - vised a scheme to

44

Em

struck her with his   cane.   But Cro - ker grabbed a   pok - er and en - gaged Sir Eus - tace   in fair fight, The
co - ver up the   crime.   A   re - cent burg - lar - y   re - called with clues which would cor - rob - er - ate the

The Abbey Grange

She was a young girl from Australia
Her first time away from home
Her name was Mary Fraser
With her trusty maid in tow
The ship, Rock of Gibraltar
Adelaide-Southampton bound
First officer, Jack Croker
Was the first male friend she found

For once in London, starry-eyed
She met Sir Eustace Brackenstall
And soon became his golden bride
And moved to Abbey Grange
Her trusty maid, Theresa Wright
Went with them down to Marsham,
Kent
Where soon their honeymoon delight
Into a nightmare changed

Sir Eustace was a drunkard
Of the most unpleasant kind
Their life at Abbey Grange was hell
But marriage vows do bind
His wife's dog with petroleum
He drenched and set alight
And threw a glass decanter
At the maid, Theresa Wright

And so Jack Croker chanced nearby
To hear of Mary's dreadful plight
He went to see her on the sly
Till she'd see him no more
About to set sail, he insisted
That she see him one last time
The girl, though she at first resisted
Opened the French door

Although their love was innocent
Sir Eustace found them there that night
He called his wife the vilest name
And struck her with his cane

But Croker grabbed the poker
And engaged Sir Eustace in fair fight
The poker found its mark
And splattered wide the husband's
brain

The maid had heard her Lady scream
And came down to investigate
Together they devised a scheme
To cover up the crime
A recent burglary recalled
With clues which would corroborate
The story Lady Brackenstall
Would lead police to fine

Inspector Stanley Hopkins
Asked if Sherlock Holmes would aid
So Holmes and Watson caught
The early morning Kentish train
The story seemed convincing
From the Lady and her maid
But beeswing in the wine glasses
Alerted Sherlock's brain

He tracked down Captain Croker
And convinced him to confess
To the truth about the poker
And his role in this piece
With Watson as the jury
And with Sherlock as the judge
The British public need not worry
Though a killer is released

Poor Mary Fraser
Fresh from Australia
Foolishly marries the vilest of men
With the help of a poker
Wielded by Jack Croker
Poor Mary Fraser is single again

The Second Stain

by Jim Ballinger

wife was at the show.) This morn-ing op-ened dis - be - liev - ing: where - ev - er did it
all the fuss is for: If that damn let - ter is ex - posed, 'twill___ cert - ain - ly mean

go? Now war.

There's been a mur-der in West
There comes a tel - e-gram from

min'ster.. Ed - uard - o Lu-cas has been stabbed in the heart.
Par is.___ Ma - dame Hen-ri Four-naye was Lu - cas-'s wife.

Though his val - et at first seemed
She's gone in-sane and that should

sin' ster,___ His al - i - bi was good, our case fell a-part.
spare us:___ She killed him on dis - cov'ring

his doub-le life.

150

151

The Second Stain

Trelawney Hope:
When I looked in my despatch-box
At eight o'clock this morning it was gone
An extremely important letter from a foreign potentate
I at once informed the Prime Minister, Lord Bellinger
At his suggestion we came to Sherlock Holmes
My name is Trelawney Hope
And hope is all that we have left

The letter came six days ago
It's never left my sight
Into the safe it straight did go
Despatch-box every night
Unguarded several hours last evening
(My wife was at the show)
This morning opened disbelieving
Wherever did it go?

Now Mister Holmes asks what in fact
Would make it so momentous
We plead Official Secrets Act
Provisions which prevent us
He calls our bluff and we disclose
What all the fuss is for
If that damn letter is exposed
'Twill certainly mean war

Lestrade:
There's been a murder in Westminister
Eduardo Lucas has been stabbed in the heart
Though his valet at first seemed sinister
His alibi was good, our case fell apart

There comes a telegram from Paris
Madame Henri Fournaye was Lucas's wife
She's gone insane and that should spare us
She killed him on discovering his double life

The case is closed, Lestrade has solved it once more
There's just one puzzle which remains
The blood did not soak through the carpet to the floor
But in the other corner was a second stain

Lady Hilda:
Mister Holmes, this is surely unfair on your part
I desired that you would keep secret my visit
Now you compromise me, do kindly depart
Don't insult me by asking "The letter, where is it?"

Mister Holmes does then threaten my husband to tell
And so I am compelled to confess my infraction
An indiscreet note into Lucas' hands fell
Which could not be redeemed save for larcenous action

And while I was performing the exchange at Godolphin
A frantic French femme fatale flew into the room
I feared for my life as she brandished a knife
When I woke the next morning the nightmare resumed

I decoyed the policeman, recovered the letter
From its hiding place wherein it had remained
Mister Holmes thinks a despatch-box return would be better
Concludes the Adventure of the Second Stain

Come, sir, there is more to this than meets the eye
How came the letter back into the box?
We also have our diplomatic secrets
That's all that Holmes is sayin'
About the Second Stain

Section 4:
His Last Bow

Wisteria Lodge

by Jim Ballinger

♩ = 100

Verse lyrics (stanzas aligned under the melody):

Mis-ter John Scott Ec-cles had sent Sher-lock Holmes a note__ Re-quest-ing an ap-point-ment to con-
fore the man could start his night's ad-ven-ture to ex-plain__ Two of-fic-ials en-tered in a
fel-low known as Hend-er-son with-in High Gab-le lived, His sec-re-tar-y al-ways by his
ci-a was an a-gent who was out to bag the Tig-er. The gov-er-ness, Miss Bur-net, was his

sult.__ "Have just had most in-cred-i-ble ex-per-i-ence", he wrote; "Gro-
hur-ry.__ One was Greg-son, Scot-land Yard, the oth-er was called Baynes, In-
side.__ There al-so was a gov-er-ness to ed-u-cate his kids,__ But
spy.__ Us-ing this ar-range-ment he had thought his chan-ces bright-er Of

tesque", as well, it verged on the oc-cult.__ At two-fif-teen his meas-ured step was
spect-or with the con-stab-l'ry in Sur-rey.__ All morn-ing they had sought him for a
all of this an e-vil past did hide.__ For he in fact was Don Mur-il-lo,
choos-ing when the dev-ious Don would die.__ But the mes-sage to Gar-ci-a was con-
il-lo and his loy-al friend made

heard up-on the stairs.__ His__ cloth-ing showed signs of neg-lect, like-wise his brist-ling hair.__ 'Cause
state-ment to ob-tain,__ And now that they had got him they'd per-mit him to ex-plain__ How
Tig-er of San Ped-ro, As__ lewd and blood-thirst-y a fel-low as a des-per-a-do, And
vert-ed to a trap.__ Des-pite his plan to be a sap-per, he be-came a sap,__ And
good their es-cape bid.__ With-in six months they met their end in ho-tel in Mad-rid.__ 'Cause

159

35 **2,3,4.**

pleas - ure._____ The din - ner was nei - ther well cooked nor well served. The serv-ant was sul - len, my
flight._____ Next morn - ing at Ox-shott, Gar - ci - a's found dead, A note in his pock - et, a
signed. At the Lodge were re - mains that a pag - an had put, And In-spect-or Baynes soon ar -

43

host was un - nerved. A note was brought in near the end of the meal_ At which he did not his dis -
hole in his head. It turned out Gar - ci - a was not who he seemed: No dip - lo - mat he, arch - i -
rest - ed the cook. But Holmes com - pre - hen-sion of da - ta was a - ble To fo - cus at - ten-tion on the

51

1.2. | **3.** | | **D.C.**

pleas - ure con - ceal.___ To Gab - le. A
tect of the scheme.___ The
house of High

Coda

54

Lodge. Yes, some-thing quite mys-ter - i - ous had hap-pened at Wist-er - i - a Lodge.

160

Wisteria Lodge

Mister John Scott Eccles Had sent Sherlock Holmes a note
Requesting an appointment to consult
"Have just had most incredible experience," he wrote
"Grotesque" as well, it verged on the occult
At two-fifteen his measured step was heard upon the stairs
His clothing showed signs of neglect likewise his bristling hair
'Cause something quite mysterious had happened at Wisteria Lodge

Before the man could start his night's adventure to explain
Two officials entered in a hurry
One was Gregson, Scotland Yard, the other was called Baynes
Inspector with the constab'l'ry in Surrey
All morning they had sought him for a statement to obtain
And now that they had got him they'd permit him to explain
How something quite mysterious had happened at Wisteria Lodge

I am a bach'lor of sociable turn, I cultivate numerous friends
One night I did see a young chap named Garcia
But who'd have known where it would end

I had him to my place, he asked me to his, located twixt Oxshott and Esher
The household was queer and it soon became clear
That the weekend would not be a pleasure

The dinner was neither well-cooked nor well-served
The servant was sullen, my host was unnerved
A note was brought in near the end of the meal
At which he did not his displeasure conceal

To bed at eleven, he popped in at one, I slept soundly the rest of the night
But when I awoke I thought it was a joke
For the household had all taken flight

Next morning at Oxshott, Garcia's found dead
A note in his pocket, a hole in his head
It turned out Garcia was not who he seemed
No diplomat he, architect of the scheme

The note which arrived near the end of the meal, the Surrey inspector did find
"Take the main stairs one flight then the seventh door right
Green and white. Godspeed. D." it was signed

At the Lodge were remains that a pagan had put
And Inspector Baynes soon arrested the cook
But Holmes' comprehension of data was able
To focus attention on the house of High Gable

A fellow known as Henderson within High Gable lived
His secretary was always by his side
There also was a governess to educate his kids
But all of this an evil past did hide
For he in fact was Don Murillo, Tiger of San Pedro
As lewd and bloodthirsty a fellow as a desperado
And something quite mysterious had happened at Wisteria Lodge

Garcia was an agent who was out to bag the Tiger
The governess, Miss Burnet, was his spy
Using this arrangement he had thought his chances brighter
Of choosing when the devious Don would die
But the message to Garcia was converted to a trap
Despite his plan to be a sapper, he became the sap
And something quite mysterious had happened at Wisteria Lodge

Murillo and his loyal friend made good their escape bid
But within six months they met their end in a hotel in Madrid
'Cause something quite mysterious had happened at Wisteria Lodge

The Cardboard Box

by Jim Ballinger

© 1993 Jim Ballinger

163

The Cardboard Box

Miss Susan Cushing got a parcel
In a cardboard box
Inside it were two tasty morsels
Laid on coarse salt rocks
A pair of human ears, unmatched
From Belfast post office dispatched
Two ears without a head attached
Inside the cardboard box

Opening the package shocked her
With the act depicted
She quickly blamed the student doctors
Whom she had evicted
The ears were not preserved but fresh
One each of male and female flesh
The savage and grotesque enmeshed
Inside the cardboard box

There had been three Cushing sisters
Susan, Sarah, Mary
But Sarah moved, the package missed her
With the message carried
It turns out Mary's husband, Jim
Had Sarah turn her wrath on him
'Twas he who sent the contents grim
Inside the cardboard box

While Jim Browner was at sea
His wife had found diversion
It was with Alec Fairbairn she
Made marital incursions
When Jim returned home by surprise
He found the lovers compromised
He acted, then sent Sarah's prize
Inside the cardboard box

Take heed, all you with spouse absent
It pays you to stay abstinent
Or else it could be your ears sent
Inside the cardboard box

The Red Circle

by Jim Ballinger

Mis-sus War-ren's pro-fes-sion was tak-ing in lod-gers In an end-less pro-ces-sion of spin-sters and cod-gers. Holmes ar-ranged an af-fair for a chap, Fair-dale Hobbs, His en-light-en-ment there got him stuck with this job. Mis-sus be.

War-ren had rent-ed her top sit-ting room At a rate much aug-ment-ed to a strang-er well-groomed. He had set as his terms he be giv-en a key, But his host-ess af-firmed he would not dis-turbed case. But be-

Sher-lock re-sort-ed to the Ag-o-ny Co-lumn Where a 'G' had ex-hort-ed to be pa-tient and so-lemn, But the next mor-ning's mes-sage set the hounds on the chase, An an-nounce-ment to pre-sage a turn in the me." It in

been sub-sti-tu-tion of lod-gers at War-ren's, And to add to con-fu-sion, the wo-man was for-eign. From a room with-out shut-ters a flash-ing they see, "It's a code." Wat-son mut-ters, "It's all Greek to

pol-i-tan mob which con-trolled New York Ci-ty, They ex-tort-ed and robbed rich in man-ners not pret-ty. In the end, thanks to Holmes we are safe in our beds From the cri-mi-nals known as the Cir-cle of

From the Red.

The Red Circle

Mrs Warren's profession was taking in lodgers
In an endless procession of spinsters and codgers
Holmes arranged an affair for a chap, Fairdale Hobbs
His enlightenment there got him stuck with this job

Mrs Warren had rented her top sitting room
At a rate much augmented to a stranger well-groomed
He had set as his terms he be given a key
And his hostess affirmed he would not disturbed be

From the very first day she had not seen a hair
Of the stranger who stayed in his room up the stairs
On occasion he'd scratch her a note what to get
Whether soap or a match or the Daily Gazette

And so Sherlock resorted to the Agony Column
Where a "G" had exhorted to be patient and solemn
But the next morning's message set the hound on the chase
An announcement to presage a turn in the case

But before they'd conducted a reconnaissance brief
Mr Warren was abducted, dumped at Hampstead Heath
Mrs Warren's home cooking of the lodger's lunch
With the aid of a looking-glass confirmed Holmes' hunch

There had been substitution of the lodgers at Warren's
And to add to confusion, the woman was foreign
From a room without shutters a flashing they see
"It's a code" Watson mutters "It's all Greek to me"

It in fact was Italian, and of danger exalted
Holmes took off like a stallion to see why it had halted
With a Pinkerton man and Lestrade they'd inspect
Found an American with a knife through his neck

Neapolitan mob which controlled New York City
They extorted and robbed rich in manners not pretty
In the end, thanks to Holmes we are safe in our beds
From the criminals known as the Circle of Red

The Bruce Partington Plans

by Jim Ballinger

25

D

Young Ca-do-gan West, a clerk at Wool-wich Ar-se-nal___ Was
Sher-lock Holmes asked My-croft for a list of for-eign spies___ And
sharp taps with the knock-er and the vil-lain made his ent-rance But

A⁷

29

found with head crushed in be-side the tracks where he did fall.___ His tick-et for the
found one where a rail-road track be-neath his win-dow lies.___ 'Twas Hu-go O-ber-
see-ing they'd sur-round-ed him he stag-gered and fell sense-less. His broad-brimmed hat flew

D

34

Un-der-ground was no-where to be seen, But se-ven of the ten plans for Bruce
stein of Caul-field Gar-dens, Ken-sing-ton And at Gol-di-ni's res-tau-rant that
from his head and his cra-vat slipped down And it was Col-onel Va-len-tine who

Bm   **E⁷**

39

A⁷

Parting-ton sub-ma-rine. There were on-ly two keys for the safe in
night Holmes met Wat-son. Wat-son came there with dark lan-tern, jem-my,
lay there on the ground.___ His dab-bling on the Stock Ex-change had

D

169

43 A7

which the plans were kept;___ One held by Sir James Wal - ters who could
chi - sel, and re - vol - ver,_____ Sher - lock said: "This case has been a
got him in the red___ And so he'd made a co - py of his

47 D ... Bm

not be a sus - pect,___ He'd spent the e - vening of the theft with friends in Bar - clay
bitch but soon I'll solve her." The two com - mit - ted bur - gla - ry and found their bird had
bro - ther's key in - stead.___ But young West was sus - pi - cious and had to be li - qui -

52 ... E7 ... A7

Square___ But died be - fore Holmes ques-tioned him con - cern - ing the af - fair.___ The
flown___ But marks of blood re - mained on win - dow - sill and steps of stone._____
da - ted, They put plans in his pock - et so he'd be in - crim - in - at - ed.___

57 Bm ... E7 ... A ... E7

o - ther key was held by Sid - ney John - son, sen - ior clerk,___ A hor - rid lit - tle
Holmes dis - cov - ered clip - ping from the Dai - ly Te - le - graph, Se - cret mes - sag - es in
Holmes made Va - len - tine write to his con - tact in Par - is,___ Who'd said he could be

170

62
A / E⁷ / A / Bm

man, he prob - 'bly stole the plans, But Holmes' de - duc - tions soon pro - duced a
code, all signed by Pi - er - rot, So Holmes put his own mes - sage in the
trouved care of Ho - tel du Louvre. And so it was the bait - ing worked, the

67
E⁷ / A / E⁷ / A / E⁷

glim - mer in the dark, The man with - out a tick - et; now there's a stick - y
pa - per for a laugh, But would the vil - lain bite? They'd wait un - til that
rest is his - to - ry, And Hu - go O - ber - stein in Bri - tish gaols did

72
A / F♯⁷ / Bm / F♯⁷

wick - et, No blood stains on the ground nor on the train were
night, And Holmes, while Wat - son frets, stud - ies Las - sus - 's mo -
time, Col - onel Val was sent to poke; with - in two years he

76
Bm / E⁷ / A / E⁷

found. One pos - si - bi - li - ty re - mained: he was on top of the
tets. They met that night at eight, to - ge - ther laid in
croaked, The plans have been re - trieved, and Sher - lock Holmes re -

171

The Bruce Partington Plans

The third week of November in 1895
London was enveloped by a dense yellow fog
Holmes studied a medieval musical archive
Having finished cross-indexing catalogues
This boredom soon was broken by a wire from Whitehall
Saying Mycroft Holmes on urgent matters soon would pay a call

Young Cadogan West, a clerk at Woolich Arsenal
Was found with head crushed in beside the tracks where he did fall
His ticket for the Underground was nowhere to be seen
But seven of the ten plans for Bruce Partington submarines

There were only two keys for the safe in which the plans were kept
One held by Sir James Walters, who could not be a suspect
He'd spent the evening of the theft with friends at Barclay Square
But died before Holmes questioned him concerning the affair

The other key was kept by Sidney Johnson, senior clerk
A horrid little man, he probably stole the plans
But Holmes deductions soon produced a glimmer in the dark
The man without a ticket: now there's a sticky wicket
No bloodstains on the ground nor in the train were found
One possibility remained: he was on top of the train
His body fell off when the train went around the bend

Someone walked off with the Bruce Partington plans
It's disaster if they reach enemy hands
And young West died falling from the train
Sherlock Holmes will get the blueprints back again

Sherlock Holmes asked Mycroft for a list of foreign spies
And found one where a railway track beneath his window lies
'Twas Hugo Oberstein of Caulfield Gardens, Kensington
And at Goldini's Restaurant that night Holmes met Watson

Watson came there with dark lantern, jemmy, chisel, and revolver
Sherlock said: "This case has been a bitch but soon I'll solve her"
The two committed burglary and found their bird had flown
But marks of blood remained on windowsill and steps of stone

Holmes discovered clippings from the Daily Telegraph
Secret messages in code, all signed by Pierrot
So Holmes put his own message in the paper for a laugh
But would the villain bite? They'd wait until that night

And Holmes, while Watson frets, studies Lassus's motets
They met that night at eight, together lay in wait
With Mycroft and Lestrade they finished off the job

Someone walked off with the Bruce Partington plans
It's disaster if they reach enemy hands
And young West died falling from the train
Sherlock Holmes will get the blueprints back again

Two sharp taps with the knocker and the villain made his entrance
But seeing they'd surrounded him, he staggered and fell senseless
His broad-brimmed hat flew from his head and his cravat spilled down
And it was Colonel Valentine who lay there on the ground

His dabbling on the stock exchange had got him in the red
And so he'd made a copy of his brother's key instead
But young West was suspicious and had to be liquidated
They put plans in his pocket so he'd be incriminated

Holmes made Valentine write to his contact in Paris
Who'd said he could be trouved care of Hotel du Louvre
And so it was the baiting worked, the rest is history
And Hugo Oberstein in British gaols did time
Colonel Val was sent to poke; within two years he croaked
The plans have been retrieved and Sherlock Holmes received
At conclusion of the story a small token from Victoria

Colonel Waters stole the Bruce Partington plans
Hugo Oberstein was a murderous man
And though nothing brings West from the dead
Thanks to Holmes we can sleep safely in our beds

The Dying Detective

by Jim Ballinger

175

176

The Dying Detective

Mrs Hudson approached Doctor Watson in tears
"For three days he's been sinking, he won't last, I fear"
He'd eschewed the attentions of medical men
Till his final relent, "Let it be Watson, then"

Watson rushed to the sick room to offer his care
A deplorable spectacle awaited him there
With the stare of a gaunt, wasted face sending chills
And flushed cheeks, crusted lips: what was causing his ills?

"Well, we seem to have fallen upon evil days,
Stay right back, if you 'proach me I'll send you away
It's a coolie disease from Sumatra I've caught
It's contagious by touch, keep away, touch me not"

Doctor Watson attempts to give medical aid
Holmes rebuffs his approach, expertise he degrades
Watson offers an infectious disease specialist
"Only one man can help: Mister Culverton Smith"

At 13 Lower Burke Street good Watson did call
Where the butler named Staples left him in the hall
When rebuffed, Watson pushed past the butler in ire
Found a yellow-faced, double-chinned man by the fire

At the name "Sherlock Holmes", Smith's demeanour did change
He enquired the state of Holmes' health in exchange
Then he flashed a malicious, abominable smile
And agreed to attend in the littlest while

Watson reached Baker Street before Smith as he said
He concealed himself behind the head of the bed
Smith arrived, laughed and sniggered at Holmes' sorry state
And he asked him if he knew how he reached this fate

'Twas an ivory box with a spring which drew blood
One just like Victor Savage received and went thud
That confession recorded, Holmes had had enough
Scotland Yard came on signal to snap on the cuffs

'Twas through fasting and make-up Holmes illness portrayed
And he'd insulted Watson to keep him away
Some nutrition from Simpson's would be most effective
Completing the cure of the dying detective

The Disappearance of Lady Frances Carfax

by Jim Ballinger

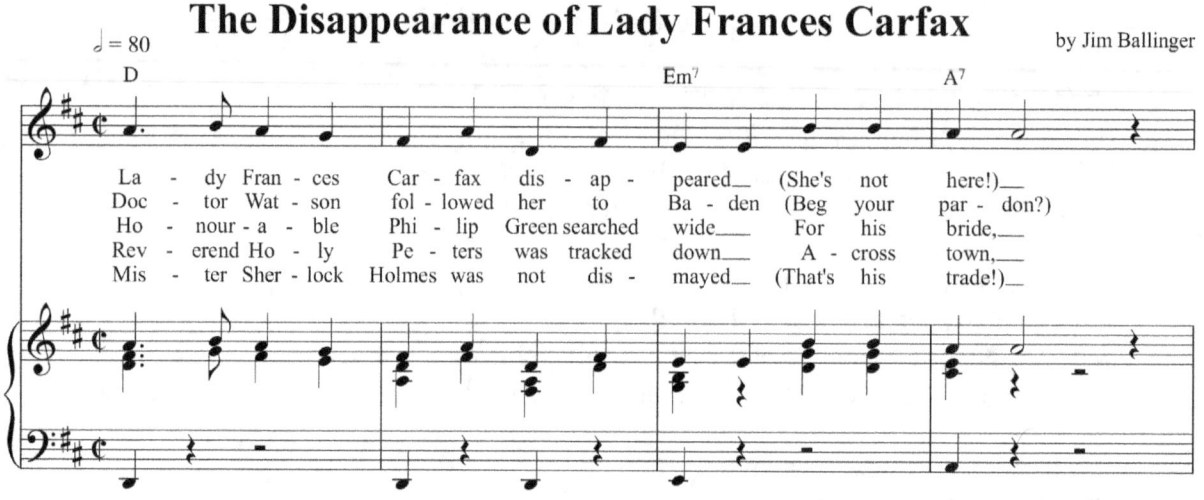

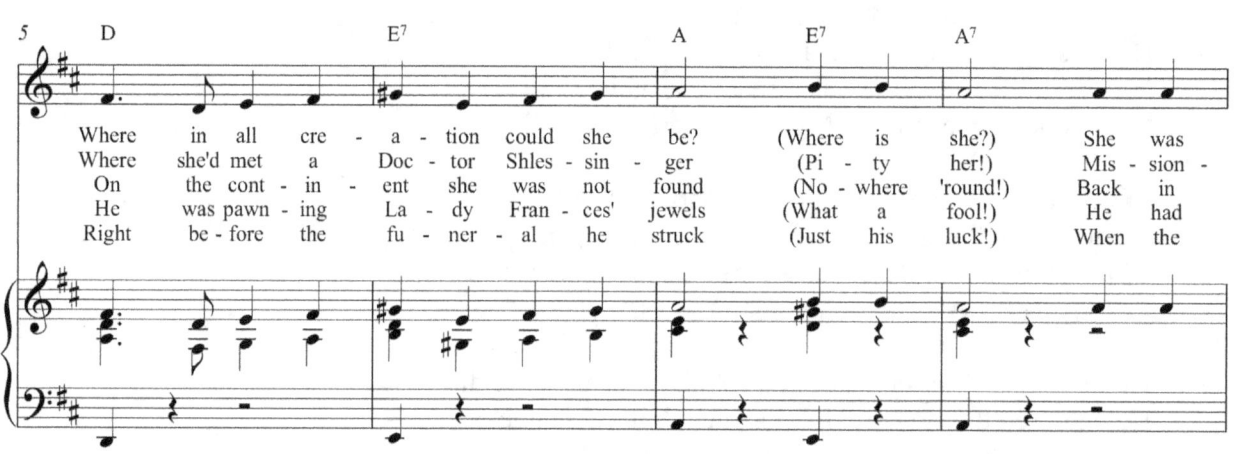

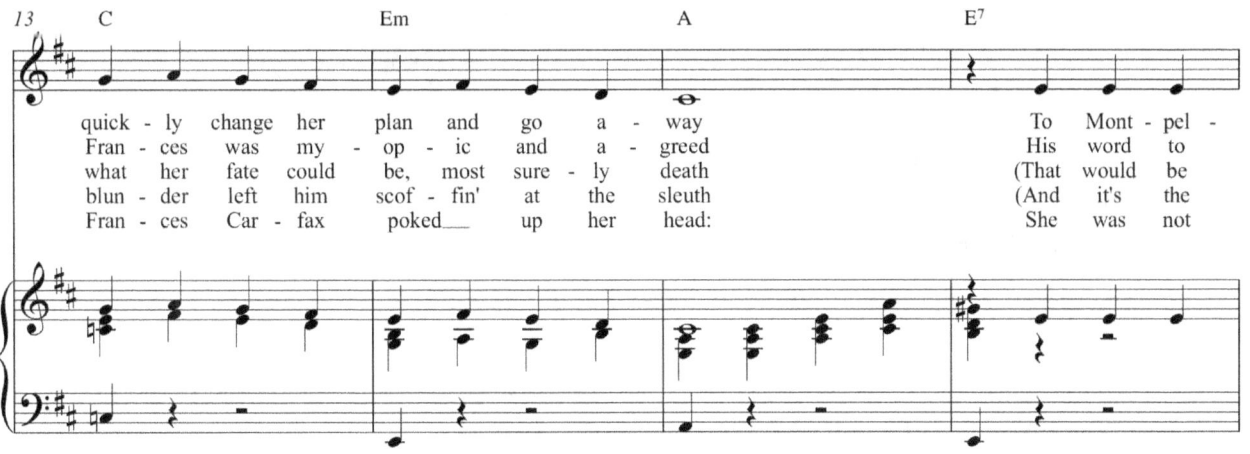

13 — Chords: C, Em, A, E⁷

quick - ly change her plan and go a - way   To Mont - pel -
Fran - ces was my - op - ic and a - greed   His word to
what her fate could be, most sure - ly death   (That would be
blun - der left him scof - fin' at the sleuth   (And it's the
Fran - ces Car - fax poked___ up her head: She was not

17 — [1,2,3,4.] A⁷   [5.] A⁷   G

lier.
heed._____   The
betht)
truth)

dead!_____   La - dy Fran - ces

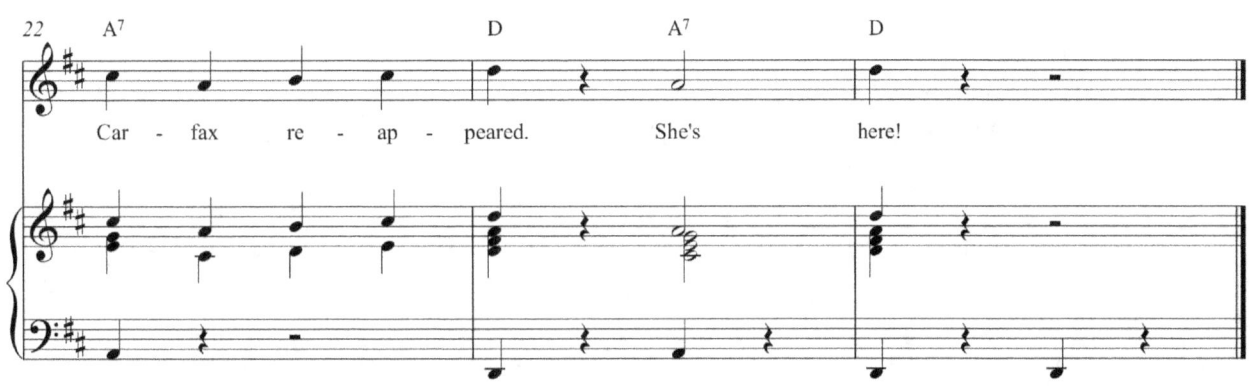

22 — Chords: A⁷, D, A⁷, D

Car - fax re - ap - peared.   She's here!

179

The Disappearance of Lady Frances Carfax

Lady Frances Carfax disappeared (She's not here!)
Where in all creation could she be? (Where is she?)
She was last seen in Lausanne
Where a tall, dark bearded man
Made her quickly change her plan
And go away to Montpellier

Doctor Watson followed her to Baden (Beg your pardon?)
Where she'd met a Doctor Shlessinger (Pity her!)
Missionary from the tropics
Mapping Holy Lands his topic
Lady Frances was myopic
And agreed his word to heed

The Honourable Philip Green searched wide for his bride
On the continent she was not found (Nowhere 'round)
Back in London she must be
With that phoney mission'ry
Wonder what her fate could be
Most surely death (That would be betht)

Reverend Holy Peters was tracked down across town
He was pawning Lady Francis' jewels (What a fool!)
He had bought a special coffin
For a nurse to shuffle off in
Holmes's blunder left him scoffin'
At the sleuth (And it's the truth)

Mister Sherlock Holmes was not dismayed (That's his trade)
Right before the funeral he struck (Just his luck)
When the coffin lid was op'd
There in chloroform well-soaked
Lady Frances Carfax poked
Up her head, she was not dead
Lady Frances Carfax reappeared. She's here!

The Devil's Foot

by Jim Ballinger

181

The Devil's Foot

Holmes was on a holiday recovering from mental strain
A cottage down near Poldu Bay, twixt roaring surf and rolling plain
The Cornish language he researched for some Phoenician trader link
Till vicar of the local church took Sherlock's powers to the brink
A man named Mortimer Tregennis, lodger at the vicar's place
Told them a tale of demon menace which turned into Sherlock's strangest case

A woman dead, her brothers wits erased
With looks of horror etched upon each face
The three had spent a whist-ful eve till after Morty took his leave
When something, somehow struck without a trace

The housekeeper slept through it all, 'twas nothing stolen, disarranged
No break-in signs, no noise, no call, no wonder Sherlock called it strange
The African explorer Doctor Leon Sterndale paid a call
To see whether the Cornish horror could be understood at all
The victims' cousin, so he claimed, returned on message from the vicar
Soon the demon struck again, M.O. the same, the mystery got thicker

For Mortimer Tregennis also died
Though broad daylight, a lamp was at his side
'Twas in this lamp that Sherlock found some traces of a powder brown
Which transformed witchcraft into homicide

The powder Holmes and Watson tested, though it almost cost their lives
The case no more had Sherlock bested, Mortimer's guilt was derived
His own death not suicide but murder by the great explorer
Radix pedis diaboli, the agent of the Cornish horror
For in killing sister Brenda, Morty tweaked her secret lover
Leon Sterndale, jungle bender, passed along the same fate to her brother

Radix pedis diaboli, devil's foot
The African witch doctors' favourite fruit
Unknown to European docs yet we have seen its highly tox-ic
Red-brown snuff-like powder, devil's foot

His Last Bow

by Jim Ballinger

185

50 C · F · Dm⁷ · G⁷ · F

lone, but ti - dy - ing up car - ries on. There's pa - pers to burn, re -
vives, he brings home the ba - con at last. The sig - nals are bought, lamp
lone, to - ge - ther the ruse they de - ployed. Though Holmes was re - tired, en -

57 C/E · Dm⁷ · G⁷ · C

ports or - ga - nise, The safe's lock is turned a - gainst pry - ing eyes. And all is in
code, se - ma - phore, Mar - co - ni, the lot, true co - pies, for sure. Von Bork blind - ly
ticed by P M He glad - ly con - spired in ser - vice a - gain. A se - cret so -

64 · F · C · F · C

rea - di - ness, ev - 'ry last thing, Once Al - ta - mont the na - val
gives out the code for his safe, And then gets a chlo - ro - formed
ci - e - ty, Buff - 'lo, New York, En route to the cap - ture of

69 G⁷ | 1.2. C | 3. C | D.C. al Fine

sig - nals does bring. The Bork.
sponge in the face. For
vile spy, Von

187

His Last Bow

Nine o'clock on August second, nineteen fourteen, cursèd year
Stand two Germans on a terrace, plotting Kaiser's reign of fear
Von Bork sent on English mission, information to Berlin
Fraternising with the natives, hunting, yachting, sportsman him

Visitor Baron Von Herling, delegation secret'ry
Checking Von Bork's preparation for return to home country
Von Herling to Carlton Terrace must return by souped-up Benz
Von Bork waits for Altamont with naval signals he will fence

Von Bork then re-enters his vast, widespread home
His family and household have gone
Save Martha, the housekeeper, he is alone, but tidying up carries on
There's papers to burn, reports organise
The safe's lock is turned against prying eyes
And all is in readiness, every last thing, once Altamont the naval signals does bring

The Irish-American agent arrives, his chauffeur for vigil is cast
He speaks and the King's English barely survives, he brings home the bacon at last
The signals are brought: lamp code, semaphore
Marconi, the lot, true copies, for sure
Von Bork blindly gives out the code for his safe
And then gets a chloroformed sponge in the face

For Altamont turns out to be Sherlock Holmes, his chauffeur is Watson, blithe boy
And Martha gave signal Von Bork was alone, together the ruse they deployed
Though Holmes was retired, enticed by PM
He gladly conspired in service again
A secret society, Buffalo, New York, en route to the capture of vile spy Von Bork

"Stand with me upon the terrace, maybe our last quiet talk
Reminisce about old cases, heed not prisoner Von Bork"
"There's an east wind coming, Watson", "I think not, it's very warm"
"It will be both cold and bitter, some may wither in the storm"

"Good old Watson, good old Watson, one fixed point in changing age
Better, stronger land in sunshine when the storm has cleared the stage"
Holmes and Watson, Holmes and Watson, ever then and ever now
Stand with us upon the terrace, Sherlock Holmes in His Last Bow

Section 5:
The Casebook of
Sherlock Holmes

The Illustrious Client

by Jim Ballinger

190

The Illustrious Client

It may be some fussy, self-important fool
It may be a matter of life or of death
Tomorrow 'twill be Sir James Damery who'll
The delicate matter explore in its depth
As Watson and Holmes wait at Baker Street's hearth
The colonel makes entrance at four-thirty sharp

Have you ever heard of one Gruner by name
Most dangerous man now in Europe his fame
The Austrian murderer, Holmes blandly asks
There's no getting past you, James Damery laughs

In Prague, Baron Gruner had bumped off his wife
A spurious accident in Splugen Pass
A technical loophole, escaped with his life
And turned up on England's green pastures at last
Where Violet de Merville fell head over heels
Remaining immune to her father's appeals

First Holmes went to Gruner's house at Vernon Lodge
Where all his entreaties the Baron has dodged
Repeated his plan to make Violet his wife
And threatened Holmes that he was risking his life

The blithe Shinwell Johnson arrived on the scene
He brought Kitty Winter, a Gruner conquest
She's caught glimpse of murder, his threats that were mean
She'd like to get one or two things off her chest
They took her to Violet who'd still not believe
That her fiancé would have ever deceived

They had to drag Kitty away by the hand
E'er she attacked Violet for loving that man
'Twas two evenings later that Gruner fought back
As Sherlock Holmes suffered a murd'rous attack

When Watson's cab arrived at 221B
As Sir Leslie Oakshott, the surgeon, departs
There is no immediate danger, says he
But scalp lacerations and bruising in parts
Holmes' head wrapped in bandages, bloody compress
Urged Watson to lay it on thick with the press

But several days later pace accelerates
It seemed Baron Gruner would sail for the States
In order to gain entry Watson must swot
Becoming an expert on Chinese Ming pots

As Doctor Hill Barton did Watson profess
To sell a Ming saucer to Gruner impressed
Who quickly saw through him, but nevertheless
Holmes managed to steal the brown book from his desk
As Gruner rushed out to the window in haste
Did Kitty throw vitriol right in his face

Despite Watson giving first aid for the scars
The once handsome face had forever been marred
At Baker Street, Holmes had already come in
"The wages of sin, Watson, wages of sin"

When Kitty was tried, well, the sentence was mild
And Holmes' charge of burglary never reached trial
And even the British law can be compliant
When object is good and Illustrious Client

The Blanched Soldier

by Jim Ballinger

Oh, my name is Mis - ter___ James M Dodd, I'm a vet - 'ran of the war. I re-
said that God - frey had gone a - way on a voy - age 'round the world, But I
dead - ly white with his ghost - ly face and he ran off in the dark. I set
Sher - lock Holmes I quick - ly came and re - count - ed these e - vents. Soon his

ceived the nod from the Mid - dle - sex squad and went off to fight the Boers. In the
had to say he'd not act___ that way, mys - t'ry had to be un - furled. So I
off in chase, search ing e - ver - y place a - round Tux - bu - ry Old Park. Though I
fer - tile brain fig - ured out___ the game but he kept me in sus - pense. And we

Corps I had a mate and God - frey___ Ems - worth was his name. Yes, Ems-
head - ed for Tux - bu - ry Old Park, his___ home up Bed - ford way, Where the
did not trace my___ friend that night, I dis - tinct - ly heard a door. In the
head - ed down to___ Tux - bu - ry, the___ col - onel aimed to call The po-

worth and Dodd, like two peas in a pod, why, we e - ven dressed the same. Then a
ma - tri - arch was an eas - y___ mark and in - vi - ted me to stay. Col - onel
morn - ing light I did search the site wait - ing for the night once more. So when
lice till he had a chance to see the one word that Holmes had scrawled. When we

194

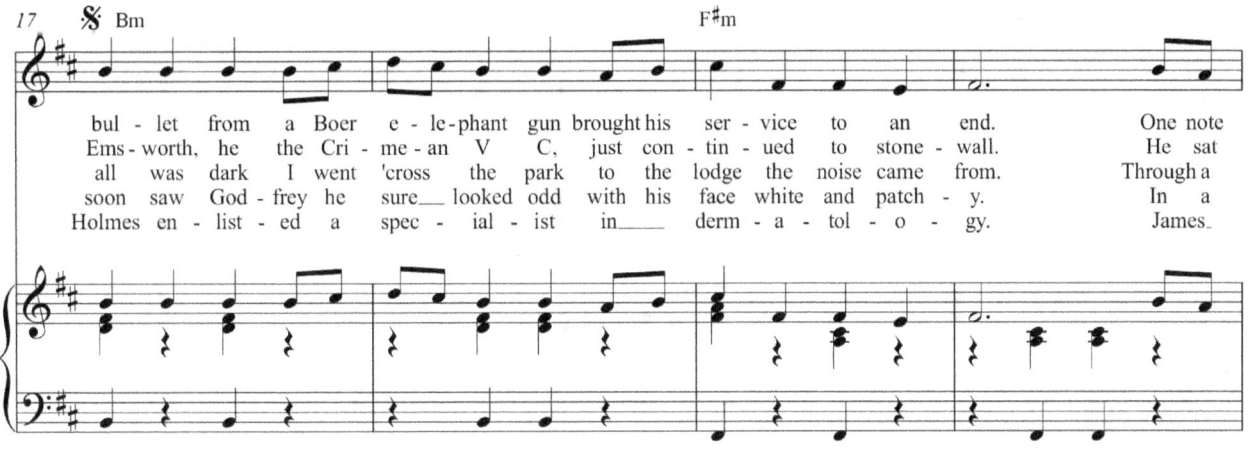

17 𝄋 Bm ... F#m

bul - let from a Boer e - le-phant gun brought his ser - vice to an end. One note
Ems - worth, he the Cri - me - an V C, just con - tin - ued to stone - wall. He sat
all was dark I went 'cross the park to the lodge the noise came from. Through a
soon saw God - frey he sure___ looked odd with his face white and patch - y. In a
Holmes en - list - ed a spec - ial - ist in___ derm - a - tol - o - gy. James___

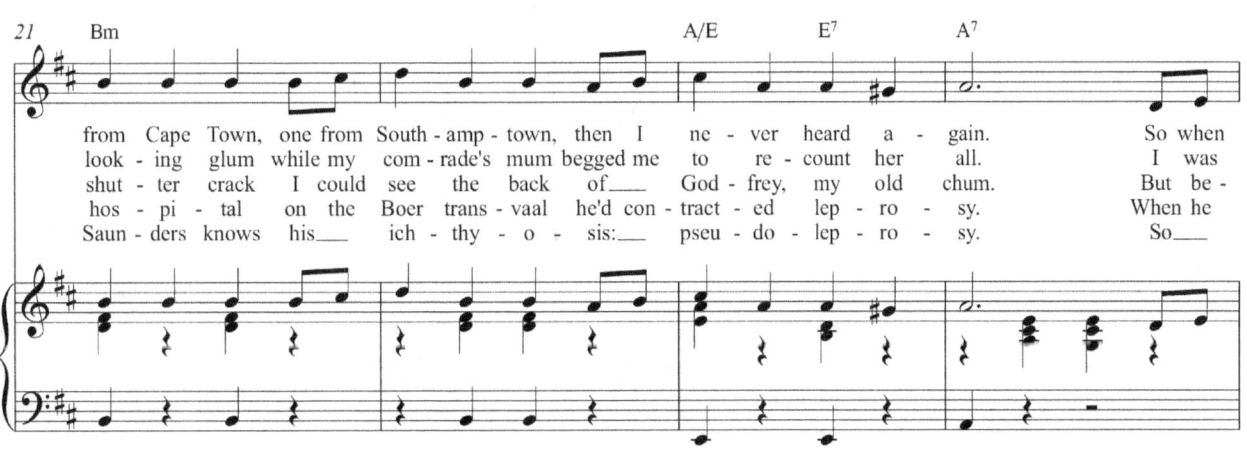

21 Bm ... A/E E⁷ A⁷

from Cape Town, one from South - amp - town, then I ne - ver heard a - gain. So when
look - ing glum while my com - rade's mum begged me to re - count her all. I was
shut - ter crack I could see the back of___ God - frey, my old chum. But be -
hos - pi - tal on the Boer trans - vaal he'd con - tract - ed lep - ro - sy. When he
Saun - ders knows his___ ich - thy - o - sis:___ pseu - do - lep - ro - sy. So___

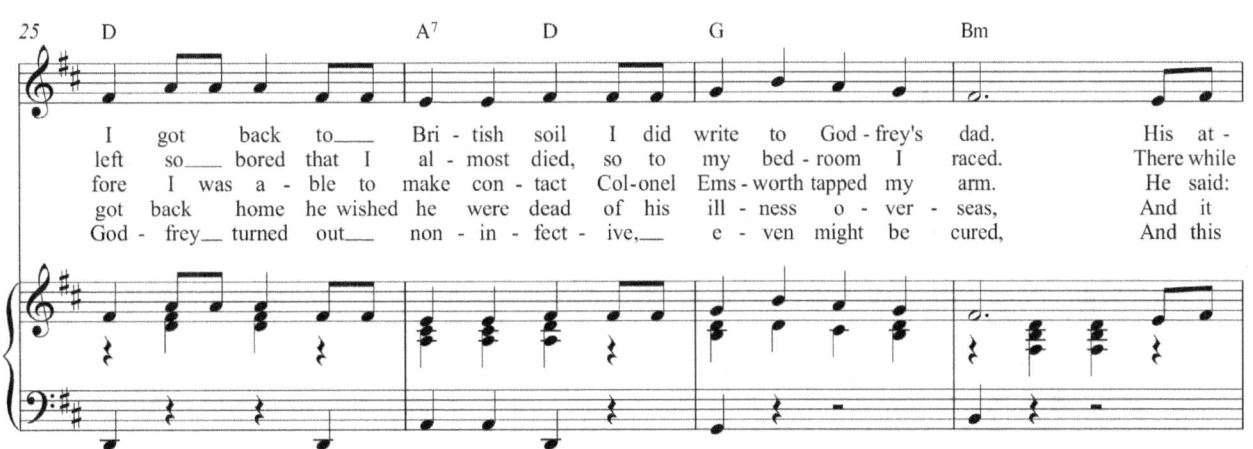

25 D ... A⁷ D G Bm

I got back to___ Bri - tish soil I did write to God - frey's dad. His at -
left so___ bored that I al - most died, so to my bed - room I raced. There while
fore I was a - ble to make con - tact Col - onel Ems - worth tapped my arm. He said:
got back home he wished he were dead of his ill - ness o - ver - seas, And it
God - frey___ turned out___ non - in - fect - ive,___ e - ven might be cured, And this

195

29

G · · · · · D G · · D A⁷

tempt to foil caused my blood to boil, yes, he real - ly made me
read - ing I looked up and es - pied my friend God - frey Ems - worth's
"Boy, get packed, and start mak - ing tracks, get your car - cass off my
could be said since it's caught in bed it's ve - ner - e - al dis -
ends pro - ject of the great de - tect - ive and the Blanched Sol -

32

1,2,3.
D

4.
D   **D.S. al Fine** 𝄋

5.
D   **Fine**

mad.   For he   ease.   But   ier.
face.   He was
farm!"   So   to

The Blanched Soldier

Oh, my name is Mister James M Dodd, I'm a veteran of the war
I received the nod from the Middlesex squad and went off to fight the Boers
In the Corps I had a mate and Godfrey Emsworth was his name
Yes, Emsworth and Dodd, like two peas in a pod; why, we even dressed the same
Then a bullet from a Boer elephant gun brought his service to an end
One note from Cape Town, one from Southamptown, then I never heard again
So when I got back to British soil I did write to Godfrey's dad
His attempt to foil caused my blood to boil; yes, he really made me mad

For he said that Godfrey had gone away on a voyage 'round the world
But I had to say he'd not act that way, mystery had to be unfurled
So I headed for Tuxbury Old Park, his home up Bedford way
Where the matriarch was an easy mark and invited me to stay
Colonel Emsworth, he the Crimean VC, just continued to stonewall
He sat looking glum while my comrade's mum begged me recount to her all
I was left so bored that I almost died, so to my bedroom I raced
There while reading I looked up and espied my friend Godfrey Emsworth's face

He was deadly white with his ghostly face and he ran off in the dark
I set off in chase, searching every place around Tuxbury Old Park
Though I did not trace my friend that night, I distinctly heard a door
In the morning light I did search the site, waiting for the night once more
So when all was dark I went 'cross the park to the lodge the noise came from
Through a shutter crack I could see the back of Godfrey, my old chum
But before I was able to make contact, Colonel Emsworth tapped my arm
He said: "Boy, get packed and start making tracks. Get your carcass off my farm!"

So to Sherlock Holmes I quickly came and recounted these events
Soon his fertile brain figured out the game but he kept me in suspense
And we headed down to Tuxbury, the Colonel aimed to call
The police till he had a chance to see the one word that Holmes had scrawled
When we soon saw Godfrey, he sure looked odd with his face white and patchy
In a hospital on the Boer Transvaal he'd contracted leprosy
When he got back home he wished he were dead of his illness overseas
And it could be said since it's caught in bed it's venereal disease
But Holmes enlisted a specialist in dermatology
James Saunders knows his ichthyosis: pseudo-leprosy
So Godfrey turned out non-infective, even might be cured
And this ends project of the great detective and the Blanched Soldier

The Mazarin Stone

by Jim Ballinger

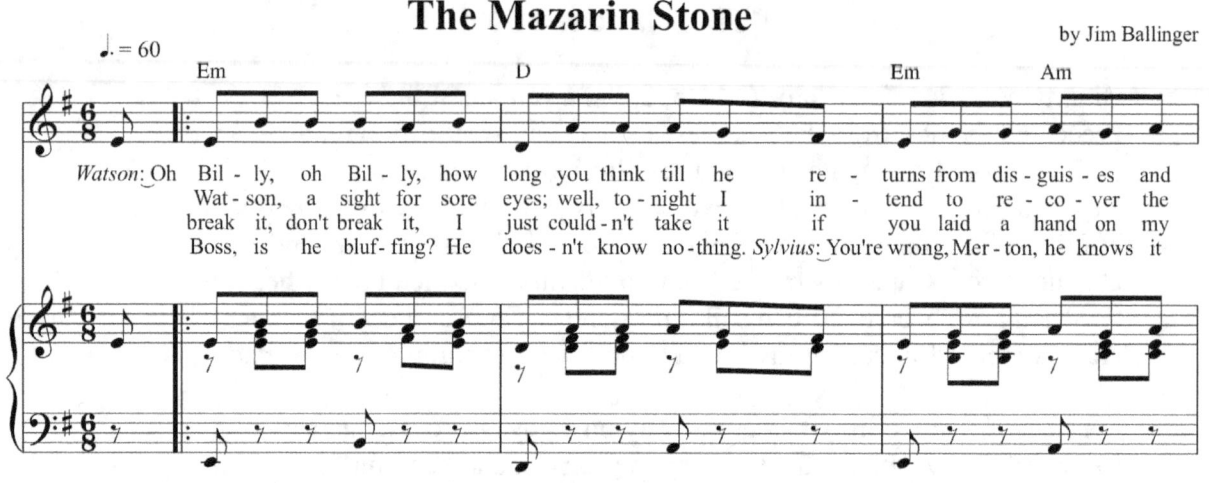

Watson: Oh Bil - ly, oh Bil - ly, how long you think till he re - turns from dis - guis - es and
Wat - son, a sight for sore eyes; well, to - night I in - tend to re - co - ver the
break it, don't break it, I just could - n't take it if you laid a hand on my
Boss, is he bluf - fing? He does - n't know no - thing. Sylvius: You're wrong, Mer - ton, he knows it

stealth?_____ Billy: Good Doc - tor, he's sleep - ing, the__ hours he's been keep - ing have
jewel._____ Al - though I'm de - light - ed the thief, as in - vit - ed, has
bust._____ My like - ness in wax can't take too ma - ny whacks be - fore
all._____ Our com - rades have squealed and now a - ny - time he'll have us

ta - ken their toll on his health._____ He works day and night with - out
come, I know he's not a fool._____ 'Tis air - guns I fear with re -
crumb - ling to no - thing but dust._____ I know all your crimes so con -
in pri - son quick - ly in - stalled._____ The rock must take flight 'cross the
Holmes: Thanks for the rock, there's no

198

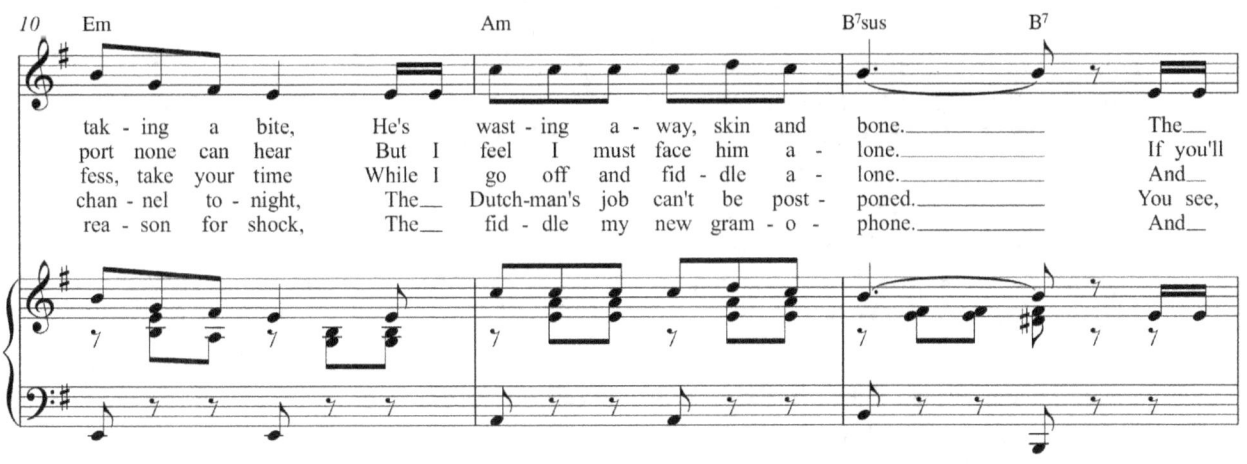

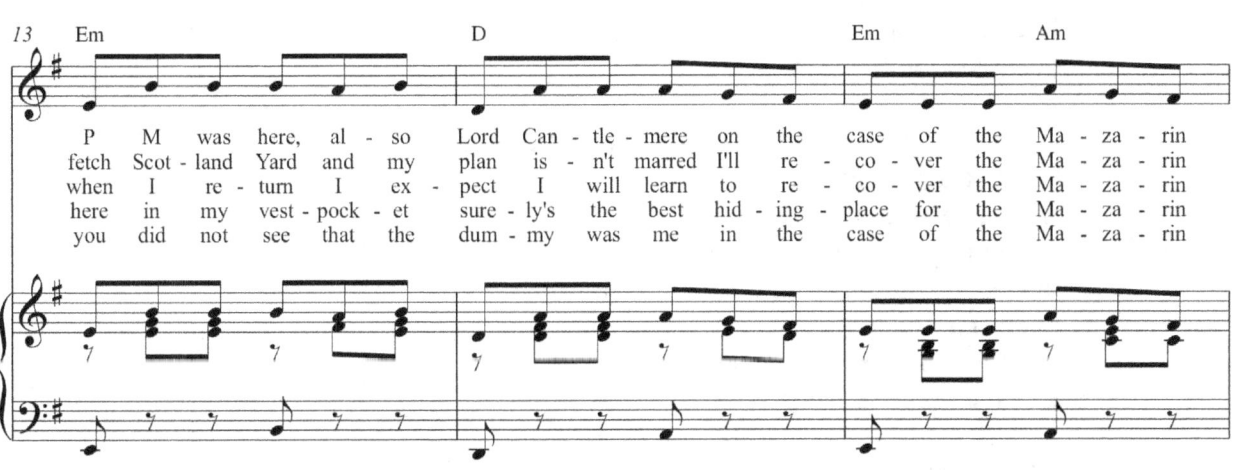

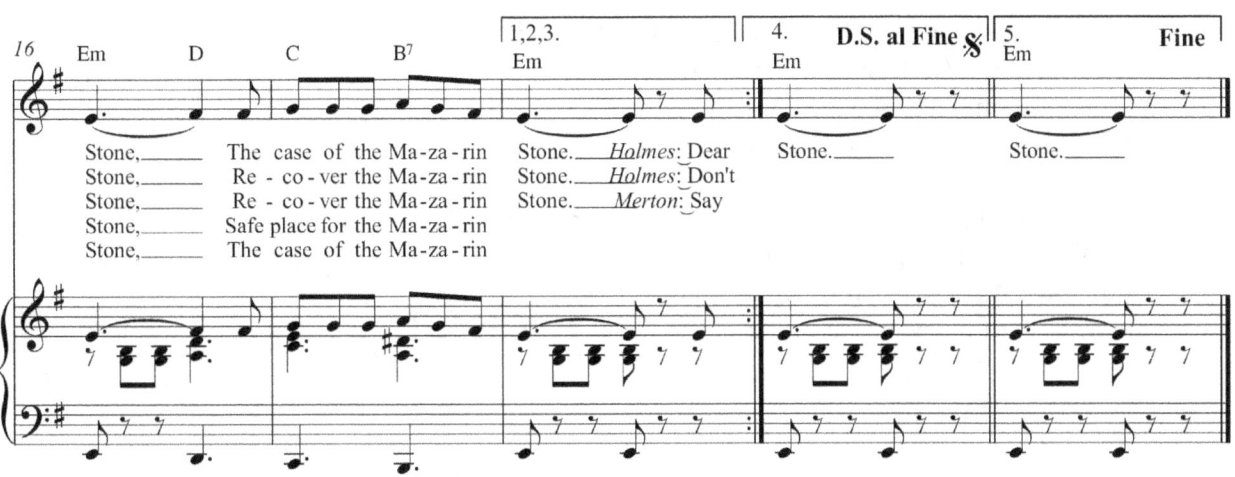

The Mazarin Stone

Watson: Oh Billy, oh Billy, how long you think till he
Returns from disguises and stealth?
Billy: Good Doctor, he's sleeping, the hours he's been keeping
Have taken their toll on his health
He works day and night without taking a bite
He's wasting away, skin and bone
The PM was here, also Lord Cantlemere
On the case of the Mazarin Stone

Holmes: Dear Watson, a sight for sore eyes; well, tonight
I intend to recover the jewel
Although I'm delighted the thief, as invited
Has come, I know he's not a fool
'Tis airguns I fear with report none can hear
But I feel I must face him alone
If you'll fetch Scotland Yard and my plan isn't marred
I'll recover the Mararin Stone

Holmes: Don't break it, don't break it, I just couldn't take it
If you laid a hand on my bust
My likeness in wax can't take too many whacks
Before crumbling to nothing but dust
I know all your crimes, so confess, take your time
While I go off and fiddle alone
And when I return, I expect I will learn
To recover the Mazarin Stone

Merton: Say, Boss, is he bluffing? He doesn't know nothing
Sylvius: You're wrong, Merton, he knows it all
Our comrades have squealed and now anytime he'll
Have us in prison quickly installed
The rock must take flight 'cross the Channel tonight
The Dutchman's job can't be postponed
You see, in my vest pocket surely's the best
Hiding-place for the Mazarin Stone

Holmes: Thanks for the rock, there's no reason for shock
The fiddle my new gramophone
And you did not see that the dummy was me
In the case of the Mazarin Stone

The Three Gables

by Jim Ballinger

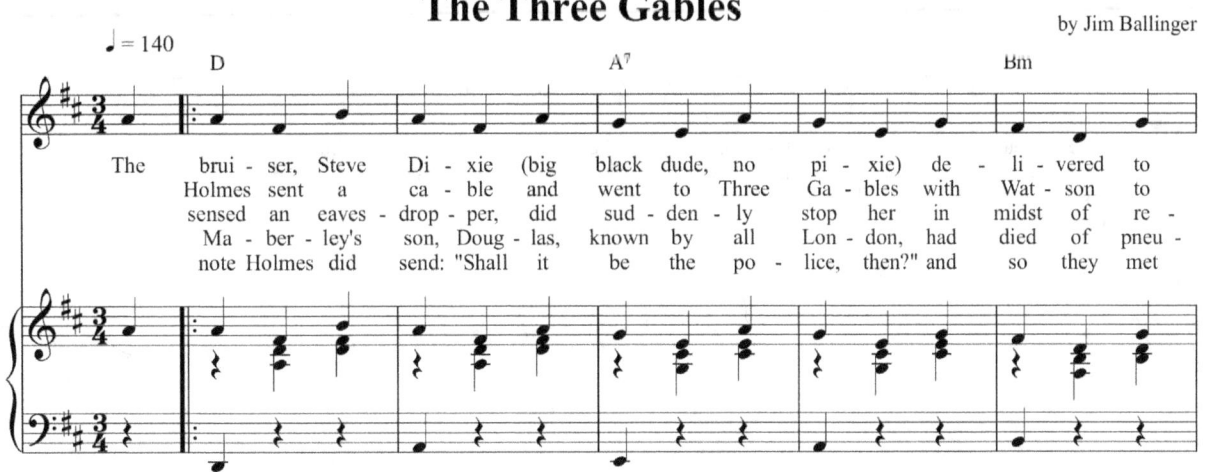

The brui - ser, Steve Di - xie (big black dude, no pi - xie) de - li - vered to
Holmes sent a ca - ble and went to Three Ga - bles with Wat - son to
sensed an eaves - drop - per, did sud - den - ly stop her in midst of re -
Ma - ber - ley's son, Doug - las, known by all Lon - don, had died of pneu -
note Holmes did send: "Shall it be the po - lice, then?" and so they met

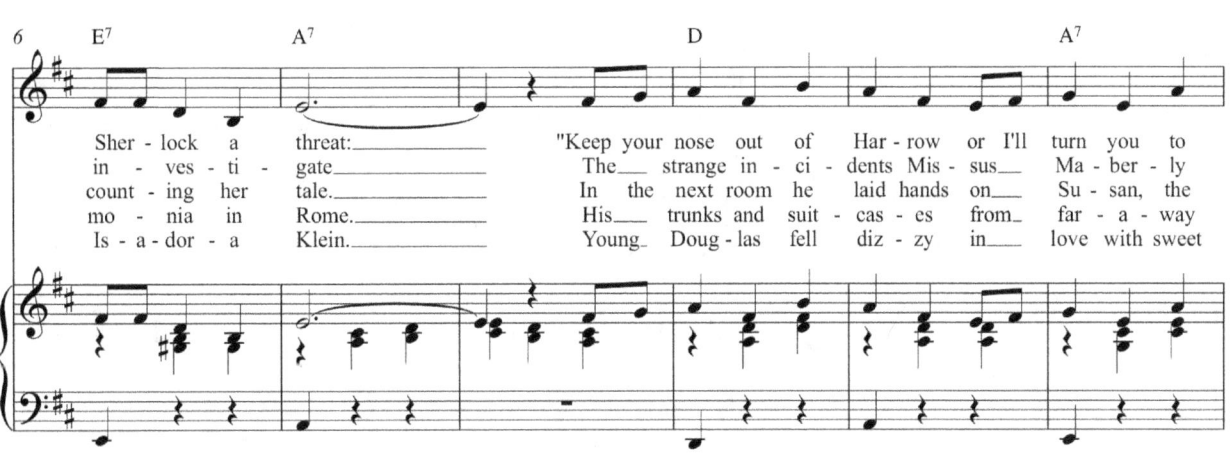

Sher - lock a threat:_____ "Keep your nose out of Har - row or I'll turn you to
in - ves - ti - gate. The strange in - ci - dents Mis - sus Ma - ber - ly
count - ing her tale. In the next room he laid hands on Su - san, the
mo - nia in Rome. His trunks and suit - cas - es from far - a - way
Is - a - dor - a Klein. Young Doug - las fell diz - zy in love with sweet

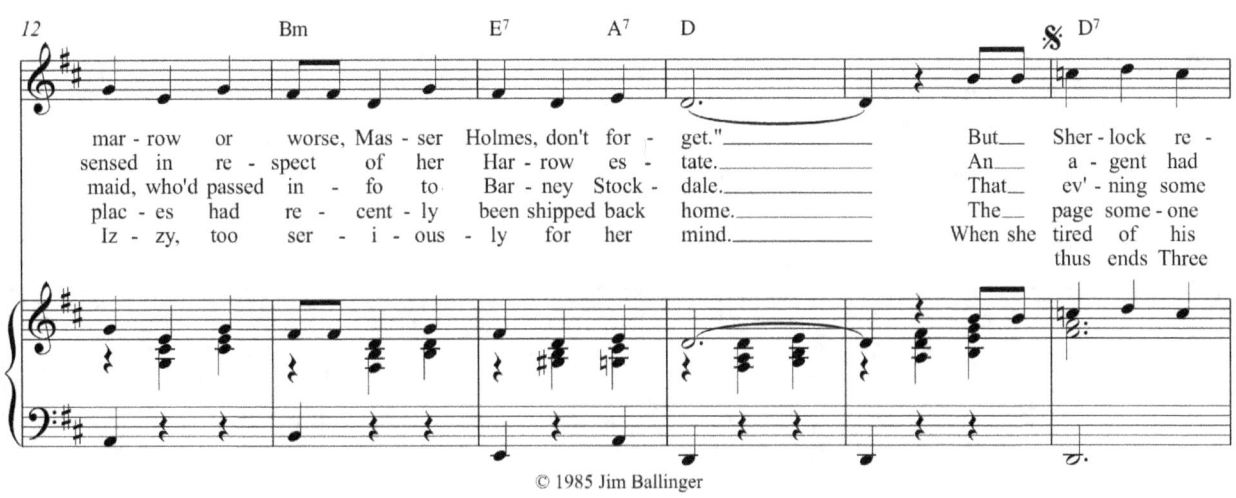

mar - row or worse, Mas - ser Holmes, don't for - get."_____ But Sher - lock re -
sensed in re - spect of her Har - row es - tate._____ An a - gent had
maid, who'd passed in - fo to Bar - ney Stock - dale._____ That ev' - ning some
plac - es had re - cent - ly been shipped back home._____ The page some - one
Iz - zy, too ser - i - ous - ly for her mind._____ When she tired of his
thus ends Three

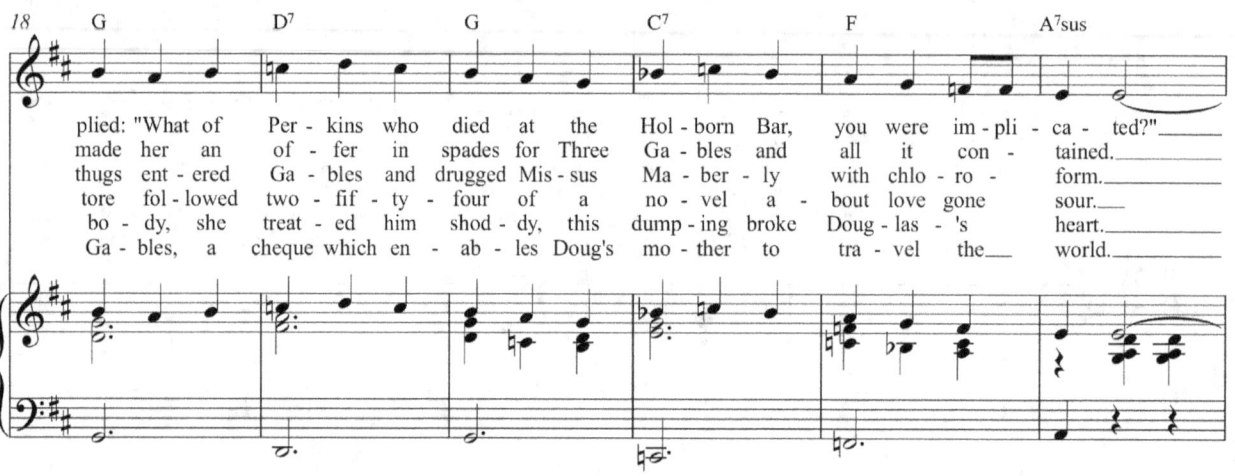

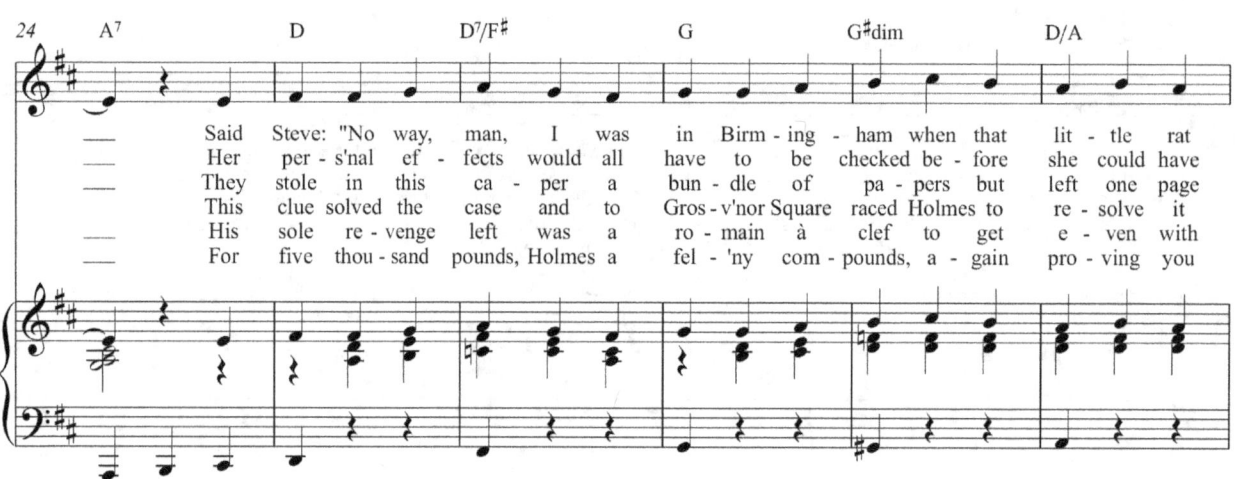

The Three Gables

The bruiser, Steve Dixie, (big black dude, no pixie)
Delivered to Sherlock a threat:
"Keep your nose out of Harrow or I'll turn you to marrow
Or worse, Masser Holmes, don't forget"
But Sherlock replied: "What of Perkins who died
At the Holborn Bar, you were implicated?"
Said Steve: "No way, man, I was in Birmingham
When that little rat got liquidated"

So Holmes sent a cable and went to Three Gables
With Watson to investigate
The strange incidents Mrs Maberley sensed
In respect of her Harrow estate
An agent had made her an offer in spades
For Three Gables and all it contained
Her personal effects would all have to be checked
Before she could have them back again

Holmes sensed an eavesdropper, did suddenly stop her
In midst of recounting her tale
In the next room he laid hands on Susan, the maid
Who'd passed info to Barney Stockdale
That evening some thugs entered Gables and drugged
Mrs Maberley with chloroform
They stole in this caper a bundle of papers
But left one page which had been torn

Mrs Maberley's son, Douglas, known by all London
Had died of pneumonia in Rome
His trunks and suitcases from faraway places
Had recently been shipped back home
The page someone tore followed two-fifty-four
Of a novel about love gone sour
This clue solved the case and to Grosvenor Square raced
Holmes to resolve it within the hour

A note Holmes did send! "Shall it be the police, then?"
And so they met Isadora Klein
Young Douglas fell dizzy in love with sweet Izzy
Too seriously for her mind
When she'd tired of his body she treated him shoddy
This dumping broke Douglas's heart
His sole revenge left was a roman à clef
To get even with this high-class tart

And thus ends Three Gables, a cheque which enables
Doug's mother to travel the world
For five thousand pounds Holmes a fel'ny compounds
Again proving you can't trust a girl

The Sussex Vampire

by Jim Ballinger

205

soon be-came mo - ther to a ti - ny son   To match a - no - ther from wife
you must re- mem - ber how he came up big   And solved the case__ known as Ma-
nurse Mis - sus Ma - son and the maid Do - lores. Re - sults we'll hear af - ter a-
wife and the hus - band have been re - con - ciled, With - in a year they had a-

num- ber one. A vam-pire on__ the loose, it seems;   A mo - ther bites her ba - by's neck; A
no -ther chorus. A vam-pire on__ the loose, it seems;   A mo - ther bites her ba - by's neck; A

fa-ther ans-wers the ba-by's screams; A night-mare from his wild - est dreams.
fa-ther ans-wers the ba-by's screams; A night-mare from his wild - est dreams.   The

til-da Briggs." Ma - til - da Briggs,   Ma - til - da Briggs,   Su - mat - ra's

206

The Sussex Vampire

Morrison, Morrison, and Dodd refer a case to Sherlock Holmes
No one thinks it even slightly odd to speak as if a vampire roams
For Robert Ferguson of Cheeseman's Manor took a Peruvian as his enamoured
She soon became mother to a tiny son to match another from wife number one

A vampire on the loose, it seems, a mother bites her baby's neck
A father answers the baby's screams, a nightmare from his wildest dreams

The hot-blooded wife is locked away after the second bloody attack
Why did she do it? she would not way nor why she assaulted step-son, Jack
So Ferguson calls his solicitors, they say, "Maybe Sherlock Holmes will take up yours
For you must remember how he came up big
And solved the case known as Matilda Briggs"

Matilda Briggs, Matilda Briggs
Sumatra's giant rat, but the world isn't ready

Holmes views the scene with his own eyes and meets all those who were involved
He sees a spaniel paralysed, Peruvian weapons on the wall
He sees the baby and the first son, Jacky,
And Watson gives comfort to the wife gone wacky
The nurse Mrs Mason and the maid Dolores,
The results we'll hear after another chorus

A vampire on the loose, it seems, a mother bites her baby's neck
A father answers the baby's screams, a nightmare from his wildest dreams

Sherlock goes for the jugular, the answer's plain for all to see
He tells Fergy, "What a mug you ar, 'twas purely sibling rivalry"
Jack used poisoning without a doubt, the horrified mother sucked the poison out
The wife and the husband have been reconciled, within a year they had another child

The vampire's back in the good old index, back where it belongs
There with Sumatra's giant rat, the clever pinch of Victor Lynch
At the ending of my song

The Three Garridebs

by Jim Ballinger

will he now sought to ful - fill in the search for the Gar - ri - debs Three._____ The sub-
traced Na - than Gar - ri - deb's place, leav - ing one more for Gar - ri - debs Three._____ From
name, sev - 'ral mur - ders his game, had cre - a - ted the Gar - ri - debs Three._____ Then
shots be - fore E - vans was caught, brought an end to the Gar - ri - debs

Three._____ For Wat - son, this case re - vealed a - no - ther face, not of

co - me - dy or tra - ge - dy,_____ For Sher - lock im - parts both great

brain and great heart in the tale of the Gar - ri - debs Three.

211

The Three Garridebs

Come and lend me an ear and I'll tell you a tale that's as corny as Kansas in June
If you'll set down your beer, wine, or brandy, or ale and I'll tell you the tale in a tune
It cost one man his mind, it cost Watson a wound, and another it cost liberty
And I hope that I'll find my guitar has been tuned for the tale of the Garridebs Three

John Garrideb claimed that he recently came from his home in the US of A
But the cut of his suit and his language to boot much extended the length of his stay
While in Kansas he'd known a substantial land owner
Who had the same surname as he
And the terms of whose will he now sought to fulfil
In the search for the Garridebs Three

The substantial corral willed by Garrideb Al was divided in three equal shares
And each third would prevail to a Garrideb male
If indeed there could be found three heirs
And so Garrideb John hunted hither and yon in the States not a one did there be
But in London he traced Nathan Garrideb's place
Leaving one more for Garridebs Three

Out of nowhere there flowered a Garrideb Howard, constructor up Birmingham way
Poor old Nathan would brave it, procure affidavit of Howard the following day
With help from Lestrade, Sherlock Holmes ascertained who John G was in reality
Killer Evans by name, several murders his game, had created the Garridebs Three

And so Sherlock Holmes mused that the will was a ruse
To entice Nathan G from his house
When the next day at five Killer Evans arrived
Holmes and Watson awaited that louse
Where a hidden trap door in the Garrideb floor and Prescott's counterfeit currency
And two quick pistol shots before Evans was caught
Brought an end to the Garridebs Three

But for Watson this case revealed another face, not of comedy or tragedy
Because Sherlock imparts both great brain and great heart
In the tale of the Garridebs Three

Thor Bridge

by Jim Ballinger

"You have heard of Neil Gib-son, the Gold King" Holmes asked Wat-son at break-fast one
ho - ur be - fore Neil's ex - pect - ed Bil - ly brought in Mis - ter Mar - low
fi - nal - ly put in ap - pear - ance, Holmes at first turned him down with - out
Gib - son was found, she had been shot, For the bul - let had gone through her
scene of the crime Holmes dis - co - vered A fresh chip on the ledge of the

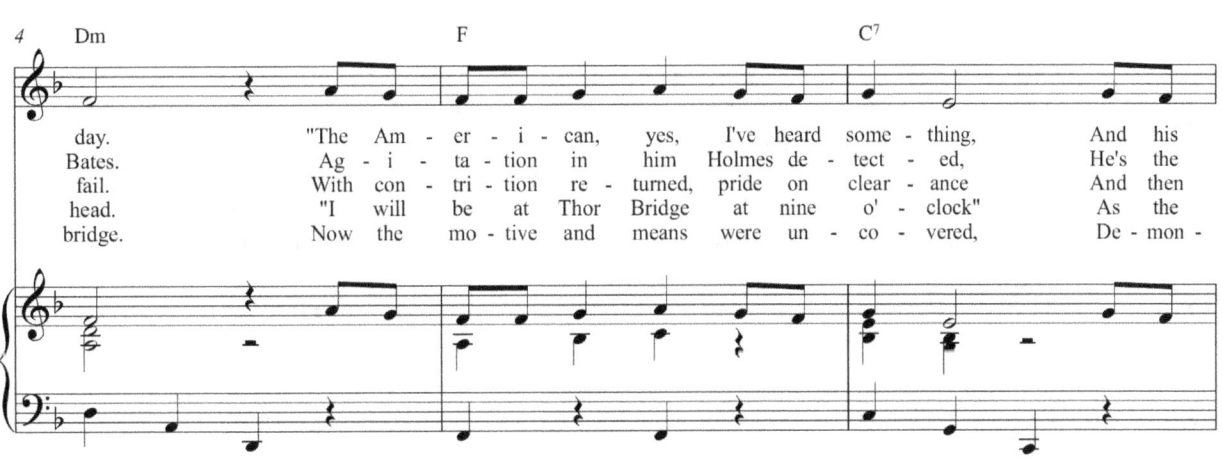

day. "The Am - er - i - can, yes, I've heard some - thing, And his
Bates. Ag - i - ta - tion in him Holmes de - tect - ed, He's the
fail. With con - tri - tion re - turned, pride on clear - ance And then
head. "I will be at Thor Bridge at nine o' - clock" As the
bridge. Now the mo - tive and means were un - co - vered, De - mon -

wife died in some tra - gic way." Gib - son wrote a lit - tle note sent from
man - a - ger, Gib - son es - tate. He's a ner - vous lit - tle mouse, fright-ened
Gib - son re - count - ed his tale. Gib - son's wife was from Bra - zil, nat - ure
note clutched in her left hand said. Grace Dun - bar did not de - ny but her
stra - ted with - out priv - i - lege. Mis - sus Gib - son's su - i - cide with a

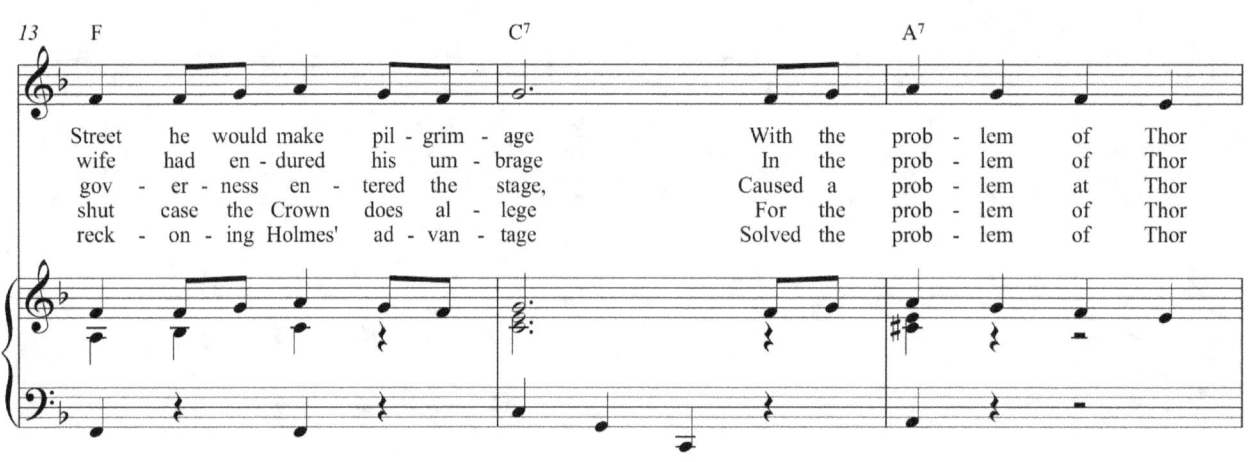

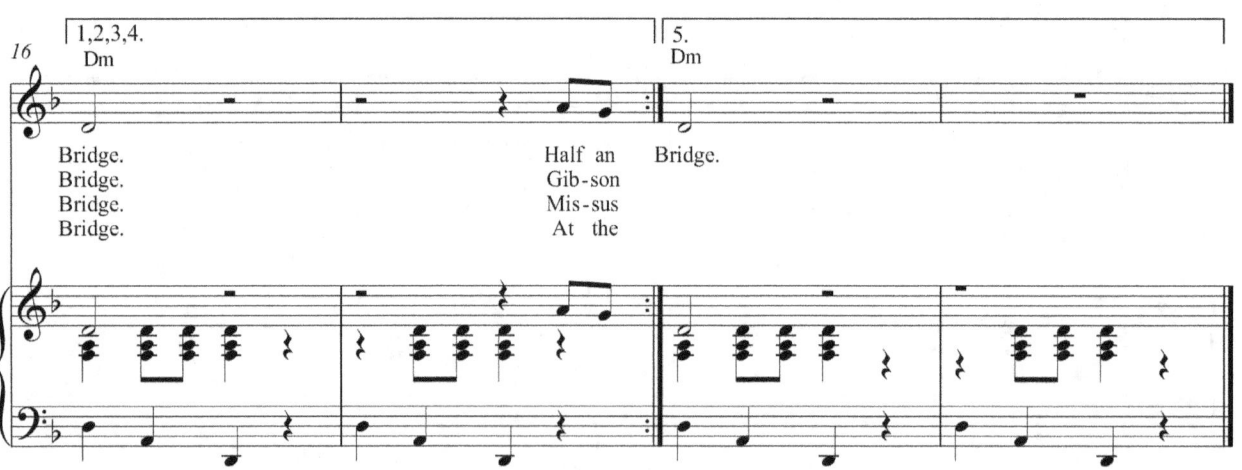

Thor Bridge

"You have heard of Neil Gibson, the Gold King,"
Holmes asked Watson at breakfast one day
"The American, yes, I've heard something and his wife died in some tragic way."
Gibson wrote a little note, sent from Claridge's Hotel
Of his bafflement he wrote, at eleven on the bell
Baker Street he would make pilgrimage with the problem of Thor Bridge

Half an hour before Neil's expected, Billy brought in Mr Marlow Bates
Agitation in him Holmes detected, he's the manager, Gibson estate
He's a nervous little mouse, frightened eyes and constant twitch
Told them Gibson is a louse and a real son of a bitch
But his wife had endured his umbrage in the problem of Thor Bridge

Gibson finally put in appearance, Holmes at first turned him down without fail
With contrition returned, pride on clearance, and then Gibson recounted his tale
Gibson's wife was from Brazil, nature tropical and hot
After twenty years the thrill had begun to fade to nought
Till a governess entered the stage, caused a problem at Thor Bridge

Mrs Gibson was found, she had been shot, for the bullet had gone through her head
"I will be at Thor Bridge at nine o'clock," as the note clutched in her left hand said
Grace Dunbar did not deny but her innocence erodes
A revolver they do find on the floor of her wardrobe
Open-shut case the Crown does allege for the problem of Thor Bridge

At the scene of the crime Holmes discovered a fresh chip on the ledge of the bridge
Now the motive and means were uncovered, demonstrated without privilege
Mrs Gibson's suicide with a gun and counterweight
And a planted pistol tried to ensure Grace Dunbar's fate
But not reckoning Holmes' advantage, solved the problem of Thor Bridge

The Creeping Man

by Jim Ballinger

♩ = 100

Verse lines under the staves:

start-ed with a dog that was en-dea-vour-ing to bite its mas-ter, new-ly home from Prague, where he had
on the prof's home-com-ing from his con-tin-ent-al tra-vel, his be-hav-iour had be-come a tang-led
night his daugh-ter got a scare, the dog was bark-ing on its chain, and clear-ly in the moon-light there was

been for a fort-night. It was res-pect-ab-le old Pres-bur-y, at Cam-ford U a prof, but what had
skein to be un-ra-velled. He be-gan re-ceiv-ing let-ters with a cross be-neath the stamp, told his as-
Fa-ther at her win-dow-pane. Her room was on the sec-ond le-vel and to reach it he had climbed the

caused the dog's ex-treme fu-ry? What sent the wolf-hound off?_____ Though
sist-ant that he'd bet-ter pass them on to him un-tamp-ered._____ There
i-vy vine, but why the de-vil? See in nine days time._____ Past

216

sixty-one years old, the good professor was so bold (and daft) as to become engaged to a girl
was a quaint carved wooden box he kept behind a cupboard's locks. The dog he sent into a craze at
midnight Holmes and Watson find Professor swinging from the vine. When tired of this he'd taunt the hound which

less than half his age. She was a colleague's daughter Alice, who at this was somewhat callous and would
intervals of each nine days. One night he was seen in the hall on hands and feet as in a crawl. When
soon escaped and brought him down. It turns out that he'd got his hands upon a source of monkey glands which

much prefer flirtation within her own generation.
his assistant offered aid, he straightened up and rushed away.
he injected each nine days to keep up with his fian-

1.2.

The creeping man.
The creeping man.

Up-
Next

217

The Creeping Man

It started with a dog that was endeavouring to bite
Its master, newly home from Prague, where he had been for a fortnight
It was respectable old Presbury, at Camford U a prof
But what had caused the dog's extreme fury? What set the wolfhound off?

Though sixty-one years old, the good professor was so bold (and daft)
As to become engaged to a girl less than half his age
She was a colleague's daughter, Alice, who at this was somewhat callous?
And would much prefer flirtation within her own generation
The creeping man, the creeping man

Upon the prof's homecoming from his continental travel
His behaviour had become a tangled skein to be unravelled
He began receiving letters with a cross beneath the stamp
Told his assistant that he'd better pass them on to him untampered

There was a quaint carved wooden box he kept behind a cupboard's locks
The dog he sent into a craze at intervals of each nine days
One night he was seen in the hall on hands and feet as in a crawl
When his assistant offered aid he straightened up and rushed away
The creeping man, the creeping man

Next night his daughter got a scare, the dog was barking on its chain
And clearly in the moonlight there was Father at her window-pane
Her room was on the second level and to reach it he had climbed
The ivy vine, but why the devil? See in nine days' time

Past midnight, Holmes and Watson find Professor swinging from the vine
When tired of this, he'd taunt the hound, which soon escaped and brought him down
It turns out that he'd got his hands upon a source of monkey glands
Which he injected each nine days to keep up with his fiancée

Elixir of eternal youth presents a danger, said the sleuth
Consumed at night while all were sleeping, the professor turned into the creeping man
The creeping man, the creeping man

The Lion's Mane

by Jim Ballinger

A re-ti-red bloke on the south-ern slope of the ver-dant Sus-sex
roy Mc-Pher-son, sci-ence mas-ter, showed his head a-bove the
then ap-proached (math-e-mat-ics coach) sent to fetch con-stab-'la-
la-dy, she was Maude Bel-la-my, by her beau-ty Holmes was
lit-tle rest, e'er the theo-ry's test, Mur-doch stag-gered through his

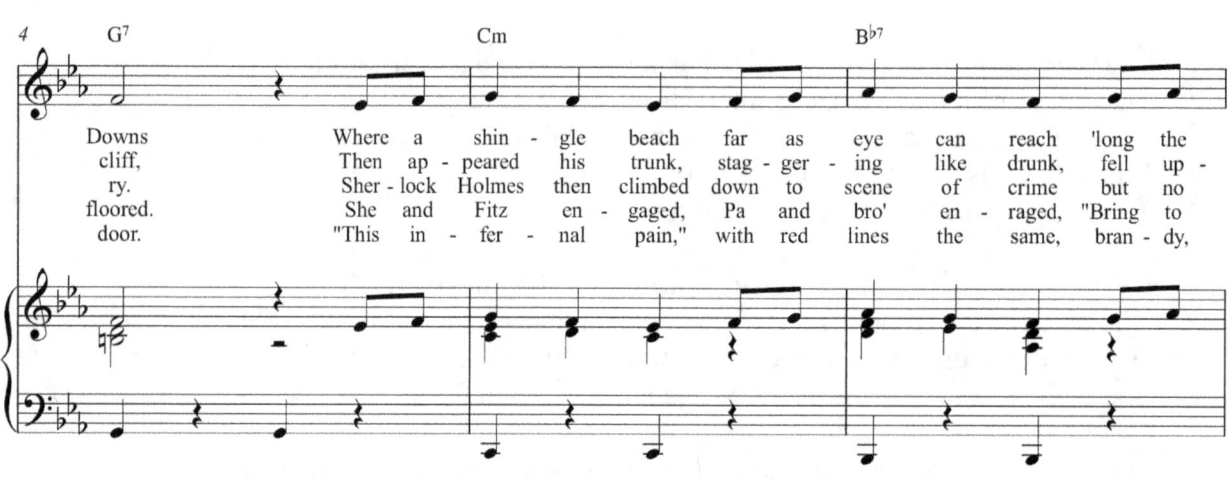

Downs
cliff,
ry.
floored.
door.
Where a shin-gle beach far as eye can reach 'long the
Then ap-peared his trunk, stag-ger-ing like drunk, fell up-
Sher-lock Holmes then climbed down to scene of crime but no
She and Fitz en-gaged, Pa and bro' en-raged, "Bring to
"This in-fer-nal pain," with red lines the same, bran-dy,

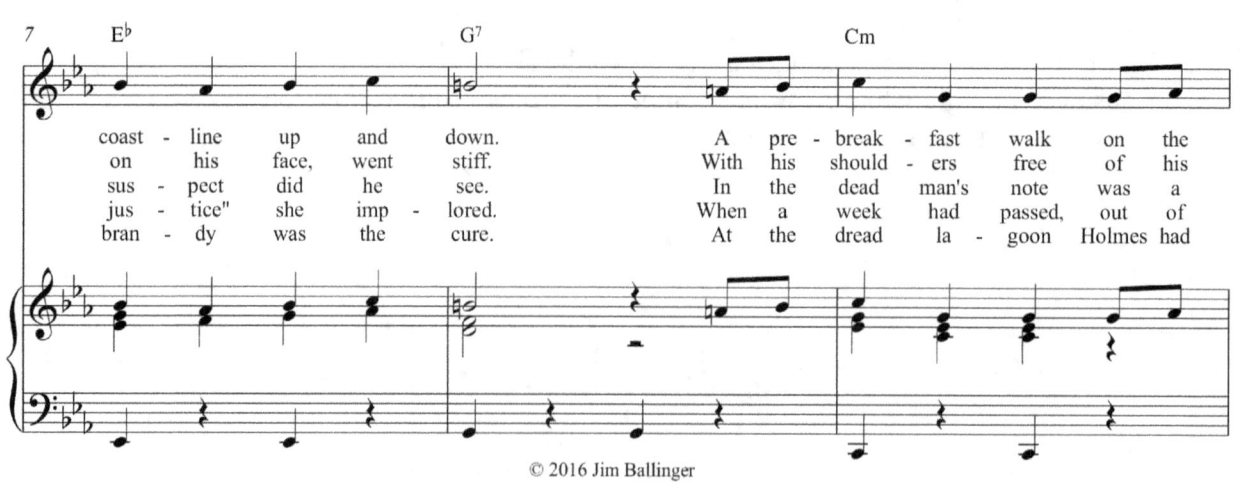

coast-line up and down.
on his face, went stiff.
sus-pect did he see.
jus-tice" she imp-lored.
bran-dy was the cure.
A pre-break-fast walk on the
With his should-ers free of his
In the dead man's note was a
When a week had passed, out of
At the dread la-goon Holmes had

220

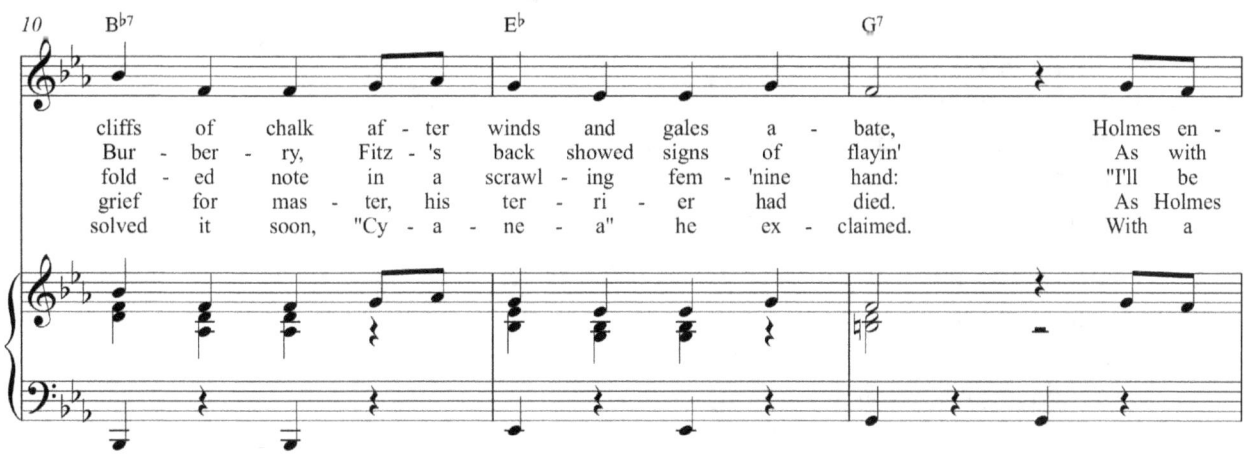

10

cliffs of chalk af - ter winds and gales a - bate, Holmes en -
Bur - ber - ry, Fitz - 's back showed signs of flayin' As with
fold - ed note in a scrawl - ing fem - 'nine hand: "I'll be
grief for mas - ter, his ter - ri - er had died. As Holmes

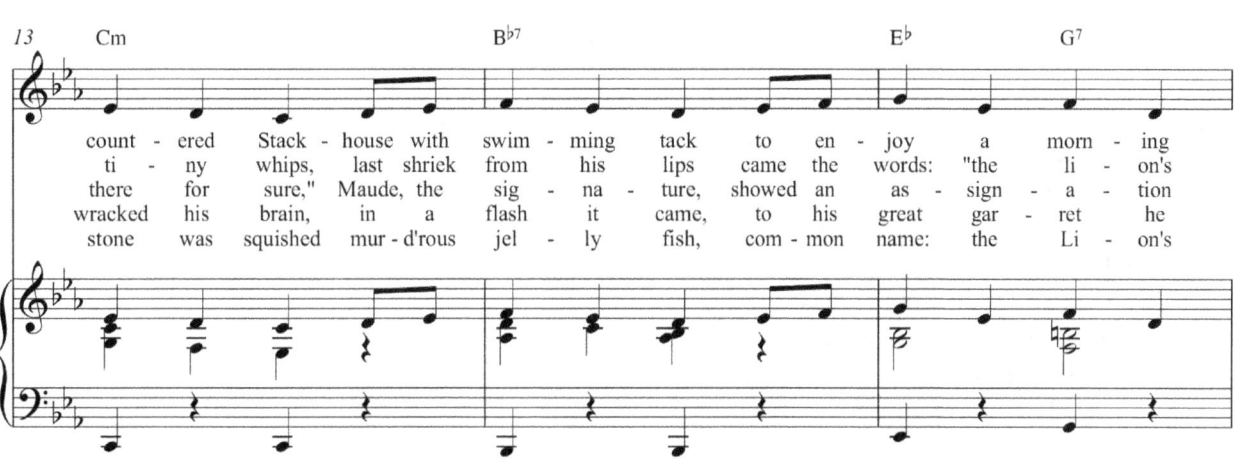

13

count - ered Stack - house with swim - ming tack to en - joy a morn - ing
ti - ny whips, last shriek from his lips came the words: "the li - on's
there for sure," Maude, the sig - na - ture, showed an as - sig - na - tion
wracked his brain, in a flash it came, to his great gar - ret he
stone was squished mur - d'rous jel - ly fish, com - mon name: the Li - on's

1,2,3,4.   5.

16

great.   But Fitz -   Mane.
mane."   Mur - doch
planned.   And the
hied.   Af - ter

The Lion's Mane

A retired bloke on the southern slope
Of the verdant Sussex Downs
Where a shingle beach far as eye could reach
'Long the coastline up and down
A pre-breakfast walk on the cliffs of chalk
After winds and gales abate
Holmes encountered Stack-house with swimming tack
To enjoy a morning great

But Fitzroy McPher-son, science master
Showed his head above the cliff
Then appeared his trunk, staggering like drunk
Fell upon his face, went stiff
With his shoulders free of his Burberry
Fitz's back showed signs of flayin'
As with tiny whips, last shriek from his lips
Came the words "the lion's mane"

Murdoch then approached, (mathematics coach)
Sent to fetch constab'lary
Sherlock Holmes then climbed down to scene of crime
But no suspect did he see
In the dead man's coat was a folded note
In a scrawling fem'nine hand
"I'll be there for sure," Maude, the signature,
Showed an assignation planned

And the lady, she was Maude Bellamy
By her beauty Holmes was floored
She and Fitz engaged, Pa and bro' enraged
"Bring to justice" she implored
When a week had passed out of grief for mast-er
His terrier had died
As Holmes wracked his brain, in a flash it came
To his great garret he hied

After little rest, e'er the theory's test
Murdoch staggered through his door
"This infernal pain," with red lines the same
Brandy, brandy was the cure
At the dread lagoon Holmes had solved it soon
"Cyanea" he exclaimed
With a stone was squished murd'rous jelly fish
Common name: the Lion's Mane

The Veiled Lodger

by Jim Ballinger

She was a wo-man, she was beau - ti - ful, Eu -
A - no - ther man then came in - to her life, 'Twas
The show was on its way to Wim - ble-don At
For se - ven years she lived be - hind a veil With

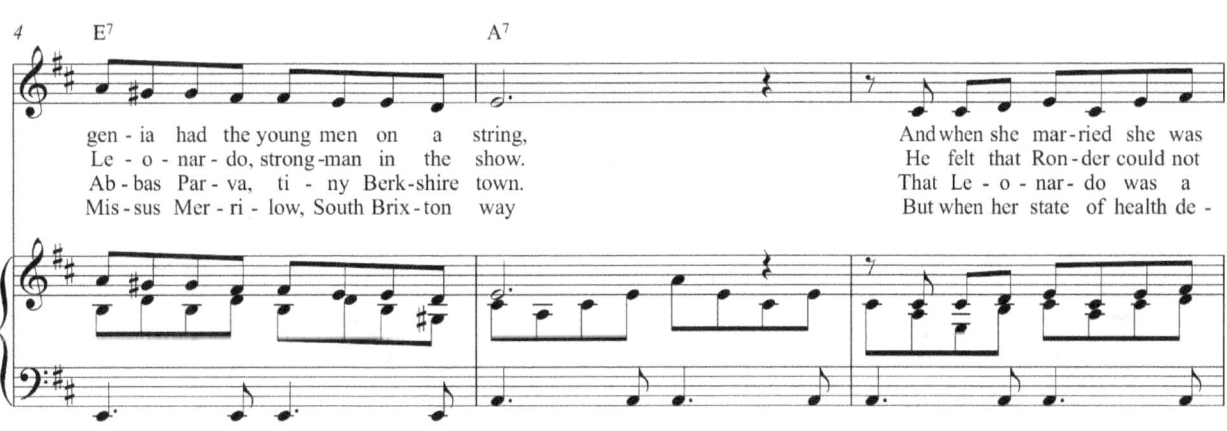

gen - ia had the young men on a string, And when she mar-ried she was
Le - o - nar - do, strong-man in the show. He felt that Ron - der could not
Ab - bas Par - va, ti - ny Berk-shire town. That Le - o - nar - do was a
Mis-sus Mer - ri - low, South Brix-ton way But when her state of health de -

du - ti - ful, Un - hap - pi - ness came with her wed - ding ring.
do a wife Such in - ju - ry and make her life so low.
nim - ble son And with the great claw he brought Ron - der down.
clined and failed Her land - la - dy to Sher-lock Holmes con - veyed

The Veiled Lodger

She was a woman, she was beautiful
Eugenia had the young men on a string
And when she married she was dutiful
Unhappiness came with her wedding ring
Her husband, Ronder, ran a circus show
And each night when he drained the bottle dry
He would mistreat her, he whipped and beat her
With such ferocity that she feared she would die

Another man then came into her life
'Twas Leonardo, strong man in the show
He felt that Ronder could not do a wife
Such injury and make her life so low
So Leonardo and Eugenia planned
How Ronder's death an accident would seem
They made a lion's paw with steel nails for claws
And with that club one pitch-dark night they did the deed

The show was on its way to Wimbledon
At Abbas Parva, tiny Berkshire town
That Leonardo was a nimble son
And with the great claw he brought Ronder down
But when they set the lion loose that night
The scent of human blood induced a fright
It sank its long and mighty teeth into Eugenia's face
And with the first of many bites her beauty was erased
But foul play was not suspected, though some odd things were detected
Leonardo left without a trace

For seven years she lived behind a veil
With Mrs Merrilow, South Brixton way
But when her state of health declined and failed
Her landlady to Sherlock Holmes conveyed
The words that brought him there to witness her
Confession after Leonardo's death
And Watson logs her "The Veiled Lodger"
Though Holmes could see her inner beauty through the veil

And Holmes received a phial of prussic acid in the mail
With unsigned note from the brave woman in the veil

Shoscombe Old Place

by Jim Ballinger

227

Shoscombe Old Place

Sir Robert's gone mad, his actions are queer
His dog since a lad he traded for beer
His sister so close now keeps to her room
And greeting morose neither horse nor groom

She drinks like a fish, a bottle a night
There's something amiss, there's something not right
He visits the crypt at midnight, the cad
Sir Robert has flipped, Sir Robert's gone mad

For this is the story as told by John Mason
Head trainer of horses at Shoscombe Park racin'
Sir Robert's indebtedness leaving him skint
His hope for the Derby the great Shoscombe Prince

The house belonged to Lady Beatrice Falder
The sister of Robert, now widowed and older
The rambling estate brought in sizeable rents
Which Sir Robert Norberton dutif'ly spent

So Watson and Holmes pursue gill and fin
By taking some rooms at Green Dragon Inn
A spaniel on lead they take for a walk
The carriage they seen the spaniel does balk

"Drive on" a voice shrieked, the coachman's whip cracked
The dog's mistress seeked, was not her in fact
"We've added a card, our hand's nearly there
We must play it hard but play it with care."

From Mason they find out Sir Robert's returning
They head for the crypt to continue their learning
The skeleton dug up has now disappeared
A coffin is opened, a recent corpse here

For Beatrice sadly had died of the dropsy
Which Holmes said required confirm at autopsy
That she was still living the world was convinced
Until Derby victory by Shoscombe Prince

With Robert's position restored by the race
Thus ending our story of Shoscombe Old Place

The Retired Colourman

by Jim Ballinger

230

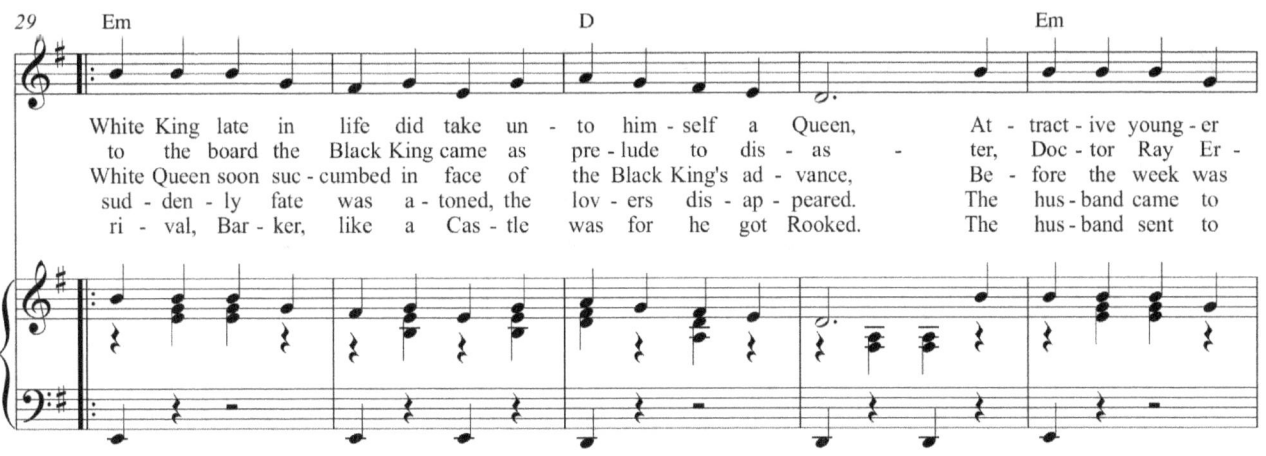

29 Em / D / Em

White King late in life did take un - to him - self a Queen, At - tract - ive young - er
to the board the Black King came as pre - lude to dis - as - ter, Doc - tor Ray Er -
White Queen soon suc - cumbed in face of the Black King's ad - vance, Be - fore the week was
sud - den - ly fate was a - toned, the lov - ers dis - ap - peared. The hus - band came to
ri - val, Bar - ker, like a Cas - tle was for he got Rooked. The hus - band sent to

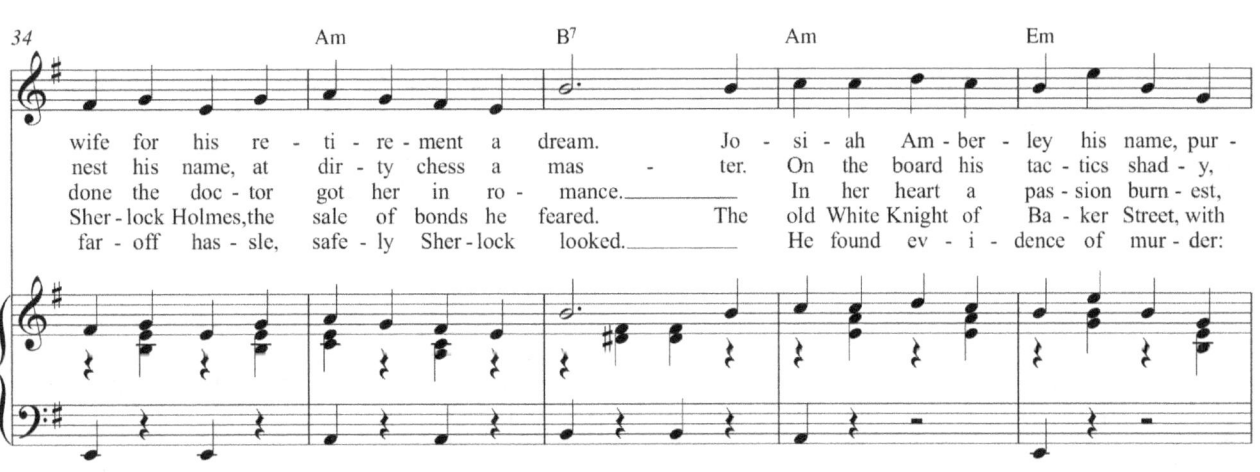

34 Am / B7 / Am / Em

wife for his re - ti - re - ment a dream. Jo - si - ah Am - ber - ley his name, pur -
nest his name, at dir - ty chess a mas - ter. On the board his tac - tics shad - y,
done the doc - tor got her in ro - mance. In her heart a pas - sion burn - est,
Sher - lock Holmes, the sale of bonds he feared. The old White Knight of Ba - ker Street, with
far - off has - sle, safe - ly Sher - lock looked. He found ev - i - dence of mur - der:

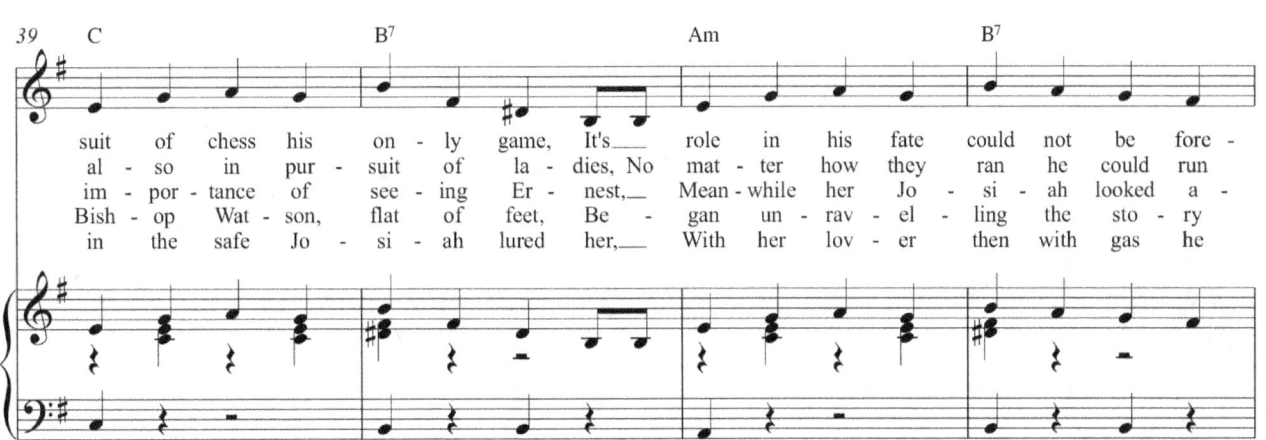

39 C / B7 / Am / B7

suit of chess his on - ly game, It's role in his fate could not be fore -
al - so in pur - suit of la - dies, No mat - ter how they ran he could run
im - por - tance of see - ing Er - nest, Mean - while her Jo - si - ah looked a -
Bish - op Wat - son, flat of feet, Be - gan un - rav - el - ling the sto - ry
in the safe Jo - si - ah lured her, With her lov - er then with gas he

The Retired Colourman

The colourman had spent his life in mixing paint-box colours
Which soon persuaded his young wife that nothing could be duller
So when the chance to paint in oils one fateful day befell her
She left her husband to his toils for a more colourful feller
The colourman whose life was spent where colour brightly blares
Had to live out his retirement on a board of sixty-four black-and-white squares

The White King late in life did take unto himself a Queen
Attractive younger wife, for his retirement a dream
Josiah Amberly his name, pursuit of chess his only game
Its role in his fate could not be foreseen

Onto the board the Black King came as prelude to disaster
Doctor Ray Ernest his name, at dirty chess a master
On the board his tactics shady, also in pursuit of ladies
No matter how they ran he could run faster

The White Queen soon succumbed in face of the Black King's advance
Before the week was done the doctor got into her p... got her in romance
In her heart a passion burnest, importance of seeing Ernest
Meanwhile her Josiah looked askance

But suddenly fate was atoned, the lovers disappeared
The husband went to Sherlock Holmes, the sale of bonds he feared
The old White Knight of Baker Street, with Bishop Watson, flat of feet
Began unravelling the story weird

The rival, Barker, like a Castle was for he got Rooked
The husband sent to far-off hassle, safely Sherlock looked
He found evidence of murder, in the safe Josiah lured her
With her lover then he cooked with gas

Amberly tried suicide but for his trial lived on
The game in which opponents died served to make him a Pawn
What have we learned from this tale? Can we avoid this fate?
In love and chess do, without fail, be sure to check your mate

Section 6:
The Novels of
Sherlock Holmes

A Study in Scarlet

by Jim Ballinger

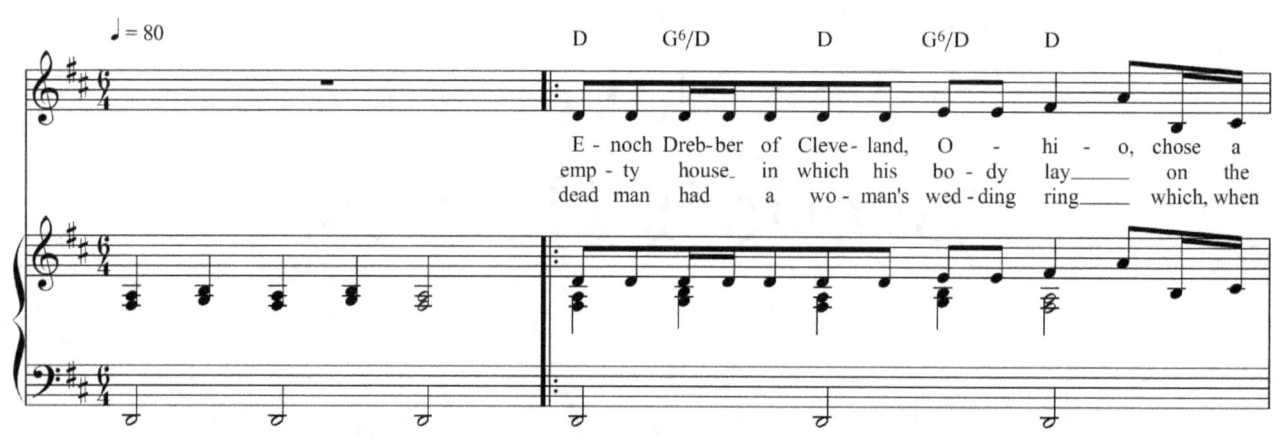

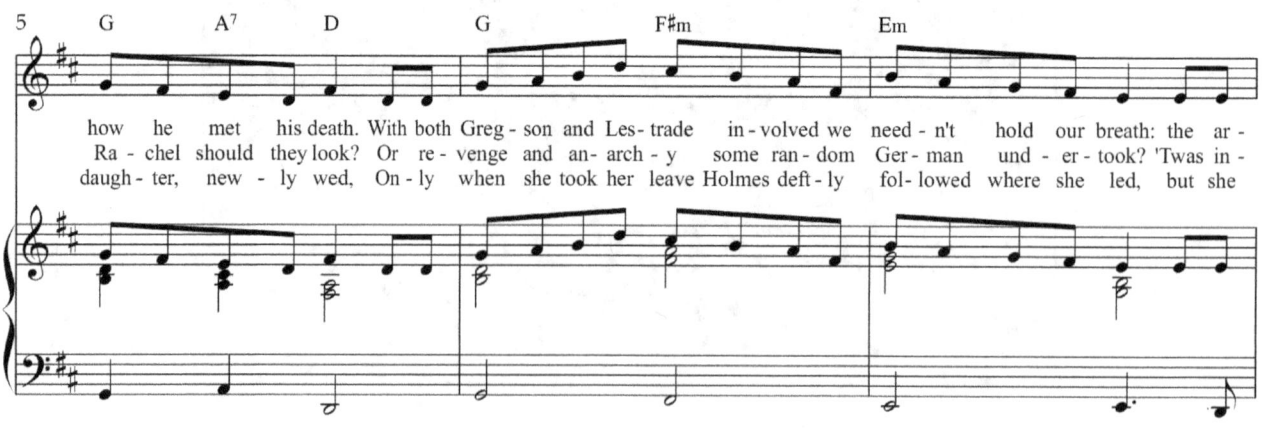

236

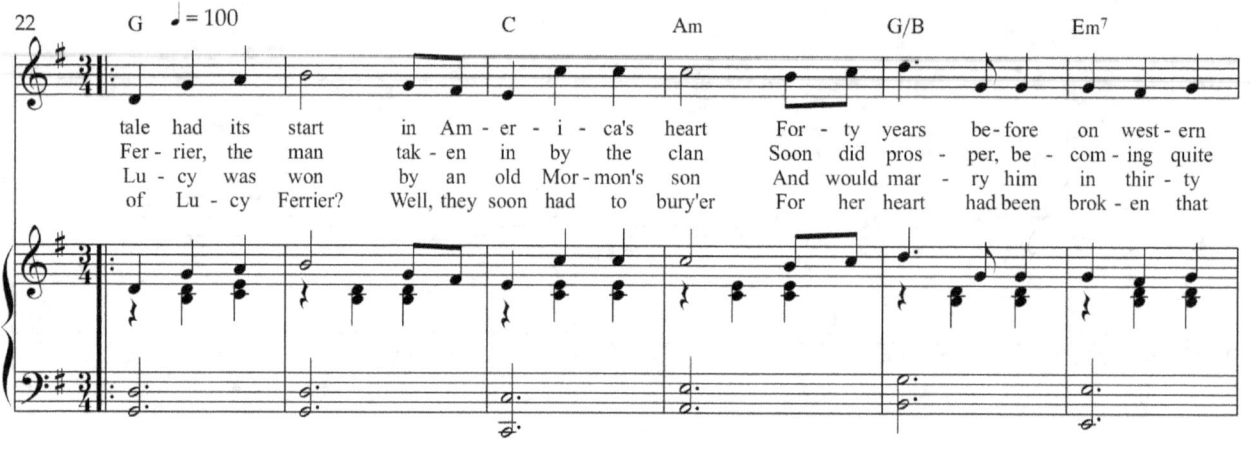

22

G ♩ = 100　　　　　　C　　　　Am　　　G/B　　　Em⁷

tale had its start in Am-er-i-ca's heart For-ty years be-fore on west-ern
Fer-rier, the man tak-en in by the clan Soon did pros-per, be-com-ing quite
Lu-cy was won by an old Mor-mon's son And would mar-ry him in thir-ty
of Lu-cy Ferrier? Well, they soon had to bury'er For her heart had been brok-en that

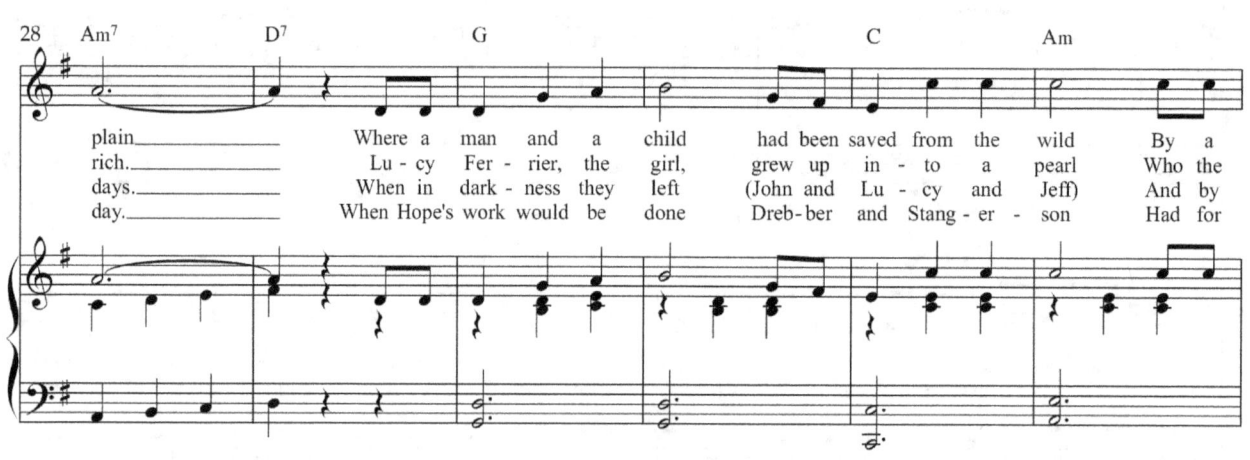

28　Am⁷　　　　D⁷　　　　G　　　　　　　C　　　　Am

plain_____ Where a man and a child had been saved from the wild By a
rich._____ Lu-cy Fer-rier, the girl, grew up in-to a pearl Who the
days._____ When in dark-ness they left (John and Lu-cy and Jeff) And by
day._____ When Hope's work would be done Dreb-ber and Stang-er-son Had for

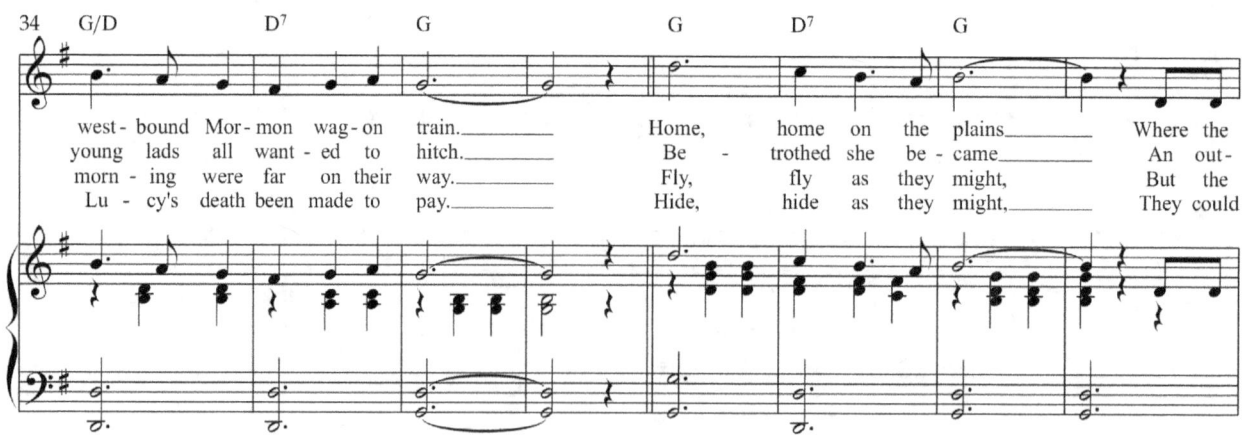

34　G/D　　　　D⁷　　　　G　　　　　G　　　D⁷　　　G

west-bound Mor-mon wag-on train._____ Home, home on the plains_____ Where the
young lads all want-ed to hitch._____ Be-trothed she be-came_____ An out-
morn-ing were far on their way._____ Fly, fly as they might, But the
Lu-cy's death been made to pay._____ Hide, hide as they might,_____ They could

238

him e - ter - nal bail, grant-ing him e - ter - nal bail. And so Hope's com - plex - ion rud - dy sig - ni -

fied a heart con - di - tion, And so a Scar - let Stud - y was in fact re - veng - ing mis - sion. The

Laur - 'ston Gar - dens mys - t'ry taxed the great de - tec - tive's brain, In Holmes'

first re - cord - ed his - t'ry straight - ened out a tang - led skein.

A Study in Scarlet

Enoch Drebber of Cleveland, Ohio
Chose a house off Brixton Road in which to die
Only he had not been robbed, no sign how he met his death
With both Gregson and Lestrade involved we needn't hold our breath
The arrests they will come soon ... and often

In the empty house in which his body lay
On the wall a message writ in blood did say
Letters R A C H E; for a Rachel should they look?
Or revenge and anarchy some random German undertook?
'Twas indeed a tangled skein ... in scarlet

For the dead man had a woman's wedding ring
Which, when advertised, to Baker Street did bring
An old woman to retrieve for her daughter, newly wed
Only when she took her leave Holmes deftly followed where she led
But she soon gave him the slip ... in spades

Gregson made his first arrest, 'twas the young Charpentier
And whose sister Drebber pressed with himself to go away
But the case got much more hairy when Lestrade arrived and said
That old Drebber's secretary, Joseph Stangerson, was dead
Once more with a message ... in blood

Near his body were some pills whose effect Holmes had to test
On a terrier who was ill and who quickly bit the dust
This discovery sealed his case and proved Lestrade and Gregson dopes
As they soon looked on the face of murderer, Jefferson Hope
'Twas signed, signed and sealed, ... and delivered

The tale had its start in America's heart
Forty years before on western plain
Where a man and a child had been saved from the wild
By a west-bound Mormon wagon train

Home, home on the plains, where the Mormons all led pious lives
Where seldom was heard a non-Biblical word
And they spent the nights counting their wives

John Ferrier, the man taken in by the clan
Soon did prosper, becoming quite rich
Lucy Ferrier, the girl grew up into a pearl
Who the young lads all wanted to hitch

Betrothed she became an outsider named Jefferson Hope
This handsome young stranger had retrieved her from danger
All too soon they desired to elope

But Lucy was won by an old Mormon's son
And would marry him in thirty days
In the darkness they left (John and Lucy and Jeff)
And by morning were far on their way

Fly, fly as they might but the Mormons were soon at their throat
John Ferrier shot dead, Lucy Ferrier wed
And poor Jefferson left without hope

What of Lucy Ferrier? Well, they soon had to bury her
For her heart had been broken that day
When Hope's work would be done, Drebber and Stangerson
Had for Lucy's death been made to pay

Hide, hide as they might, they could not escape him who they loathed
For Hope sprang eternal to revenge their infernal
Acts upon his friend and his betrothed

He eventually caught up to them in London
And where finally revenge was with poison done
But his revenge was shorter for on his first night in gaol
He went and ruptured his aorta, granting him eternal bail
Granting him eternal bail

And so Hope's complexion ruddy signified a heart condition
And so a Scarlet Study was in fact revenging mission
The Lauriston Gardens mystery taxed the great detective's brain
In Holmes' first recorded history straightened out a tangled skein

The Sign of Four

by Jim Ballinger

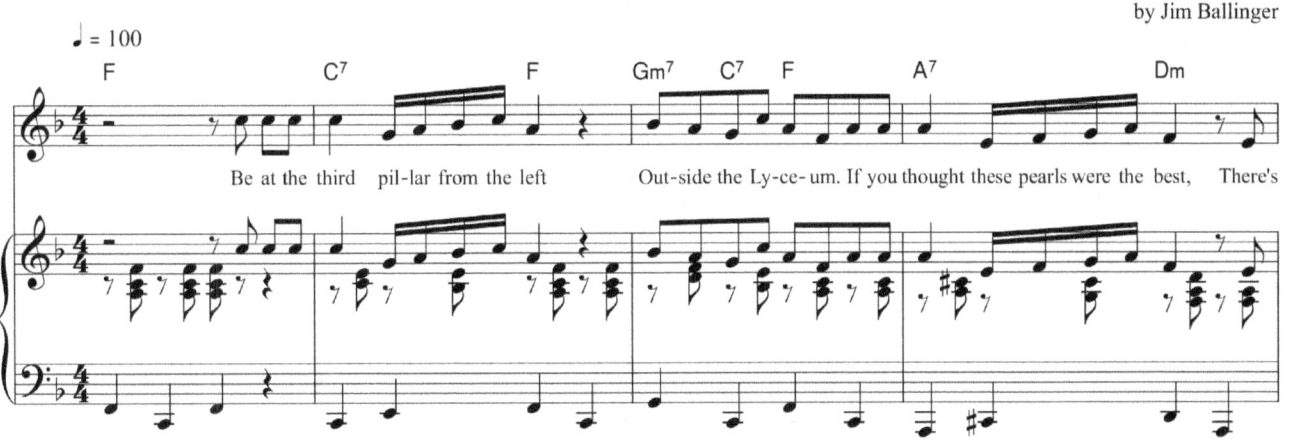

Be at the third pil-lar from the left   Out-side the Ly-ce-um. If you thought these pearls were the best,   There's

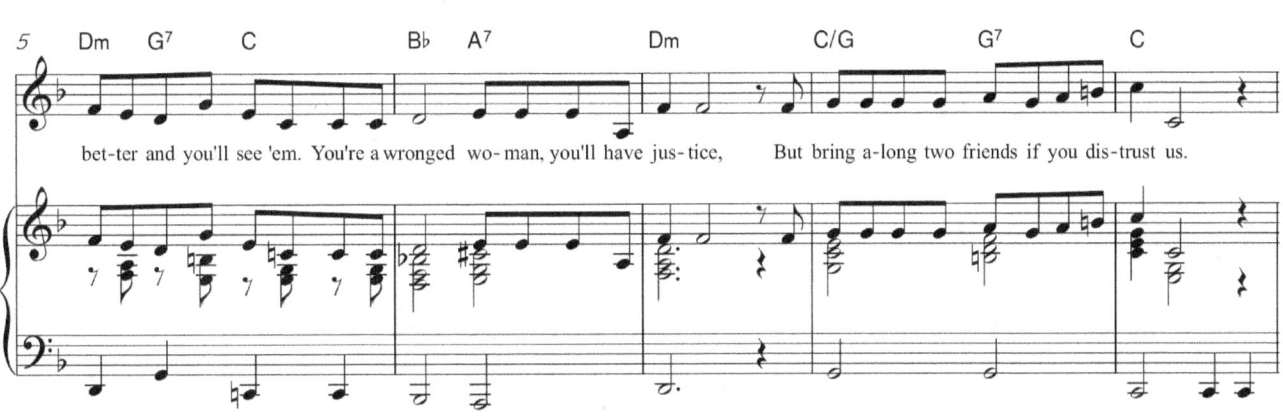

bet-ter and you'll see 'em. You're a wronged wo-man, you'll have jus-tice,   But bring a-long two friends if you dis-trust us.

That's how Holmes and Wat-son   And Ma-ry Mor-stan   Came to meet Thad-de-us Shol-to.   It
a-no-nym-i-ty___   For six years run-ning   Thad-deus sent Ma-ry a pearl.___   Bro-

243

Four. In Four. Sher-lock Holmes was in luck Be-cause the thief had stepped in cre-o-sote And
Bak-er Street__ Ir-reg-u-lars, That gang of juv-en-ile de-lin-quensts

his ac-com-plice left foot-prints as well. 'Twas half the size of a man's: "A child has done this hor-rid thing." Holmes
Searched a-long the ri-ver long and hard. Dis-guised as an old sea-man, Holmes in search of launch-es went And

has an ex-plan-a-tion but won't tell. With aid of bor-rowed mutt named To-by, Trail of cre-o-sote they fol-low
found Au-ror-a hid'n a Jac'b-son's yard. And that night a po-lice launch chased Au-ror-a at a break-neck pace And

Down to where it ends be-side the Thames, Then as-cer-tained they must look for a
Ton-ga's blow-pipe played its fi-nal song. But when Au-ror-a ran a-ground The

The Sign of the Four

Be at the third pillar from the left outside the Lyceum
If you thought these pearls were the best, there's better and you'll see 'em
You're a wronged woman, you'll have justice
But bring along two friends if you distrust us

That's how Holmes and Watson and Mary Morstan came to meet Thaddeus Sholto
It seems that Sholto's father and Mary's father had been in India together
But Sholto had returned out of India with a treasure
Poor Morstan kicked the bucket long before he'd had his measure
But Sholto joined him not long after showing his displeasure
At wooden-legged men, (he sure distrusted them)
He was found in final rest with a note pinned on his chest:
The sign of the four

In anonymity for six years running, Thaddeus sent Mary a pearl
Brother Bartholomew did not approve: Don't waste these jewels on a girl
But now Bartholomew has discovered the full treasure
The attic space at Pondicherry Lodge, which he did measure
But when the group to Norwood got they found to their displeasure
With brother Bartholomew dead, a poisoned thorn in his head
And the treasure taken away where a hastily scrawled note did say:
The sign of the four

Sherlock Holmes was in luck because the thief had stepped in creosote
And his accomplice left footprints as well
'Twas half the size of a man's, "A child has done this horrid thing"
Holmes has an explanation but won't tell
With aid of borrowed mutt named Toby, trail of creosote they follow
Down to where it ends beside the Thames
Then ascertained they must look for a speedy steam launch named Aurora
But to find it Holmes would need some friends

The Baker Street Irregulars, that gang of juvenile delinquents
Searched along the river long and hard
Disguised as an old seaman, Holmes in search of launches went
And found Aurora hidden at Jacobson's yard
And that night a police launch chased Aurora at a breakneck pace
And Tonga's blow-pipe played its final song
But when Aurora ran aground the treasure chest was empty found
And Mary's rich inheritance was gone

.

Jonathan Small recounted his tale about the Agra treasure
Mary Morstan, beautiful and pale, took Watson's hand with pleasure
This news was greeted by Holmes with distain
He soon would drown his sorrows in cocaine
'Twas seven percent strong or maybe more
The doldrums after the Sign of the Four

The Hound of the Baskervilles

by Jim Ballinger

249

some jok-er has walked off with Sir Hen-ry's old black boot.

When
Sir
There
When

Wat-son and the Bar-on-et reach the an-ces-tral house___ Just who is there to care in it? Why,
Hen-ry has a pas-sion for his neigh-bour's love-ly sis-ter, The neigh-bour's teeth were gnash-in' when Sir
al-so was a-no-ther man who lived up-on the Tor,___ Be-sides the con-vict bro-ther of E-
Holmes and Wat-son leave on pres-sing bus-'ness in Lon-don.___ Sir Hen-ry is quite peeved but goes to

Bar-ry-more and spouse.___ Then Wat-son meets their neigh-bour on a walk up-on the moor.___ And
Hen-ry fin'-lly kissed her.___ Back at the Hall the plot thick-ens with Bar-ry-more at night.___ They
li-za Bar-ry-more.___ The old a-ban-doned huts were where he lived, a house of stones. Wat-son
dine at Sta-ple-ton's.___ De-ci-ding he should walk home 'cross the mo-or through the fog,___ Sir

Sta-ple-ton, the nat-ur-'list Cyc-lop-i-des de-tours.
won-der what the dick-ens was he do-ing with that light.
went com-plete-ly nuts when he dis-co-vered Sher-lock Holmes.
Hen-ry was soon stalked by a huge phos-phor-es-cent dog.

His
The
A
It

250

32 — B♭ ... E♭ ... B♭

sis - ter, Ber - yl, thought that Wat-son was young Bask-er - ville,___ And warn-ing him of per - il if__ he
can-dle was a bea-con for a con-vict on the moor. Es - cap - ee they were seek-in', bro' of
wo-man, Lau-ra Ly - ons, by her fa-ther, Frank-lin, shunned, The clue which Holmes en - twi - nes both Sir
took the work of five bul-lets to save Sir Hen-ry's life, Then to the House of Mer - ri - pitt, re -

35 — E♭ ... Gm ... Dm

stayed a-gainst her will. But on her bro-ther's re - turn there's a mel - an-cho - ly sound: 'Twas the
Mis - sus Bar-ry-more. On edge of Grim-pen Mi - re they are stopped short by a sound Start-ing
Charles and Sta - ple - ton,___ And as their plan is closed they hear an a - go - ni - sing sound. Wear-ing
lease Sta - ple-ton's wife.___ But Sta - ple - ton mis-stepped his route, was swal-lowed by the mire. And they

38 — A⁷ ... | 1,2,3. ... Dm ... E♭ ... F

boom-ing of a bit - tern or the howl - ing of a hound?
deep, then ris-ing high - er like the cry - ing of a hound.
Hen - ry's cast-off clothes Sel - den is brought down by the hound.
found Sir Hen-ry's old black boot, in

42 — | 4. ... Dm ... G ... D

side it the name Meyers. Meyers. Meyers.

The Hound of the Baskervilles

This was a dog that did something in the night
As poor old Sir Charles Baskerville has dropped dead of fright
His nephew from the colonies, Sir Henry, has arrived
He'll need the help that Doctor Mortimer gives to survive
He's followed by a bearded man while on his London roams
A man who tells the cabbie that his name is Sherlock Holmes
A warning message cut out of The Times, Holmes is astute
And some joker has walked off with Sir Henry's old black boot

When Watson and the Baronet reach the ancestral house
Just who is there to care in it? Why, Barrymore and spouse
Then Watson meets their neighbour on a walk upon the moor
And Stapleton, the natur'list, Cyclopides detours

His sister, Beryl thought that Watson was young Baskerville
And warning him of peril if he stayed against her will
But on her brother's return there's a melancholy sound
'Twas the booming of a bittern or the howling of a hound?

Sir Henry has a passion for his neighbour's lovely sister
The neighbour's teeth were gnashin' when Sir Henry finally kissed her
Back at the Hall the plot thickens with Barrymore at night
They wonder what the dickens was he doing with that light?

The candle was a beacon for a convict on the moor
Escapee they were seekin', bro' of Mrs Barrymore
On edge of Grimpen Mire they are stopped short by a sound
Starting deep, then rising higher like the crying of a hound

There also was another man who lived upon the Tor
Besides the convict brother of Eliza Barrymore
The old abandoned huts were where he lived, a house of stones
Watson went completely nuts when he discovered Sherlock Holmes

A woman, Laura Lyons, by her father, Frankland, shunned
The clue which Holmes entwines both Sir Charles and Stapleton
And as their plan is closed they hear an agonising sound
Wearing Henry's cast-off clothes Selden is brought down by the hound

When Holmes and Watson leave on pressing business in London
Sir Henry is quite peeved but goes to dine at Stapleton's
Deciding he should walk home 'cross the moor through the fog
Sir Henry was soon stalked by a huge phosphorescent dog

It took the work of five bullets to save Sir Henry's life
Then to the House of Merripit, release Stapleton's wife
But Stapleton mis-stepped his route, was swallowed by the mire
And they found Sir Henry's old black boot, inside it, the name Meyers

The Valley of Fear

by Jim Ballinger

28 Gm / Dm / C⁷

Por - lock, an un - der - ling   far down the chain,   Was in con - tact with Holmes, it ap -
Ce - cil John Bar - ker, oc - cas - ion - al guest,   Who had known Doug - las   back in the
ter - rib - ly jeal - ous con - cern - ing his wife;   If   a man spoke to   her he'd ex -
would-be as - sa - sin was   shot in the face,   They had switched his clothes   so   it ap -

31 F / D⁷ / Gm / Dm

pears._____   'Twas from him that the cod - ed   in - scrip - ti - on came,   In - tro -
States._____   And   so this was the cast on the   ev - ening in quest - ion, E -
plode._____   But she'd gath - ered tales of his Am - er - i - can life   And the
peared_____   It was Doug - las who died and his   bo - dy re - placed   In the

34 Bb / C / Dm / Dm / Gm⁶

duc - tion   to Val - ley   of Fear.   (3) They de - ciph - er with Whit - a - ker's
vents which the mys - t'ry   cre - ate.   (6) At   a quart - er to twelve when the
curse which on his should - ers rode.   (9) "Will we nev - er get   out   of the
end   of   the Val - ley   of Fear.   (12) For the Scow - rers of   Ver - mis - sa

257

38 Dm / Gm⁶ / Dm / C⁷ / F

old al-man-ac,   Not the new one, too up-to-date, how   There is
first a-larm shrilled,   Ser-geant Wil-son was quick off the mark.   Ce - cil
Val-ley of Fear?"   Bo-dy-mas-ter Mc-Guin-ty was named.   Wat-son
Val-ley had been   In-fil-trat-ed by Pink-er-ton's man.   In the

41 Gm⁶ / A⁷ / Gm⁶ / A⁷ / Gm⁶

dan-ger may come ve-ry soon, an at-tack   On one Doug-las of Birl-stone had
Bar-ker said Doug-las was bru-tal-ly killed,   'Twas a tra-ged-y ter-rib-ly
strolled in the gar-den and hap-pened to hear   As the wid-ow and Bar-ker en-
guise of Mc-Gin-ty, who's act-u-al-ly   Bird-y Ed-wards, he up-set their

44 A⁷ / Gm / Dm

died.   But no soon-er had Sher-lock de-ciph-ered the code   Than In-
dark.   Bar-ker, Wil-son, and Doc-tor Wood ent-ered the room   Where had
flamed.   Holmes sus-pect-ed the two a con-spi-ra-cy hatched   For their
plans.   Their ar-rest and con-vic-tion put price on his head,   So to

The Valley of Fear

Like an old married couple at breakfast they sat
With a note from Fred Porlock in hand
Holmes examined the envelope, writing, and flap
The Greek "e" with the flourish would stand
"You have heard me speak of Moriarty," said Holmes
"He's as famous to criminals as…"
"As my blushes," said Holmes? "To the public unknown."
What a pawky humour Watson has

Moriarty, the schemer, greatest of all time, organiser of all deviltry
And controlling the underworld with just his mind, what a genius professor was he
But this Porlock, an underling far down the chain
Was in contact with Holmes it appears
'Twas from him that the coded inscription came, introduction to Valley of Fear

They decipher with Whitaker's old almanac, not the new one, too up-to-date, how
There is danger may come very soon, an attack
On one Douglas at Birlstone House now
But no sooner had Sherlock deciphered the code than Inspector MacDonald came by
But on seeing the message, "It's witchcraft," he quotes
Mister Douglas of Birlstone had died

Holmes and Watson, together with Inspector Mac from Victoria Station depart
They reach Birlstone in Sussex (it's just down the track)
And are met by White Mason with cart
Soon ensconced at the inn they can hear the details of a case most remarkably queer
It's a real downright snorter, the press will hightail to the case of the Valley of Fear

For John Douglas had taken the Manor House o'er and inserted himself in the town
California the source of his fortune (gold ore), and a much younger second wife now
Also Cecil John Barker, occasional guest who had known Douglas back in the States
And so this was the cast on the evening in question events which the myst'ry create

At a quarter to twelve when the first alarm shrilled
Sergeant Wilson was quick off the mark
Cecil Barker said Douglas was brutally killed, 'twas a tragedy terribly dark
Barker, Wilson, and Doctor Wood entered the room
Where had happened the fatal event
Douglas clad in a dressing gown lay in the gloom with a shotgun across his chest leant

For the drawbridge was up, blocking means of escape
Did the murderer wade 'cross the moat?
On the floor near the corpse where a card of white lay where VV341 someone wrote
On the dead man's right arm was the mark of a brand
And his gold wedding ring disappeared
In the corner were boot prints where someone did stand
It grew deeper, the Valley of Fear

Interviewing the witnesses, details emerged of the past life that Douglas kept hid
'Twas a secret society harbouring the urge to see Mister John Douglas stone dead
He was terribly jealous concerning his wife, if a man spoke to her he'd explode
But she'd gathered tales of his American life
And the curse which on his shoulders rode

"Will we never get out of the Valley of Fear?" Bodymaster McGinty was named
Watson strolled in the garden and happened to hear as the widow and Barker enflamed
Holmes suspected the two a conspiracy hatched, for their story was clearly fake news
The most vital of evidence: dumb-bell unmatched
Holmes continued to follow the clues

When an evening alone in the study Holmes planned for the genius loci believed
With a borrowed umbrella from Watson at hand, the lost dumb-bell he safely retrieved
Unto Barker they wrote that the moat would be drained
Then concealed themselves well and observed
After hours of waiting a yellow light came from the study and justice was served

Holmes cried "Now!" and they rushed to the study wherein
They found Barker with bundle resumed
When the widow arrived in a state of chagrin
Non-dead Douglas emerged from the gloom
For his would-be assassin was shot in the face
They had switched his clothes so it appeared
It was Douglas who died and his body replaced in the end of the Valley of Fear

For the Scowrers of Vermissa Valley had been infiltrated by Pinkerton's man
In the guise of McGinty, who's actually Birdy Edwards, he upset their plan
Their arrest and conviction put price on his head, so to England he soon disappeared
But it was Moriarty who wanted him dead at the end of the Valley of Fear
Enigmatic epistle Holmes opened with dread
"Dear me, Mister Holmes, dear me!" it said

Lasting Impressions

by Jim Ballinger

Lasting Impressions

Consulting detective, the first of his kind
The wisest and best man that we'll ever find
Intently pursues
The minute, vital clues
Which make the onlookers seem blind
He leaves a lasting impression in each of our minds
A lasting impression in each of our minds

Retir'd army surgeon, the sweetest of men
Precisely the person you'd pick as a friend
Not luminous, quite
Yet conductor of light
The stories he masterf'ly told
He leaves a lasting impression in each of our souls
A lasting impression in each of our souls

The Woman, he called her, alone of her sex
Adventuress, she left the master sleuth vexed
She wished him "good night"
Then astutely took flight
The fruit of her wit and her art
She leaves a lasting impression in each of our hearts
A lasting impression in each of our hearts

An ophthalmic surgeon, no patients to see
He picked up his pen and became history
As fresh from the page
He evoked bygone age
Forever eighteen ninety-five
He leaves a lasting impression in each of our lives
A lasting impression in each of our lives

He leaves a lasting impression in each of our minds
A lasting impression in each of our souls
A lasting impression in each of our hearts
He leaves a lasting impression in each of our lives

List of First Performances

Title	Written	Premiere	Venue*
The Adventures of Sherlock Holmes			
A Scandal in Bohemia	May86	24May86	Hungarian Village Restaurant
The Red-Headed League	Sep 86	13Sep86	Metro Toronto Library
A Case of Identity	Jun 07	17Nov18	SM: Chez Alberstat. Dartmouth
The Boscombe Valley Mystery	Dec 86	8Dec86	Metro Toronto Library
The Five Orange Pips	Jan 16	15Sep19	SM: Split Crow Pub, Halifax
The Man with the Twisted Lip	Apr 87	25Apr87	Metro Toronto Library
The Blue Carbuncle	Jun 87	21Jun87	Carleton Inn
The Speckled Band	Sep 87	12Sep87	Metro Toronto Library
The Engineer's Thumb	Oct 87	23Oct87	Engineers Club
The Noble Bachelor	Nov 87	5Dec87	Metro Toronto Library
The Beryl Coronet	Mar 88	19Mar88	Metro Toronto Library
The Copper Beeches	Apr 88	23Apr88	Metro Toronto Library
The Memoirs of Sherlock Holmes			
Silver Blaze	Jun 16	30Oct21	YouTube
The Yellow Face	Sep 88	18Sep88	Royal York Hotel
The Stock-Broker's Clerk	Oct 88	22Oct88	Metro Toronto Library
The "Gloria Scott"	Mar 89	4Mar89	Metro Toronto Library
The Musgrave Ritual	Nov 88	3Dec88	Hart House
The Reigate Squires	Apr 89	29Apr89	Metro Toronto Library
The Crooked Man	Jan 16	6Nov21	YouTube
The Resident Patient	Sep 89	9Sep89	Metro Toronto Library
The Greek Interpreter	Jul 16	6Nov21	YouTube
The Naval Treaty	Dec 89	9Dec89	Metro Toronto Library
The Final Problem	Mar 90	17Mar90	Metro Toronto Library
The Return of Sherlock Holmes			
The Empty House	Jul 16	13Nov21	YouTube
The Norwood Builder	Jun 81	13Jun81	Plaza II Hotel
The Dancing Men	Jan 83	29Jan83	Old Mill
The Solitary Cyclist	Jan 81	31Jan81	Old Mill
The Priory School	Dec 83	3Dec83	Enoch Turner Schoolhouse
Black Peter	Apr 81	25Apr81	Harbour Commission Building
Charles Augustus Milverton	May83	7May83	Debates Room, Hart House
The Six Napoleons	Sep 83	25Sep83	Ryan's Restaurant
The Three Students	Sep 91	7Sep91	Metro Toronto Library
The Golden Pince-Nez	Oct 91	26Oct91	Heliconian Hall
The Missing Three-Quarter	May82	8May82	Metro Toronto Library
The Abbey Grange	Sep 82	24Sep82	Arts and Letters Club
The Second Stain	May92	30May92	St Andrew's Presbyterian Church

His Last Bow

Wisteria Lodge	Mar 93	20Mar93	St Matthew's United Church
The Cardboard Box	May93	15May93	Manor Road United Church
The Red Circle	Sep 93	18Sep93	Hart House
The Bruce-Partington Plans	Oct 81	24Oct81	HMCS York
The Dying Detective	Jul 16	25May19	SM: St Joseph's Square, Halifax
Lady Frances Carfax	Oct 84	13Oct84	St Paul's Bloor Street
The Devil's Foot	Oct 82	29Oct82	Enoch Turner Schoolhouse
His Last Bow	Dec 17	4Dec21	Bootmaker Zoom

The Casebook of Sherlock Holmes

The Illustrious Client	Aug 16	4Dec21	YouTube
The Blanched Soldier	Mar 85	23Mar85	Metro Toronto Library
The Mazarin Stone	Sep 85	28Sep85	Metro Toronto Library
The Three Gables	May85	25May85	Arts and Letters Club
The Sussex Vampire	Mar 82	13Mar82	Metro Toronto Library
The Three Garridebs	May84	27May84	Le Rendez-Vous Restaurant
Thor Bridge	Aug 16	11Dec21	YouTube
The Creeping Man	May93	15May93	Manor Road United Church
The Lion's Mane	Aug 16	11Dec21	YouTube
The Veiled Lodger	Dec 81	12Dec81	Metro Toronto Library
Shoscombe Old Place	Feb 17	11Dec21	YouTube
The Retired Colourman	Mar 83	12Mar83	Metro Toronto Library

The Novels

A Study in Scarlet	Mar 86	4Dec21	Bootmaker Zoom
The Sign of the Four	Apr 86	19Apr86	St Paul's Bloor Street
The Hound of the Baskervilles	Oct 92	3Oct92	Arts and Letters Club
The Valley of Fear	Apr 17	18Dec21	YouTube

Other

Lasting Impressions	Jun 97	28Jun97	Arts and Letters Club

*All premieres took place at meetings of the Bootmakers of Toronto unless otherwise indicated: SM, Spence Munros of Halifax

Acknowledgements

To my Father, who gave me my first book of Sherlock Holmes stories. Little did he know what an obsession he was kindling

To my Mother, who encouraged me to join the Bootmakers of Toronto. Little did she know how it would change my life

To my Grandmother, who told me of rushing home from church on Sunday evenings in the 1930s to listen to Sherlock Holmes on the radio

To my other Grandmother, who, when I told her I had written a song, said "I hope I hear it on the radio some day"

To Deborah, who gave me the support and space to complete this project

To my friends in the Bootmakers of Toronto and the Spence Munros of Halifax, who gave me encouragement and laughed at appropriate times

To successive Meyers of the Bootmakers of Toronto, who indulged me over the past 40 years

To Cameron Hollyer and successive curators of the Arthur Conan Doyle Collection at the Metropolitan Toronto Reference Library, now Toronto Central Library

To Mark Alberstat who brought this project to fruition

To MX Publishing and Steve Emecz, who took on this project

To George Vanderburgh, who published my first collection, *Singalong with Sherlock Holmes*

To an unknown winemaker in Chateauneuf du Pape, whose product launched the final Baker Street dozen songs

About the Author and Editor

Born in Toronto, **Jim Ballinger** was introduced to the Sherlock Holmes stories as a pre-teen. Some years later the chance purchase of Baring-Gould's *Sherlock Holmes of Baker Street* reinforced that interest. His first contact with the Sherlockian movement was a public forum with the Bootmakers of Toronto held in conjunction with a run of *The Incredible Murder of Cardinal Tosca* at the St Lawrence Centre in Toronto. He joined the Bootmakers in 1978, the Sherlock Holmes Society of London in 1984, Capital Holmes in 1987, and the Spence Munros of Halifax in 2017. With the Bootmakers he received the True Davidson Memorial Award for 1981, the rank of Master Bootmaker in 1984, and the Warren Carleton Memorial Award for 1995. His first musical collection, *Singalong with Sherlock Holmes*, was published by the Metropolitan Toronto Reference Library/Battered Silicon Dispatch Box in 1995. In non-Sherlockian life, he earned a doctorate in radiopharmaceutical chemistry and had a career in nuclear medicine of more than three decades in hospitals in Ontario and in Britain. Indeed, for 14 years he lived 10 km south of 221B Baker Street. Jim and Deborah returned to Canada in 2017 and are now living in Halifax.

Mark Alberstat has been a Sherlockian for decades and is the author and editor of many articles and books including *Canada and Sherlock Holmes*. He was first introduced to the world of Sherlock Holmes through the two-volume Doubleday set of stories that his father owned. After discovering the world of Sherlockian societies and being spurred on by legendary Sherlockian John Bennett Shaw to start his own club, Mark has never looked back. The Spence Munros of Halifax is not only his home society but the club he started as a teen and continues to this day with Mark at the helm as the Colonel. Mark is co-editor, with his wife JoAnn, of *Canadian Holmes*, the quarterly journal of The Bootmakers of Toronto. Mark lives in Dartmouth.

Index of Story Titles

About MX Publishing

MX Publishing is the world's largest specialist Sherlock Holmes publisher, with over four hundred titles and two hundred authors creating the latest in Sherlock Holmes fiction and non-fiction.

Our largest project is The MX Book of New Sherlock Holmes which is the world's largest collection of new Sherlock Holmes Stories – with over two hundred contributors including NY Times bestsellers Lee Child, Nicholas Meyer, Lindsay Faye and Kareem Abdul-Jabbar. The collection has raised over $85,000 for Stepping Stones School for children with learning disabilities.

Learn more at www.mxpublishing.com

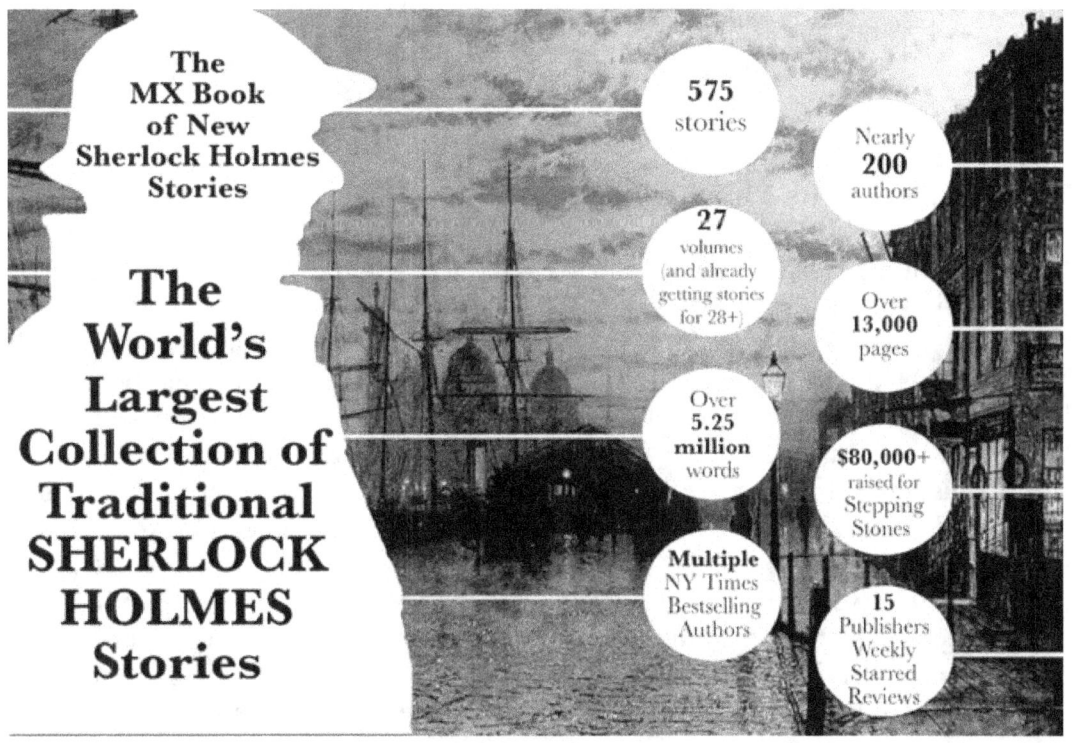

(as of May 2021 – more volumes on the way!)

Also From MX Publishing

In addition to fiction and non-fiction, MX has published several Holmes adaptations for the stage.

The Hound of The Baskervilles: A Sherlock Holmes Play

Laughter, intrigue and suspense are evoked in equal measure by this fast-paced dramatisation of the classic Sherlock Holmes mystery. Originally scripted for open-air performance in the promenade style, the action kicks off with an amusing, rustic, Victorian melodrama; but thereafter it is the brooding presence of Dartmoor which lies at its dark centre. Over the purple heather, the granite tors and the sucking bog of Grimpen Mire, comes a parade of colourful characters to confuse and disturb the courageous soul of Doctor Watson, sent by Holmes to scout for some solid facts behind the highly mysterious death of Sir Charles Baskerville. Fresh-faced from Canada, the new baronet, Sir Henry Baskerville, - You can cut the Sir ! - is having none of the old world superstition surrounding the ancient curse on his family; yet it slowly becomes apparent, even to his no-nonsense mind, that a very real threat is lurking on Baskerville Moor. And, what is more, it leaves footprints... Playwright Simon Corble gives Conan Doyle's original tale some highly inventive twists in order to create an engaging drama that has delighted audiences and received glowing reviews wherever it has been staged since 1995. In print for the first time, the action leaps off the page at even the most casual reader and, if you think you know exactly how it is going to end...the female of the species has a surprise in store. Hell hath no fury, Watson. Quite, Holmes.

Also From MX Publishing

In addition to fiction and non-fiction, MX has published several Holmes adaptations for the stage.

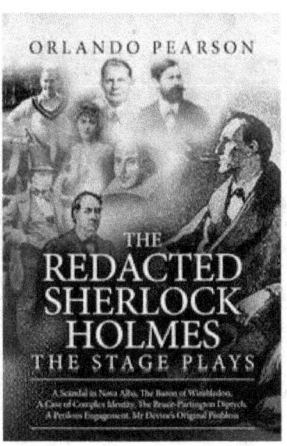

The Redacted Sherlock Holmes – The Stage Plays

Dramatisations of the works of Arthur Conan-Doyle, Shakespeare, Sophocles, and of Orlando Pearson.

A Scandal in Nova Alba – Did Macbeth really kill King Duncan? Sherlock Holmes investigates.

The Baron of Wimbledon - The story of a true German hero of the Nazi period. And a jaw-dropping revelation about the relationship between Sherlock Holmes and Irene Adler.

A Case of Complex Identity - Arthur Conan Doyle's A Case of Identity. And its shocking sequel, The Camberwell Tyrant.

The Bruce-Partington Diptych - Arthur Conan Doyle's espionage story, The Bruce-Partington Plans and its realpolitik inspired sequel, The Sleeper's Cache, featuring Mycroft as well as Sherlock Holmes.

A Perilous Engagement – more Machiavellian machinations as we see that there can be a whitewash at Whitehall.

Mr Devine's Original Problem - Sherlock Holmes is consulted by the most illustrious client of all.

Pearson's plays are ideal for private reading, Zoom broadcasting or production on stage or in the classroom with forces small or large.

Also From MX Publishing

In addition to fiction and non-fiction, MX has published several Holmes adaptations for the stage.

Don't Go Into The Cellar, Mr Holmes! - Sherlock Holmes Stories Re-Imagined for the Stage

This book contains five scripts, three of which I owe a great debt of gratitude to Tony Reynolds as they are adaptations of stories taken from his wonderful book of Sherlock Holmes stories 'The Lost Stories of Sherlock Holmes' – The Adventure Of The Medium, The Giant Rat of Sumatra and The Adventure of The Amazonian Explorer.

As for the others, "Holmes Alone" is a light-hearted romp, that borrows elements and characters from several other Conan Doyle tales. "The Mazarin Malediction" is my attempt to embellish that oft-maligned story, "The Mazarin Stone". Almost always it's this story in particular that is singled out for harsh criticism. Yet I have always enjoyed the tale, and the others in the collection entitled "The Case-Book of Sherlock Holmes". "Malediction" is my homage to ACD's original, written and performed with great affection and enjoyment.

To paraphrase Sir Arthur Conan Doyle. I have wrought my simple plan if I brought one hour of glee to the Sherlock fan, and the Doyle devotee.

Also From MX Publishing

In addition to fiction and non-fiction, MX has published several Holmes adaptations for the stage.

The Curse of Sherlock Holmes

The acclaimed National Theatre actor Robert Stephens said to the star of Granada TV's Sherlock Holmes; Jeremy Brett; 'Do not undertake the role of Sherlock Holmes. He will be your undoing'. 'You must drop it Mr. Holmes, you really must. It will be your undoing' said Professor James Moriarty upon his first encounter with Sherlock Holmes. Somewhere between the fact and fiction Sir Arthur Conan Doyle's greatest creation stole the soul of Jeremy Brett, the actor who would become the embodiment of the Baker Street sleuth. The Curse of Sherlock Holmes follows Jeremy as he fights for his sanity…. His life. This is the full script of the play by Dhanil Ali.